ROYALLY TRICKED

MISHA BELL

♠ Mozaika Publications ♠

Published by Mozaika Publications, an imprint of Mozaika LLC.
www.mozaikallc.com

Cover by Najla Qamber Designs
www.najlaqamberdesigns.com

Photography by Wander Aguiar
www.wanderbookclub.com

e-ISBN: 978-1-63142-690-2
Print ISBN: 978-1-63142-691-9

Chapter One

I tighten my grip on the knife. "Hold still."

My victim—I mean my friend Waldo, the spectator—looks uneasy. "Are you sure about this?"

It takes all of my acting skills to let just the right amount of doubt appear on my face. "Just don't jerk your hand away."

He's holding his palm against mine, as though we've been glued together in the middle of an awkward high five. My hand is gloved, of course.

I glance around. We're alone in the outdoor seating area of the coffee shop, and the pedestrians passing by on the street aren't paying us any attention.

Too bad. I love an audience.

As I hoped, Waldo mistakes my gawking for nervousness, and his hand trembles.

Am I a bad friend for enjoying this so much?

Dumb question. That's like asking if I'm a bad

sister for putting my twin's hand into warm water that night when she happened to wet her bed "for some reason."

I'm just a fun friend. And a fun sister.

I glare at the back of my gloved hand to make my victim more nervous. "I'm going for it… now."

Matching actions to words, I lift the knife in a wide, dramatic arc, channeling the shower scene from *Psycho*.

Waldo snatches his hand away before the blade reaches its target.

Whew. This wouldn't have worked if he hadn't chickened out.

I go through with the stabbing motion and yelp in fake pain before doing the sneaky move to complete the illusion.

The resulting picture speaks for itself: the knife is buried to the hilt on one side of my gloved palm, with the blade sticking out of the other side.

Waldo gapes at it, his thin face almost as pale as mine—and as part of my stage persona, I haven't let the sun touch my skin in years.

I take his reaction as a compliment. He must believe I actually pierced my hand. The reality is different, of course. The blade that was sticking out of the knife is now hidden in the hollow hilt, and the blade that's protruding from my palm is held in place by a powerful magnet inside my glove.

"Wait a second," Waldo says, his breathing steadying. "There's no blood."

Before he can use more pesky logic, I triumphantly "rip" the knife out and claim to have healed my hand with a magic word.

"That was obviously an illusion," he says, peering at the knife.

I hide it in my pocket. "You sure?"

He grabs my wrist to inspect the glove. It's intact, and I dropped the magnet in my pocket when I hid the knife, so as we say in my profession, I'm clean.

"Let me see the knife," he demands.

I pull out the normal knife hidden in my pocket next to the gimmicked one.

Waldo examines it, looking more confused by the second. Finally, he utters every magician's favorite eight words. "I have no idea how you did that."

I grin. "Then you might be even more surprised by this." I take a red-striped watch out of my pocket. "I believe this is yours."

Gasping, he snatches his possession away. "How did you do that?"

"Extremely well," I deadpan.

"Holly?" an unfamiliar male voice says from the street.

I glance at the newcomer, and suddenly, it's my turn to gape.

I didn't realize this kind of masculine perfection existed outside of Hollywood.

Chiseled features. A Roman nose. Vaguely feline hazel eyes that zero in on my face predatorily, making me feel like an about-to-be-devoured gazelle.

I swallow the overabundance of saliva in my mouth with a loud gulp.

The stranger's broad-shouldered, muscular torso is clad in a tight white t-shirt, and despite the raggedy jeans riding low on his narrow hips, there's something regal about him—an impression supported by the strange design on his belt buckle. It resembles a crest that a medieval knight might put on his shield.

I've been told I compare people to celebrities too much, but it's hard to do with this guy. Maybe if the love between Jake Gyllenhaal and Heath Ledger in *Brokeback Mountain* had borne fruit?

Nah, he's even better-looking than that.

Realizing that I'm staring at his face too intently for it to be considered polite, I drop my gaze lower and notice that he's holding two leather straps in his fists. Leashes, presumably.

Half expecting to see willing sex slaves on the other end of those leashes, I instead find two weird dogs.

At least I think the creatures are dogs.

One sports black-and-white spots that make it look like a panda. Actually, given the creature's ginormous size, I can't rule out the possibility that it *is* a bear. And, if looking like an endangered ursine species wasn't odd enough, the beast is wearing goggles.

Is it because of bad vision, or is the panda about to go snowboarding?

The second creature is eyewear-free and reminds

me of a koala, just much bigger and with a lolling canine tongue.

I force my gaze back to their ridiculously handsome owner. "Hey," is all I can manage. My overactive hormones seem to have robbed me of the ability to speak.

The stranger narrows those hazel eyes. "You *are* Holly, right?"

This is your chance, my inner magician pipes up. *Trick the hot stranger. Fool his pants off.*

Banishing lust with a heroic effort of will, I inwardly rub my hands together, à la evil villain. Until I adopted my current pale-skinned, raven-haired stage persona, I was mistaken for my identical twin on a regular basis, even by people closest to us. Our oval-shaped faces are exactly the same, right down to sharp cheekbones and a strong nose. I was literally born for this particular deception.

Adding the slightest touch of poshness to my voice, I say, "Who else would I bloody be?"

There. If he knows that Holly has a twin named Gia (as in, me), he'll voice that guess now and I'll stand down.

Maybe.

I bet I can bluff him out even if he does know I exist.

He stares at me intently. "You've changed your hair."

"*Addams Family* cosplay," I say in my best Morticia Addams voice. It's not my most convincing lie, but the guy looks like he's about to buy it anyway. Then I see a problem. Waldo, who's blinking in confusion, is about to speak. I kick his leg under the table and cheerfully ask the stranger, "Have you met Waldo?"

I'm hoping the hottie will extend his hand and introduce himself, thus letting me learn his name.

My evil ploy is thwarted by the panda. It pulls on the hottie's pant leg with its teeth. Seeing this, the koala does the same on the other side, except its movements are clumsy, puppy-like, leaving a hole in the pants.

If this is how the dogs get his attention, no wonder he wears something so raggedy. Also, yuck. I hope he washes that dog saliva off his pants ASAP.

"One second, guys," the stranger says to his furry friends in a warm, paternal tone that tugs at something in my chest. "Can't you see I'm talking to Holly?"

Score! He believes I'm Holly.

Looking up from the dogs, the stranger gives Waldo a once-over. Does he also think my friend looks like Willem Dafoe, only when he played Aquaman's mentor, not the Green Goblin from *Spider-Man*?

Before I can ask, the stranger's gaze returns to me. "That's not your boyfriend."

I blink. He knows Holly's boyfriend? Where does my sister find all these hunks? This one is even hotter than her Alex.

"Indeed," I say, channeling her again. "This bloke is just a *friend* friend."

The stranger's wicked smirk is like a flick on my clit. "I don't think men and women can be just friends."

They so can. My sisters and I have been friends with one particular guy forever, and he's never made a move on any one of us. Granted, he's gay, but still.

Waldo stands up, all wounded dignity. "Look, chum, I'm allergic to dogs, so if you don't mind..."

"Chum?" The stranger's feline eyes are mocking as they capture mine. "See? He doesn't like me horning in on his territory."

The heat that flashes through my body is no longer lust. The nerve on this guy. "I'm nobody's territory." And certainly not Waldo's. He's never made a move on me either, not in the entire eighteen months we've known each other.

Waldo's face reddens, and he tightens his grip on the knife that he never gave back.

Seriously? Can testosterone make you *that* stupid?

"She's right, chum," Waldo says in his most menacing voice, which, if we're honest, sounds a bit like he's doing a Cookie Monster impersonation. "You'd better skedaddle."

The stranger curls his upper lip at him. If he's aware of that knife, he doesn't show it. Another testosterone-poisoning victim, no doubt.

"Skedaddle?" He looks back at me. "Where did you find this Waldo?"

Okay, that's it. I'm the only one allowed to make "Where's Waldo?" jokes at my friend's expense.

The hot stranger has just crossed a line.

I push my chair back and rise to my full five-foot-five height. "How about 'get the fuck out of here?' Is that a better choice of words for you?"

This is when the panda growls at Waldo—a threatening sound one wouldn't expect to come out of such a cute, if overlarge, dog. It reminds me of this news report about a man who tried to hug a panda at the zoo, only to end up in the hospital after the frightened bear mauled him.

Paling, Waldo sets the knife on the table. There are clearly at least ten brain cells inside that thick skull of his.

The stranger pats the bespectacled beast's head and murmurs something soothing in a language that sounds Eastern European.

Huh. He didn't have any accent when he spoke to me, but English must be his second language. Otherwise, he wouldn't address his dogs in that foreign tongue.

Crap. With our luck, the hottie is some Russian mobster.

"Sit down," I hiss at Waldo, and to my relief, he does as I say.

Make that twenty brain cells.

The stranger's beautiful eyes roam over my face before narrowing again. "You're not Holly. She's nice." A touch of that wicked smirk returns to his lips, and his voice deepens. "Whereas *you* are naughty."

That does it. No more Mrs. Nice Magician.

I slowly saunter over to him.

Although… maybe this isn't such a good idea.

Now that I'm closer, I realize just how tall he is. And wide-shouldered. The giant dogs threw off my perspective, creating a visual illusion that their owner was normal-sized. He's not. Worse yet, he smells divine, like ocean surf and something ineffably male.

A trick under these conditions will test all of my abilities.

Hold on. Will the dogs get mad that I'm so close?

As if reading my mind, the stranger gives them a stern command, and they sheepishly fall behind him.

Was that command intended to make *me* want to behave like a good, obedient bitch? Because I kind of want to.

No, screw that. I'm sticking with my plan, which requires me to get within pickpocketing distance.

"Do you want to see just how naughty I can be?" I ask in the sultriest voice I can muster.

Is it normal for human eyes to go all slitty like that, as if he were a lion?

"How naughty is that, *myodik*?" the stranger murmurs.

Did he just say "me dick?" Nah. It was something in whatever language he used with the dogs. Still, his dick is now firmly on my mind, which doesn't help the hormonal overload situation.

Forcing away the X-rated images, I purposefully lick my lips. "I'll steal your wallet. Or your watch. Your choice."

The supposed choice is misdirection, obviously. My real target is neither of those things, but he doesn't need to know that.

His nostrils flare as his gaze drops to my lips. "Is it stealing if you warn me?"

If it were possible for me to forget my concerns about germs and consider placing my lips on someone else's, I'd do that now. It's the strongest such urge I've ever felt.

"What's the matter?" I say breathlessly. "Chicken?"

He pats the right pocket of his jeans. "How about you steal my wallet?"

I take in a steadying breath. "Thanks for showing me where it is."

Before he can reply, I delve into that pocket. I need major misdirection for what I'm really trying to steal.

By Houdini's eyebrows, is that what I think it is?

Yup. There's no mistaking it. As I brush my gloved fingers over the wallet, I feel something else behind the fabric of the pants.

Something big and very hard.

Well. Someone is overly happy to be pickpocketed.

Maybe he *was* saying "me dick" before?

I do my best to hold his gaze and not clear my suddenly dry throat. "Can you feel me stealing it?"

As I speak, I work on unclasping the fancy buckle—his belt being my real target.

His lids lower to half-mast, and his voice deepens

further. "Your nimble fingers are exactly where I want them."

Crap. Between my gloves and his ridiculous sex appeal, I'm having trouble with the clasp.

But no. I can't get caught. That would be like revealing a magic secret—the biggest taboo I can think of.

"These fingers?" I ask huskily and gently stroke his hardness through the layers of fabric, using the misdirection this slutty move creates to pull harder on the clasp with my other hand, finally opening it.

I'd like to see David Blaine do *that.*

The stranger's low, guttural groan is animalistic and makes my nipples so hard they feel on the verge of turning inside out. He now looks like a lion about to pounce.

Gulping, I yank my hand out of his pocket and try to give him a sneaky smile. It comes out faltering instead. "I changed my mind. I'll steal your watch."

I grab his wrist and give it a tight squeeze while pulling out the belt with my other hand.

Yes! Got it. Hiding the belt behind my back, I pout at the watch. "On second thought, I think I'll let you keep your possessions."

He looks triumphant, probably convinced that his sex appeal has defeated my pickpocketing skills. Since it almost did, I can't really fault him for thinking it.

I carefully back away. "Oh, by the way, did you lose this?"

I show him my prize.

Eyes wide, he shifts his gaze back and forth between my hand and his pants.

"How?" he asks.

The question is music to my ears.

"Extremely well," I say, but I can't manage my usual bluster.

He extends his hand to get the belt back. "You're a dangerous woman."

Two things happen simultaneously as I step toward him to return the belt.

The panda tries to get his attention again by pulling on his left pant leg. Not wanting to be outdone, the koala does the same thing on the right side—only this time, there's no belt holding the pants up, and they slide down.

All the way down.

Fuck. Me.

The biggest erection in the history of phalluses juts out and—though this could be my imagination—winks at me.

He's been commando all this time?

Me dick indeed.

I gape at the ginormousness. Even though I touched it and felt its size when I was rummaging in his pocket, I never would've imagined it like this.

Smooth. Straight. Delectably veiny. It just begs to be touched, or sucked, or licked—but I can't for reasons that are difficult to recall right now.

A concealed carry license should be required to pack that kind of heat. And also whatever license you need to operate heavy machinery. And a hunting license. Maybe even a 007-style license to kill—

Behind me, I hear Waldo gasp. Poor thing. I bet even *he* is ready to get on his knees for a taste, and to the best of my knowledge, he's straight.

I can't tear my gaze away.

If that cock were a magic wand, it would be one of the Deathly Hallows—the one Voldemort wielded at the end. And if it were a banana, it would be just the right-sized snack for King Kong.

The stranger should be turning red with embarrassment and scrambling to cover himself, but instead, a cocky smirk lifts the corners of his lips. "Like what you see?"

I do. So much so I want to pull out my phone and take a selfie with it.

To my huge—and I do mean *huge*—disappointment, he pulls up his pants. His voice is husky. "Like I said. Naughty. Very naughty."

Snatching the belt from my nerveless fingers, he loops it back into his pants and saunters away with his dogs, leaving me standing there, mouth agape.

"Can you believe that guy?" Waldo asks somewhere in the distance, his tone outraged.

No. I can't.

I can't believe what just happened, period.

All I know is this wasn't what I had in mind when I set out to fool that guy's pants off.

Chapter Two

The rest of the outing with Waldo happens in a fog. I'm pretty sure he spends at least twenty minutes railing against the stranger's balls—literal and figurative—but I only half listen. As soon as is socially acceptable, I make an excuse to leave and rush home to videocall my twin.

Since the mystery guy knows her, she must know him too.

Entering my room, I scan it for a place to set up my phone where my sister won't see the magician paraphernalia scattered all over. I don't want her coming here in person and going Marie Kondo on my ass.

There.

I walk up to Manny, the mannequin I practice my tricks on—of the magic variety, that is. Taking off Manny's expressionless head, I set my phone in his neck and dial Holly.

No answer.

Crap.

I call her without the video. Same result.

Switching to text, I ask her to call me as soon as she's available and wait.

And wait some more.

Tired of waiting, I decide to distract myself. But with what?

Usually, I use every spare moment of my life to practice magic, but the mystery guy's cock has reminded me of a project I've been working on from time to time—a type of exposure therapy meant to one day allow me to become intimate with a man.

Fine. I admit it. I might have an itsy-bitsy problem. I don't just have trouble shaking hands without gloves. I also have an issue with more intimate touching, not to mention bodily fluid exchanges of any kind.

This isn't great for a magician, or a human. If I wanted to be a detective à la Adrian Monk, though, I'd be golden.

On the bright side, my chances of getting dysentery are slim to none.

It all started in my childhood when I witnessed something horrible, an incident I've been calling The Zombie Tit Massacre.

My parents own a farm where they rescue all sorts of animals, and they had the bright idea to give shelter to a bird that goes by the scientific name of *Parus major*, more commonly known as *The Great Tit.*

This bird has another name as well—the Zombie Tit. The reason for the latter is what you'd expect. In the wild, these birds are thirsty for brains—bat brains, to be exact. But as it turns out, they're not super picky and will eat the brains of other birds too, including chickens, which is what I walked into on that fateful day.

Bloody chickens with their brains viciously pecked out.

Blood and brains everywhere.

A satisfied Zombie Tit.

I almost lost my voice from screaming.

There were actually two of us traumatized on that day. My sister Blue, one of the sextuplets and thus younger and more impressionable, came upon the bloody scene first. She's afraid of birds to this very day. Maybe also tits, as in boobs. I've never asked.

Me, I'm okay with birds. And tits. But I am grossed out by blood and brains, and that aversion has since transferred to all bodily fluids and, by extension, germs.

So, yeah. If the concept of kissing is unfathomable to me, various sex acts are even more so.

With a loud sigh, I grab my laptop and open the first porn site I find.

Am I ready for this?

I take a deep breath and slowly let it out.

What I'm about to do is called systematic desensitization, and the idea behind it is as the term implies: if I see acts that scare me in a calm, controlled environment, I might be able to work up the courage to deal with the real thing.

Hey, it works for spider and snake phobias.

I start with videos of people kissing.

Keep calm. Don't think about salivary microbiota. Or tongue microbiota.

The problem is, no one merely kisses in porn. They suck each other's faces in a way that reminds of the monsters from *Alien*. In general, watching porn does for me what horror movies must do for everyone else.

Speaking of horror, time to up the ante.

I start with a vanilla sex scene. The story here is he's a pizza delivery guy and she can't help but seduce him.

Yeah. Sure. That's likely.

Watching them undress is okay. They don't kiss, which is good—not for their fictional relationship but for my squeamishness. However, as I watch a condomless cock go into the actress's opening, my heart rate kicks up again, and not due to sexual arousal.

Fuck. Am I hyperventilating?

Breathe. In. Out. It's not happening to me. The people in the video are consenting adults. Also, porn stars get tested regularly, so what's the worst that could happen?

My mantras aren't working. I can think of a handful of STDs that have an extremely short incubation period, yet according to my research, porn stars test themselves only about twice a month. Simple math says that if they shoot enough scenes, they could get infected.

Somehow, I manage to even out my breathing.

Good. I'm ready for more.

I click on a video featuring a kink that's particularly disturbing to me—a golden shower.

The story here is she's a MILF and he's her son's best friend. Which makes no sense. Shouldn't she be his urologist or something? Also, MILF stands for Mom I'd Like to Fuck, so in this case, shouldn't she be a MILPO, as in Mom I'd Like to Pee On? Or MILPOM—Mom I'd Like to Pee On Me?

In any case, this really amps up the therapeutic value of this session. Once I can tolerate watching something like this, I might be ready for first base in the real world.

Hopefully. Maybe.

As soon as the video starts, the feeling that I'm watching a horror flick intensifies.

Some people believe that urine is sterile, but that doesn't make sense. When someone has a UTI, what do the doctors look for in their urine sample? Bacteria. Would that work if the stuff was really sterile? Nope.

I get halfway through the video before I have to shut it off. Not quite there yet, I guess.

I chew on my lip, debating ending the therapy session here, but I decide to brave one more thing.

Bukkake.

It's a Japanese word that translates to "eye

herpes." At least that's what I assume because bukkake is an act where a huge number of men collectively ejaculate on someone—a woman in the version I'm about to watch.

The story in this video is that she's the naughty stepsister—a very popular porn theme on this site.

But hold up. Forgetting the fact that some of the guys are way too old to still live at home, how did this fictional family end up with fifty stepsons and one stepdaughter in the first place?

Once the actual bukkake starts, I find it hard to watch.

Maybe if I fast-forward a little?

Nope.

Worse.

They're keeping a digital count in the corner of the video that tells the viewer how many times the guys have already come, as well as the number of times the actress has swallowed—and we're up to sixteen cum splashes and ten gulps.

Shouldn't this look like a horror flick to everyone? Unlike with a regular facial, the woman's face is completely covered in creamy liquid, creating a grotesque effect.

Strangely, I don't get the feeling that the actress is being exploited, though she might very well be. Maybe it's because she looks like she's having a great time, while the faceless men just rub one off mechanically and without any enthusiasm—like it's a chore.

I wonder how much it would cost to hire so many

dudes if you wanted this done privately at your house. Also, is this actually fun for straight men to watch? I'm not an expert, but it seems like cocks and man-jizz are the main course here, with a girl almost as an afterthought. Also, does the actress skip a meal after this scene? Just how nutritious is that stuff? Can a vegan consume it?

Side note: none of these cocks look as nice as the one the mysterious stranger was packing. In fact, none of the porn shlongs I've ever seen can compare.

Wait. I'm cheating. I disassociated from the video. I have to pay close attention to the screen and work on calming down to get any therapeutic effects.

I open my eyes *Clockwork Orange*-style and gape at the binge coming and drinking.

Now the panic sets in.

Just like with urine, if a guy has a UTI, semen can be contaminated with bacteria. With that many guys, the chances of a bad outcome increase proportionally.

I turn the video off and even out my breathing.

Am I ready for the hardest part of the therapy?

I go to the target category and do a double take. There's a video called *Analysis*. Do people get off on analyzing things?

Nope. It's actually Anally Sis, another stepsister situation.

Fine. At least this has a more realistic stepsibling ratio. I start watching and force myself to gape at the gaping orifice on the screen.

Yep. There it is. Ass to mouth—a practice I find creepier than Freddy Krueger, Michael Myers, The Babadook, and even Pee Wee Herman.

Slow breathing isn't helping me at all now. This is how someone with a clown phobia must feel while watching *It.*

The receiver must be super clean.

Nope. Not helping.

The giver must have an extremely well-developed immune system.

Nope.

I turn the video off.

Can't watch it. Not ready.

Hey, at least I didn't scream. Or have a heart attack. The first time I learned what "toss the salad" meant, I gave up eating all salads for about a year.

Shutting my laptop, I work on calming myself.

Maybe this was a bad idea. Maybe I don't want my twin to tell me who the guy is. What's the point? It's not like I can do anything with him. It might just be frustrating to—

My phone rings.

As I nearly trip on my way back to my mannequin, I admit to myself that I *do* want to know who he is.

Which is why it's a great relief that it's my twin, Holly, who's calling.

Chapter Three

All but bouncing from eagerness, I accept the video call.

"Hiya," Holly says, a warm smile illuminating the face we share.

Hmm. Is that a look of post-coital bliss? That would explain why it took her so long to call me back.

As is often the case, she's poshly clutching a steaming cup of tea, her pinky out. The large room behind her is unfamiliar. She's probably at her boyfriend's house—further supporting my coitus theory.

"Hey," I say, peering at the top of her head. "Did you color your hair?"

Usually, all that stands out when I look at my twin are our similarities. This time, though, I focus on the subtle differences, especially in our faces, and it leads me to think that the mysterious stranger might've been right after all. Compared to the guilelessness etched into Holly's innocent features, I just might look a bit naughty.

Then again, so might a nun.

My twin picks up a strand of her hair and frowns at it. "It's the same color it's always been. Why do you ask?"

I steal the wallet from Manny's back pocket with a smooth motion that a normal human hopefully wouldn't notice. "It looks redder to me for some reason."

She shakes her head.

I grin. "Maybe you finally washed it?"

She blows exasperatedly on her tea, and I can see that she's itching to roll her eyes. "Perchance you've forgotten what our natural hair color is at this point?"

"I have my pubes to remind me." I sneak the wallet back into Manny's pocket, a technique called put-pocketing. "And there's no hint of red there."

She loses her fight against the eyeroll. "I—that is, *we*—only have that red tint on the head, and only in certain light, which might be why you haven't noticed it."

I shrug. "It makes you look like Cate Blanchett at the beginning of *Elizabeth*."

She looks unsure if she's been insulted or not, which is strange given how much she likes anything British. Her slightly squinty eyes seem to indicate she's taken offense in the end. "Well, *you* look like Cate Blanchett as Hela in *Thor: Ragnarok*."

"I'll take that as a compliment. That woman looks

more amazing the older she gets, and that particular character was totally badass."

She shakes her head. "Wasn't she evil?"

My grin turns devious. "Was she? She was the firstborn, so that made her the rightful heir to the throne. Are you saying she didn't deserve to rule Asgard because she was a woman?"

"A bloodthirsty woman."

I steal the wallet again. "Her father raised her to be a conqueror, but then flip-flopped on foreign policy before banishing the poor woman. Why? She's no worse than Loki, yet he was allowed to stay."

Holly's blowing on the tea is almost violent now. "Did you call me because you wanted to start a random debate?"

Since I've done that in the past, I don't feel too insulted. "No." I glance at my door to make sure it's closed, since I don't want one of my roommates to overhear the next bit. "I ran into someone you know and wanted to ask you about him."

She puts her cup down and drags the phone closer to her face. "A *him*?"

Huh. The sneaky expression that twists her features makes it seem like I'm staring into a phone-shaped mirror.

I put-pocket the wallet. "Yup. A male of the *Homo sapiens* species."

I describe him and the details of our meeting, and when I get to the part where I saw his enormous magic wand, she spits out her tea.

"So," I say when she gets herself under control. "He knew about your boyfriend, so it's someone you've—"

"I know exactly who he is."

A downright mischievous expression is on her face now. Is that what I look like most of the time? If so, I'd better keep it in check during my magic performances.

She picks up her cup again, blows on the liquid exaggeratingly slowly, and takes a leisurely sip.

I sigh. "Are you going to make me beg?"

She swallows her tea with relish. "Why do you want to know?"

It's my turn to roll my eyes. "To paraphrase Leonardo DiCaprio in *Django*: when I first saw him, he had my curiosity. But after I saw his fully erect cock, he had my attention."

"Fine. It was Tigger." She peers at me intently over her cup. "Remember?"

I stare back uncomprehendingly. "Remember what? Is he a big fan of Winnie the Pooh?"

She chuckles. "I thought something similar when I first heard that nickname. I suspect he was dubbed that because he bounced around a lot as a kid."

Oh. Well, he can bounce—or pounce—on me anytime he wants. "What is it that I'm supposed to remember?"

The tea receives another exasperated-sounding blow. "That I offered to set you up with him."

"You did?"

"Yeah." She takes a dainty sip. "You refused. Said he sounded like a manwhore."

"Oh." On pure autopilot, I steal Manny's watch as I strain my memory. "Do you mean your new bestie's boyfriend's brother's cousin?"

Until recently, I was worried that my twin was anti-social. For years, I've been her best and only friend, while she's been one of my many. I was pleasantly surprised when she met a guy and became close with his sister—and I'm not jealous of their friendship at all. Not even when she waxes ecstatic about how beautiful, smart, and inspirational said new BFF is, and how cool her dildo-making business is. My sis even received something like a friendship bracelet from her new friend—except it was a dildo.

She looks longingly at her diminishing tea. "He's not a cousin, but yeah, that's the guy."

I sneak the watch into Manny's left pants pocket. "Is this the guy who tried to dance with you?"

"Indeed. I figure that means he finds our face attractive."

I narrow my eyes. "Isn't he also the one who dry-humped your boyfriend's mother?"

She snorts, and it's a marvel the tea doesn't pour out of her nose. "They just danced, and *she* dry-humped *him*."

Sounds plausible. If I were a middle-aged woman, he'd make a cougar out of me in a heartbeat. Then again, I'd find him delectable at any age, even—

"So." Now Holly looks so much like our mother I

half expect her to spout off tips on how to achieve a proper orgasm. "Do you want an introduction?"

Do I?

The memory of the porn debacle is back with a vengeance. To calm myself, I steal the wallet again. As casually as I can, I say, "No, thanks."

The disappointment on her face is pure Octomom. "Why not?"

"Because he's still a manwhore?"

The full truth is obviously subtler than that. Holly doesn't know about my intimacy issues. Back in high school, I created one of my best illusions: I made all seven of my sisters believe I was sexually active when I was anything but. If I'd told them the truth—that my perfectly reasonable germ avoidance has prevented me from so much as kissing a boy—they would've mocked me until our parents put me in therapy. Fluid exchange is sacrosanct for our Octomom, as well as Octodad. Granted, Holly wouldn't have mocked me, but she can't keep a secret to save her life, so I fooled her along with the sextuplets.

Now that we're grown, I'm too ashamed to admit even to her that I still haven't kissed anyone. No one knows that I'm a virgin—one who broke her hymen with a dildo many years ago, but still.

"If you're after some casual rumpty-tumpty, you won't find a better match." She puts her teacup down.

"Rumpty-tumpty? Is that another version of 'shag?'"

Holly attended college in the UK and came back

sounding like a character in a Jane Austen novel, providing me with the joy of making fun of her for a while. Now she's lost the accent but still drops an occasional (and usually charming) Britishism, so I don't get to mess with her as much as I'd like.

She makes a circle with her right index finger and thumb, then pierces it with her left middle finger. "Baking the potato, putting the bread in the oven, planting the parsnip, a cucumber in—"

"Stop," I say sternly. "My food choices are limited as is."

She looks smug. "I bet he would be up for a one-night stand."

Sure. Great idea. Lose virginity to a sex god and be ruined for any other man for the rest of my life. Not that he would even want to be used in such a fashion, not to mention—

"If it helps," my sister whispers conspiratorially, "he's a prince."

"Excuse me?" I shove the wallet into Manny's pocket without any stealth and thumb up the volume on my phone. "What did you just say?"

"It's called *velikiy knyaz* in his homeland," she says. "Which translates to something like a Grand Prince."

Her face is earnest. Either she's suddenly mastered the art of lying, or she's telling the truth. Or maybe she's finally re-watched one too many episodes of *Downton Abbey*.

"He's a prince?" I say incredulously. "An actual prince?"

"Indeed." She hands her cup to someone outside the view of the camera and says something (probably in Russian) that sounds like, "*chai.*" Looking back at me, she says, "If you married him, you'd be a princess."

As she says that, I see a Disney-esque montage playing out. Me bursting into a song about how badly I want to become a renowned illusionist. Me talking to my (likely animal) sidekick, who'll sound just like a famous comedian. Me having the one true kiss with the prince—

"Here," a male voice says with a slight Russian accent as a giant hand holding a steaming teacup appears in the video.

I was right. She's at her boyfriend's place.

"*Spasibo*," she says with an adoring grin.

So she *can* speak Russian now. Cool. If I'm lucky, she'll develop a Russian accent as well, and I'll get to tease her about it.

Cradling her tea, she peers into the camera. "Didn't you hear me? You could be a bloody princess."

I pinch the bridge of my nose, too distracted by the topic at hand to make fun of that "bloody." "This doesn't make any sense. Who is royal nowadays? And if he really is a prince, why does his nickname reference a tiger? Wouldn't a lion make more sense? As in king of the jungle?"

"Maybe in Ruskovia, they think tigers are kings of the jungle." She gives her new cup a disturbingly seductive-looking blow.

Is she putting on a show for her beau?

Then I register the country she mentioned, and my right eyebrow shoots up. "He's a prince of Ruskovia?"

That makes sense, as much as meeting a real-life prince could make any sense. It explains the Eastern European language he spoke in to his dogs, and the design of his belt buckle—that was probably a family crest. It may even explain the cocky attitude.

She nods. "You've heard of Ruskovia?"

Is that a dig at my lack of a college degree?

I steal Manny's wallet, a feat no college can prepare you for. "Of course. My favorite female illusionist resides there. Rasputina. Have you heard of her?"

"From you, I think." She pointedly looks at my hair. "Wasn't she the one you stole this vampire guise from?"

"No," I say indignantly.

I didn't steal it. I was inspired by it. In general, I adore Rasputina. If I had to sleep with a woman—gun to the head scenario—I'd choose *her*.

I put-pocket the wallet once more. "My stage persona is closer to that of Criss Angel, with some Winona Ryder from *Beetlejuice* thrown in."

"Sure," Holly says. "In any case, you and Tigger would make a cute couple."

I snort. "Why would he even need me? Has he run out of women in his homeland?"

"I have no clue, but if you decide to do anything more than just sleep with him, you should know that he's a daredevil." She proceeds to tell me about his crazy stunts—with BASE jumping being the tamest thing on the list.

"Don't worry," I say when she's done. "I'm not going to do anything with him at all."

Having said that, if my twin's goal was to scare me from wanting the man, the list of activities he's into has had the opposite effect. I'm now picturing Tigger as the Most Interesting Man in the World, à la the Dos Equis beer commercials. I can practically hear the voiceover guy saying, *"His only regret is not knowing what regret feels like. He's won the lifetime achievement award... twice."*

"You know," Holly says. "If you did go out with him, it would make your upcoming get-together with our parents that much easier."

Houdini help me. I totally forgot about that. Not long ago, Holly owed me a favor, and I asked her to grab lunch with our parents in my stead—a task she managed to screw up, badly. Now, besides fending off the parental units' prying concerns about my dating life, I have to hear Octomom's lamentations about that (pretty tame) deception.

Oh, and this reminds me: Holly still owes me one. I'll have to make sure to collect.

"You *are* seeing them, right?" she asks guiltily. No doubt her thoughts went in the same direction as mine.

I sigh. "Of course. But I'm not telling them anything about Tigger. The last thing I want is for Octomom to try to breed me."

My twin cringes.

Ah. Right. She doesn't like it when I call our mother Octomom, and not because of inaccuracy—Mom birthed the two of us and then our sextuplets sisters, not octuplets. No, Holly just doesn't like the number eight. Or nine. Or six. She prefers primes, like five. I bet if she'd had foresight when the two of us were hanging out in Mom's uterus together, she would've choked me with her umbilical cord to make sure the total number of Hyman siblings ended up being seven. She's also the only one of us who wouldn't have minded Mom spawning three more siblings to make it eleven.

7-Eleven must be a heavenly place for her.

"When are you meeting them?" she asks.

"In a few days."

She chuckles. "Good luck."

"Thanks." I sneak Manny's wallet out of his pocket once more. "I'll need it."

She nods at someone outside my view—no doubt her boyfriend. "I'd better go."

"One last thing," I say. "Is the Ruskovian language similar to Russian?"

"I think so. Why?"

I scratch the back of my head. "I'd like to know what *me-dick* or *me-o-dick* means."

She grins. "Do you mean *myodik*?"

"I think so."

"In Russian, it means *little honey*," she says in a professorial tone. "Probably the same in Ruskovian."

Wow. Either she's learned all the words related to teatime, or her Russian vocabulary is already sizable. Either way, that accent is just around the corner.

A male voice says something on her end that I don't quite catch.

"Ah. I'm being told you don't call a woman *myodik* in Russia," she explains. "Honey is a masculine noun."

"It is?"

Does that mean I look masculine to him?

She sighs. "Don't get me started on this. Russian is a hard language to learn."

"But why is honey masculine? The bees that make it are female, so why should their excretions swap genders?"

She nods enthusiastically. "There's no logic to bodily fluids in Russian, period. Blood is female, sweat is male, poop is neuter. Why?"

Eww. I grimace and shake my head. "I'm still on honey. It's a liquid, so shouldn't it be gender fluid?"

She groans. "The one that bugs me the most is flowers. Why are they masculine? They're shaped like vaginas and usually contain both sex organs. And not to stereotype, but it's women who like flowers, not men." A male laugh sounds behind the camera, so my sister looks at the source and pointedly asks, "Why is the moon feminine, but the sun neuter? Why are spoon and fork feminine, but knife masculine?"

"They just are," he says. "Not my fault, *kroshka.* You don't have to learn it."

"There," she grumbles. "*Kroshka* means *breadcrumb*, and it's female. Bread itself is male. A slice of bread is also male, but as soon as you get down small enough, the gender changes?"

"Hey, I'll let you get back to linguistics," I say and reach toward my phone to terminate the call.

"Wait, sis, I'm sorry." Holly looks back into the camera. "Want to say hi to my Russian teacher?"

I nod, and her beau, Alex, comes into view.

I've met him before, but damn. Good for Holly. She's got herself one impressive specimen. I bet that's what Henry Cavill would look like if he were cast as the *Red Son*—a version of Superman whose space crib crash-landed in Soviet Russia instead of Kansas.

Is it weird to feel an ego boost from knowing that a man like that would date a woman with my face?

"Hey," I say to him. "Do you have any new Russian jokes?"

He flashes a sexy grin. "The door rings. Young Vovochka opens it and sees a young man with a bouquet. He stares at him thoughtfully and says, 'You've been visiting my sister quite a bit lately. Don't you have your own?'"

After the chuckles over the joke die down, we say our goodbyes. Both of theirs are in Russian.

Chapter Four

The temptation to look up Tigger online after that call is strong, but I fight it. Nothing good will come from learning more about him or his better-than-in-porn dick.

Since he's a prince, I'm hereby dubbing it His Royal Hardness.

Taking my phone from Manny's neck, I reattach his head. To distract myself from thoughts of Tigger and his royal appendages, I put on the CGI movie version of *The Lion King*. All that stuff about Disney and giant cats has kindled the urge to watch it.

Midway, I pause and look up an important question: who would win in a fight, a lion or a tiger?

My research reveals that tigers are stronger and larger than lions. However, lions hunt in prides, while tigers are solitary creatures, so if they met in nature, the fight wouldn't be fair. If that's true, why is the lion considered the king? Shouldn't it be the tiger? Actually, if strength is the deciding factor, it should be the elephant, or better yet, the killer whale.

Lions must know the right people, like the folks at Disney.

I continue with the movie but soon realize that watching it was a mistake. A song is now stuck in my head, only in my version it's Tigger who sleeps in the mighty jungle tonight. Sleeps with me, preferably.

No. Must not think of him.

Must think of something else.

Anything else.

Oh, I know. Maybe it's the Russian joke that primed me, but it seems like there are incest shenanigans in *The Lion King*. Take Simba and Nala. She might be his sister or his cousin. After all, the only males in the movie are Mufasa and Scar, and they're brothers. Not to mention, the females in a lion pride are usually related. What is a Disney lion marriage like, anyway? In nature, the male lion sleeps with every female in the pride. Do they have an open marriage in *The Lion King* as well?

Thinking of feline royals lets a certain prince sneak back into my consciousness, along with His Royal Hardness.

Ugh. Seems that dwelling on lion sex has only made me hornier.

Time for a bigger movie distraction: *The Illusionist*, *The Prestige*, or *Now You See Me*.

I put on *The Illusionist*, but that's yet another mistake. There's a prince, and though he's a villain, his presence reminds me of Tigger—not to mention that the evil prince's name is Leopold. He's probably Leo to his friends, and Leo is Latin for lion, so not all that far from tiger.

Giving up on movies, I practice some sleight of hand.

Nope. Makes me think of him. Or at least my hand on His Royal Hardness.

Desperate, I fire up my computer—the greatest time-suck device known to humankind—and open an app created for me by my sister Blue, the other trauma victim of The Zombie Tit Massacre. I use the app to modify some images of shirtless guys on popular internet platforms by replacing the man nipples with the nipples of female porn stars.

Why? Because it's funny to me, plus I support the Free the Nipple movement, though not enough to put my nipples where my mouth is by going topless in a public place.

Maybe one day. Maybe if I get the chance to do a large stage performance, I can make my nipples "disappear."

Crap. Now I'm wondering what Tigger's nipples look like, and which female porn star's nipples they resemble the most, if any.

My phone pings with an incoming text.

Serendipity.

I was just using Blue's app, and here she is, asking to have lunch in the near future.

That's great. Blue is one of my favorite sextuplets.

Besides having lived through The Zombie Tit Massacre with me, she has a passion for spycraft, which is surprisingly similar to magic.

I tell her that I'm game to eat, and she tells me where—a restaurant that has no fowl on the menu—and when.

Speaking of food, I'm starving.

Entering the kitchen, I grab some oat milk from the fridge and a box of Frosted Flakes from the pantry. This is to be a breakfast-for-dinner day, a common occurrence for me and the rest of my starving artist roomies.

I plop down at the table and begin to shovel in the food, only to pause as I notice the front of my cereal box.

This is just grrrrrreat. Tony the Tiger reminds me of Tigger too.

Must divert thoughts now.

Why is a tiger a spokesman for carbs? Shouldn't he work for a steakhouse chain instead? Also, wouldn't grrr be an expression of tiger anger? Tony sounds happy, so shouldn't he be purring?

Do tigers purr?

Nope. According to a quick Google search, when happy, tigers chuff, which sounds like a snort and is done by blowing through their nostrils.

"Hey." A familiar voice drags me away from the allure of my phone's screen.

"Hey yourself." I grin at my roommate and friend, who's known in the magic world as La Profesora.

That's because her father was a famous Spanish magician known as El Profesor, and also because when it comes to card magic, she could teach a graduate-level course.

The name on her birth certificate is Clarisa, but she prefers to go by the more American-sounding Clarice—maybe because she can hear slaughtered lambs screaming at night à la the eponymous heroine of *Silence of the Lambs*.

Why else would she name her cat Hannibal?

Despite her name, she doesn't look like Jodie Foster, the original Clarice, or Julianne Moore, the recast one. The actress she reminds me of most is Penelope Cruz, specifically her character in *Pirates of the Caribbean*, right down to the pirate-style shirt, waistcoat, and feather-capped hat that makes everyone think she's on her way to a steampunk convention.

Knowing my issues, Clarice blows me an air kiss, and I return it. She then joins me in the cereal-for-dinner meal, only in her case it's Captain Crunch—no doubt because she has a similar fashion sense to the mascot.

"Want to see something I've been working on?" she asks.

She let me perform for her for an hour yesterday, so it's only fair to let her practice on me. "Sure. Just as long as I don't have to touch anything until I'm done eating."

She takes out a deck of cards and gives them a real-looking shuffle. "Think of a card."

Wow. Only the best of the best card magicians begin a trick by asking you to merely *think* of a card. Most others have you pick one.

"I have one in mind," I say as I think of the Three of Spades.

"Now think of a number," she says.

I feel chills running down my body. If this is going where I think it's going, my mind will be blown.

"Got one," I say with great hesitation as I settle on seventeen.

"I'm going to put the cards face down on the table," she says. "When we get to your number, say stop."

No fucking way.

She starts to put the cards down one at a time.

I count until we get to my number and say, "Stop."

How could that be the card I merely thought of? No way. She's about to make things more complicated or something.

But no.

She turns the card over, and it's the fucking Three of Spades!

I feel an overwhelming sense of awe. It takes me back to my childhood, when I first got fooled by a magic trick and became hooked for life.

In the next moment, however, possible ways she might've done it pop into my head, ruining the moment. Maybe she primed me to think of that card and number? Or used some kind of subliminal messages to somehow *Inception* them into my brain?

But when? How?

I'm back to having no clue, and though she'd probably tell me how she did it if I asked, I don't want to do so—in part because I'd have to reveal some big secret of mine in reciprocity, but also because it's more fun not knowing.

Sometimes.

"That was amazing," I say. "You really are La Profesora."

She beams and lovingly gathers the cards before hiding them in her pocket.

The rumor among us, her roommates, is that she sleeps with a deck of cards in her hand and another under the pillow. If she had a vibrator in the shape of a deck of cards, I wouldn't be surprised either. If there is such a thing as a card-sexual, she is it.

"So," Clarice says, looking extremely uncomfortable. "This month is my turn to collect the rent money."

And just like that, any warm afterglow after her miracle is gone.

It's been a while since I've had anything resembling a paying gig.

"How bad is it this month?" I ask tentatively.

She sighs. "Without your share, we won't make the payment on time, and the landlord will evict us for sure. We've already been late five times."

Yep. As bad as I feared. My cereal suddenly tastes like the box it came in.

"I'll call my TV contacts," I say. "Maybe someone needs something?"

Even though the thing I want most is to perform myself, I've been earning some cash by consulting for successful magicians who are too busy to come up with new tricks for their repertoire.

"Thank you." She stands up. "I really like living with all of you guys."

I nod solemnly. My roommates are mostly magicians, but we also have a mentalist—which is pretty much the same thing—a juggler, a contortionist, and even a comedian. All are women I like a lot and don't want to see become homeless, especially because of *my* money problems.

She leaves, and I empty my bowl. Then I drop it in the dishwasher and run back to my room to make calls and send emails.

Hours later, I have to admit to a sense of impending doom.

There doesn't seem to be any work for a not-so-famous magician.

Maybe I should get a muggle job after all? Something like a stewardess, a bank teller, or a panda breeder? Are those hard to get?

One thing's for sure: given how my exposure therapy has been going, the world's oldest profession is out for me. Stripping wouldn't work either. The metal poles those brave women climb seem like they'd have more germs than the handrails in the NYC subway, and *those* cooties are on the verge of becoming sentient.

I sigh, loudly.

If we get evicted, I'll not only screw myself over but also the people closest to me outside of my family.

Speaking of family, maybe I could beg my sisters or parents for money?

No. No way. I've been cursed with too much pride. Besides, family money comes with too many strings attached. Octomom, for example, would demand I pay her back with a grandchild or two.

Yeah, no, thanks. I'll find some gig, even if it means teaching teenage boys the basic principles of magic or selling trick decks of cards in a magic shop.

Wait a second. I never checked to make sure Clarice's deck was regular. She always claims to use normal cards, but isn't that what she'd say regardless?

In any case, with teaching in mind, I navigate to my YouTube channel and look at the comments under my most popular video, the one where I "held my breath" under water for twenty minutes.

As you'd expect on the internet, ninety-nine percent of the comments are extremely rude, with the most popular topic being how fuckable I look in the swimsuit I wore for the stunt.

Yeah, that's what's interesting. My boobs, not my ability to be without oxygen. Not that I was without oxygen for real, but still.

The good news is there's still that one percent of

teens who want to know how I did what I did. For their sake, I record a video where I offer my magic tutoring services and post it in the hopes that someone's parents are rich.

Time to sleep. Except when I get in bed, I have trouble falling under—thoughts of eviction are interspersed with the memories of Tigger's eyes… and other parts. Like His Royal Hardness.

Hmm. Should I play with myself to get that off my mind?

To get in the mood, I put on some sexy music—"The Final Countdown" by Europe. Though this song was used in *Arrested Development* to mock magicians, I love it anyway.

Next, I take out my trusty dildo from my nightstand and give it a narrow-eyed look. *You're too small. And too plain. I'm suddenly in the mood for something much bigger… and more regal.*

Hey, I can picture the poor dildo replying. *It's not the size of the ocean that matters, but the vibrations of the waves.*

Nope.

I grab my laptop and email my twin, asking for a link to the website where her new best friend sells her toys. I want to buy the biggest dildo she's got.

After I click "send," I realize my mistake. I need rent money, and frivolous shopping—along with a lack of magic gigs—is why I'm in trouble in that department.

Oh, well. My tiny dildo will have to do.

Call me tiny one more time, and I'll short-circuit myself.

I turn on the vibration and think about Tigger's chiseled features.

Boom. I come in record time.

See. Tiny but mighty.

Basking in the orgasmic afterglow, I fall asleep quickly, but my dreams are strange. One reminds me of *Donnie Darko*, except instead of a giant rabbit, there's Batman's Joker. After that, I dream of Jake Gyllenhaal delivering a baby fathered by Heath Ledger.

Chapter Five

The first thing I do the next morning is take my laptop to the coffee shop from the other day.

It's *not* a ploy to bump into Tigger again. The internet here is faster than at my house, that's all.

Sadly, no job prospects have shown up despite all the calls and emails I've sent out.

Also, no Royal Hardness—not that I'm here for that reason.

Since I shouldn't spend my sparse money on eating out, I head home for a quick lunch and look for employment for the rest of the day.

The next day, I go to the coffee shop once more—again not in the hopes of bumping into Tigger.

I'm job searching. That's all.

Sadly, no leads on said jobs again. With a heavy heart, I apply for a waitressing position at the coffee shop and a few other restaurants nearby, only to be rejected on the spot due to lack of experience.

Damn my teenage self for spending all my summers practicing magic instead of getting the usual jobs.

I'm about to head home when I get a text from my twin:

Bella and I will be in your neck of the woods. Can we stop by?

I tell her that they can and hurry home.

By the time I've finished dinner, I've forgotten about my sister's text—that is, until someone knocks on my bedroom door.

"Yeah?" I open the door and see Harry standing there.

One of my favorite roomies, Harry reminds me of Meg Ryan in *When Harry Met Sally*, only with round spectacles. Unfortunately, she violently refuses to answer to Sally. Born Harriet, she claims she goes by Harry because of the famous magicians Harry Houdini and Harry Blackstone, but given her glasses, I strongly suspect it's actually because of Harry Potter.

Until I met her, the name Harry had brought to mind Octodad—since Harry is his first name—but it suits my roommate better. Not for the first time, I wonder if my grandparents realized that naming their son Harry with the last name of Hyman makes him sound like the virginal membrane of a yeti. Then again, he deserves it for naming my poor twin Holly, as Holly Hyman also sounds like the virginal membrane, only that of a maiden goddess. And don't even get me started on Blue and some of the other sextuplets.

If they weren't screwed up from jostling for space in one uterus, their names would surely do the trick.

"Someone's here for you." Harry sounds miffed about having to be the butler, so I make sure to thank her before I rush to the door.

There, waiting for me, is Holly, and with her is a woman who looks to have stepped out of a fashion magazine.

This must be Bella, my twin's new best friend.

Damn. She *is* as gorgeous as my sister has been saying. Reminds me of Angelina Jolie in *Maleficent*. Actually, since she's Russian, shouldn't she remind me of Angelina Jolie in—spoiler alert—*Salt*?

"You guys totally are twins," Bella says, her gaze darting from my face to my sister's.

Hmm. Zero accent.

"Yeah," Holly says. "Except she was raised by vampires."

I roll my eyes. "At least I wasn't raised at Downton Abbey… by Mary Poppins."

Bella grins at me. "Your sister *is* supercalifragilisticexpialidocious."

I return the grin. I can understand Holly's girl crush now. If Bella were a magician, she'd join Rasputina as a woman I'd sleep with—again, under a gun to the head scenario, of course.

"Give it to her," Holly whispers to her BFF.

Was it my earlier thought, or did that sound vaguely sexual?

"Ah, right." Bella brings forward the briefcase she's been holding. It looks a lot like the one that projected a golden glow when Jules opened it in *Pulp Fiction.*

Wait. Is the lid decorated with hand-drawn genitalia?

Before I can ask, Bella opens the case and I stare at the contents in morbid fascination.

Dildos.

Colorful dildos.

Bulbous dildos.

Thin dildos.

Small dildos.

Large dildos.

Huge dildos… and even a few obscenely ginormous.

Silicone dildos.

Glass dildos.

Metal dildos.

Even something that looks to be made of wood, but hopefully isn't, because splinters in the hooha do not sound fun at all.

Holly must mistake my expression because she sounds guilty as she says, "I mentioned your email to Bella, and she wanted to give you a nice selection."

"Right," I say, still scanning the phallic goods on display.

"They all vibrate," Bella says, her tone turning salesy. "All work with the Belka teledildonics app too, so you can have your boyfriend please you remotely."

If I had a boyfriend—and a very specific person comes to mind—I'd want to enjoy His Royal Hardness instead of a dildo, like the hoi polloi.

"Just pick already," my twin says, a light blush touching her cheeks.

Oh. She thinks having a woman I've never met bring this over is embarrassing for *her*?

Also, "pick" makes this whole thing sound like a card trick.

"Pick a dildo, any dildo."

Someone does.

"Now remember your dildo."

They memorize the dildo.

"Now let's hide the dildo in any woman in the audience."

They do.

With great gravitas, the magician locates the woman and pulls out the dildo without taking off her panties. "Is this your dildo?"

My twin looks at me worriedly. "I think her brain crashed from the indecision."

I shake my head and grab the dildo that's closest to His Royal Hardness in size and shape, only bright red. And hey, that might be the color of the Ruskovian flag. "This one. How much do I owe you?"

Bella closes the briefcase with a loud thud. "It's a gift."

"A gift?" Holding the dildo by the shaft, I wave it in the air. "Isn't this how you make your living?"

She winks at me. "If you feel like you owe me, you can tell me what you think of it. Like a beta tester."

Great. That should be a fun conversation.

Then an idea occurs to me.

I can pay her for the dildo with my art and get some priceless performance experience while I'm at it.

Holly frowns. I think she knows where my mind has gone—a feat of twin pseudo-telepathy. I can't blame her for not being enthused. She was there when I was only starting out as a magician, so she's sat through tedious tricks that are not at all like the fun masterpieces I perform nowadays.

"How about I show you some magic," I say to Bella in a voice that might be a touch too seductive.

Her eyes light up. "Seriously?"

"Yep." I usher them into the living room. "Give me a sec."

I rush to my room, leave the dildo there, and grab some props.

When I come back, I do a half hour show for Bella, who turns out to be the perfect spectator: oohing and ahhing at all the right moments and asking, "How did you do that?" like she really means it.

It doesn't take long before my roommates swoop in and begin to perform their own stuff for her, which Bella takes in like a kid at a candy factory on Halloween.

Even my jaded-with-magic twin seems to have a good time.

After Harry finishes performing her signature rope trick, Bella thanks us all profusely, gifts every one of the performers a dildo, and leaves with my twin in tow.

"*That's* what stood out to you?" I ask Clarice, nodding at the dildo she chose—the polished wooden one.

She shrugs. "Fits with my stage persona."

There might be some logic there. Pirates have peg legs that are made of wood, so I guess if they used dildos, said dildos would also be made of wood. Their users would no doubt call them woodies and scream "argh, matey, faster, faster" in the throes of passion.

I grin. "So you're going to add a wooden dildo to your act?"

She lifts her chin. "You have to *live* your stage persona at all times."

With that sage lesson from *The Prestige* firmly in our minds, we all scatter to our separate rooms.

I smile as I lock my door. To slightly paraphrase Forrest Gump's Mama, life is like a briefcase of dildos—you never know what you're going to get.

Before testing out the new toy, I decide to be good and check for job prospects one more time.

Yes! The email sitting in my inbox is from a form on my website, one that's only used by prospective clients or folks from the media, like Waldo.

I look at the "from" field and see the name listed as Anatolio, with no last name.

Hmm. Doesn't sound familiar.

I read the first line and cringe: "*Dear Amazing Hyman.*"

Stupid Waldo.

He covered my breath-holding performance for his magazine and dubbed me that way in his article, claiming that it was my stage name, which it wasn't until then. To this day, Waldo claims he didn't intend to be mean. Hyman is my last name and lots of magicians use the "Amazing" adjective in their stage names, like the Amazing Kreskin or the Amazing Randi.

Amazing Hyman is much worse, though. It makes me sound like a virgin superhero, or like something someone might say in an infomercial selling virgins as sex slaves or dragon sacrifices. The fact that I *am* a virgin (hymen intact or not) just makes it worse.

Fine. Whatever.

I read the rest of Anatolio's short message. He says that he saw my YouTube performance, was impressed, and now wants to discuss a related opportunity.

Intriguing. Especially because of the last line:

This is a serious proposal. Money is no object. Please set a time and place where we can meet.

He sounds like a man who gets what he wants.

I hit "reply" and ask him if he'd meet me at the

coffee shop I've been frequenting—a public place, in case he's a creep.

Before I can close my laptop, I get a reply:

How about tomorrow morning at 10?

That's before my lunch with Blue, but two hours should be enough to talk business so I agree.

Who is he?

I look up magicians by the name of Anatolio, but the search doesn't yield any results. Maybe he isn't a magician? Hey, not everyone is perfect. What's key is that I get good sleep tonight, so I can wow this potential client into a large fee tomorrow.

Since a liaison with a dildo helped me sleep the night before, I decide to use the same strategy tonight. Plus, I'm dying to test out my new silicone friend.

First things first. I sterilize the dildo as well as I can, then put a condom on it, just in case.

When I get back to bed, I glance at my old dildo guiltily.

Oh, don't worry about me. Just let my batteries run out and toss me in the garbage. I never expected loyalty from someone as shallow as you.

With a shrug, I look at the new dildo.

Very nice. Bella is a great designer. I like it so much, in fact, that I decide to give it a name. If I'm going to anthropomorphize my toys, I might as well go all the way.

How about Royal Hardness?

No. That's taken. I'm thinking the Regent.

How about Prince Regent?

Done. I download the necessary app to enable Prince Regent's vibration.

As I get myself off, I try not to think of Tigger, especially of his hazel eyes, his broad shoulders, or his—

Never mind.

I let myself fully visualize the Ruskovian prince and come with a bang before falling asleep with a goofy grin on my face.

Chapter Six

I'm at the coffee shop ten minutes early, since the last thing I want is for my roommates and me to get evicted because of my tardiness.

Grabbing a table outside, I sip my iced latte and look at the passersby.

"Hello," says a familiar sexy male voice.

I look up and nearly choke on my latte.

It's Tigger in all of his Most Interesting Man in the World glory. Unbidden, the words of the commercials come to me: "*He once had an awkward moment, just to see how it feels. In museums, he is allowed to touch the art. His lovemaking has been detected by a seismograph.*"

Actually, he's even hotter than I remember, probably because he's dressed much nicer without his dogs around.

His tiger eyes glint deviously. "Fancy meeting you here."

I jump to my feet and execute a mocking curtsy. "Your Royal Heinie. It's an honor and a privilege."

He smirks. "Sounds like I've made an impression on you."

I roll my eyes theatrically. "Easy there, *Tigger*."

"See." The smirk turns cocky. "You've asked your sister about me."

Crap. He's got me. I blame hormones.

Suddenly feeling thirsty, I take a huge gulp of my latte. Can you get dehydrated if your lady parts produce too much juice? Asking for a friend.

He sits at my table.

"What are you doing?" I ask sternly.

"Joining you. Obviously."

Unbelievable. "How big is your fucking ego?"

He glances down. "Everything is proportional."

Great. Now I have the image of His Royal Hardness in my mind's eye. And my mind's mouth.

"That seat is taken."

There. I'm proud of how steady my voice is.

His eyebrow lifts. "By whom?"

I narrow my eyes. "None of your business."

"Oh, I think it's very much my business."

The nerve! "Seriously. Leave."

He crosses his arms over his chest. "Where is Waldo?"

I can't bring myself to get mad this time. If someone gave me a dollar every time I used that exact phrase to tease my friend, rent wouldn't be a problem.

Still, I keep my tone stern. "He's at home, not that it's any of your business either. Where are your dogs?"

"Also at home. I don't take them to business meetings." He looks at me pointedly.

Business meetings.

My fingers feel icy despite the gloves.

He can't be.

Can he?

"Ah." This time, his smirk is self-satisfied—like that of a cat who finally ate an annoying canary. "You're beginning to catch on."

My molars grind together. "What's your real name? It's not Tigger, obviously."

"How rude of me." He extends his hand. "Anatolio Cezaroff, at your service."

Anatolio. As in the name from the "client's" email.

In stunned silence, I shake his hand.

Even though there's a glove between us, a zing spreads through my body, swirls around, and settles in my nether regions.

Damn. If one of those *Predator* creatures were to look at me with their heat vision, I'd be lit up like a horny Christmas tree.

With great effort, I snatch my hand away. "Why the farce?"

He cocks his head. "Whatever do you mean?"

"Why didn't you say we've met when you emailed me? Do you even have business to discuss, or is this some joke?"

"Oh, I need your unique skills, I assure you," he says.

Either his poker face is the best I've seen, or he's telling the truth.

"Whatever it is, it had better be magic related."

His eyes glint. "It is."

Hmm, okay. "It will cost you… a lot."

"I told you, money is no object."

I take in a deep breath and let it out slowly. If it weren't for my dire financial situation, I'd dismiss him outright, but as things stand, I need to see if he could actually be a path to avoid eviction. "Okay. If we're going to be working together, what do I call you? Anatolio? Your Majesty? Assh—"

"You can call me whatever you want… except Nate."

I grin despite myself. "How about Tony? You know, like the tiger?"

"If that means you'll work with me, be my guest—though I prefer simply Tigger." He leans in. "That's what people close to me call me."

Oh, yeah. I want to be close to him. In fact, I want to throw myself at him, head first.

No, vagina first.

I swallow my drool. "Tigger works. Now, what is it that you want?"

He looks longingly at my cup.

I heave a sigh. "Do you want to get a coffee first?"

He nods.

"Then go," I say in an imperious tone before realizing I might sound like his mom.

"You want a refill?" he asks.

When I shake my head, he strides off.

I take my phone out and type "Anatolio Cezaroff" into Google.

Wow. My sister wasn't kidding.

Besides being a prince, he's famous for his stunts. There are mentions of racing (motorcycle, car, and speedboat), tightrope walks, rock climbing (with and without gear), extreme surfing, and snowboarding.

Maybe he *is* the guy from those commercials. Maybe he "once won the Tour-de-France but was disqualified for riding a unicycle."

He's coming back with a cup, so I quickly hide my phone.

He gracefully folds his muscular body into his seat and takes a sip as I watch his lips hungrily. "Believe it or not, I came across you online before we met," he says. "I was searching 'how to hold my breath for a long time' and saw your YouTube video. I wasn't internet-stalking you, specifically."

I'll go with *not* believing that, but I let him keep talking.

"I'm not sure if your sister mentioned it, but I like to do fun excursions from time to time, and my next one is a free dive into Dyrka," he says. "Have you heard of it?"

I shake my head.

Fun excursion? It *is* just like in those ads: *"He*

played a game of Russian Roulette with a fully loaded magnum, and won."

"Dyrka is a famous underground lake in my homeland," he explains. "Scuba gear is forbidden there. Any of this ring a bell?"

I shake my head again. "I only know two things about Ruskovia: my favorite magician lives there, and one of their princes is full of himself."

His smirk is back. "You've met my brother Kaz?"

"No. Why? Is he even more full of himself than you?"

He sips his coffee while I try to be subtle about my fixation on his lips. "Kaz is short for Kazimir," he says, "which means 'a great and mighty destroyer of peace.' Now add in the fact that he owns the biggest chain of hotels in the world and that he's a prince."

"What does the name Anatolio mean?" I ask in the snarkiest tone I can manage. "I bet it's 'Roses stop to smell *him*.'"

"No," he says, and if he realizes I just quoted a Dos Equis ad, he doesn't show it. "My name means 'one who comes from the East.'"

"Is that how you got your nickname—Tigger? Lots of tigers in the East."

"How about we get back to the business at hand," he says. "In case it wasn't obvious, I want to free dive in the Dyrka."

"Free dive. As in 'dive without breathing gear.'"

"Exactly," he says. "So you can see why I've come to you."

No. "Yes," I lie. I have no clue how I'm supposed to help with him with something like that.

Then it hits me.

My video. He saw me hold my breath for twenty minutes and thinks I can teach him how to do that for the free dive.

"I want to hold my breath for ten minutes," he says, confirming my suspicion. "I want you to be my breathing coach."

I take a huge gulp of my latte to give myself a chance to gather my thoughts.

There's a problem.

A big one.

I have no clue how to genuinely hold my breath, at least for any longer than ninety seconds. That video wasn't real. I mean, I was in the water and all that, but I was merely creating an illusion of not breathing for twenty minutes. I wasn't hardcore enough to do it for real, like David Blaine claims to have done.

My methodology was similar to the way the Masked Magician did it on his TV show: a breathing tube concealed in the water, a hidden oxygen tank, and a lot of acting. What made my version better was that it didn't require me to have a creepy mask on, and that I was using my own bathing-suit-clad body as misdirection instead of objectifying an assistant.

It was a stunt to impress Waldo's newspaper, nothing more. I got the idea while watching *Now You See Me*—specifically, the scene where Isla Fisher was "eaten by the piranhas."

I didn't want to even think about doing that stunt for real because of how dangerous it is. Doing a real stunt is how the wife of Hugh Jackman's character died in *The Prestige*. Okay, that's fiction, but lots of real magicians have died doing water escapes. And I don't want to die yet.

It's too sad to drown as a virgin.

"So," he says. "Will you do it?"

I audibly swallow my drink as my inner magician awakes.

Who cares if you faked it? Let him think you did it for real. That's fooling him twice. You need rent money, and you'll be able to brag that a prince is your client.

He gives me a panty-incinerating smile. "Just say yes."

"Yes," I parrot, though I'm not sure what I'm agreeing to—teaching him or becoming Mrs. Tigger. No, *Princess Tiggress.*

"Great," he says. "How about we have our first lesson at Chelsea Piers Fitness? I'll get you access."

"Why?" I ask.

He frowns. "They have a pool."

I shudder. "A public pool? Why don't we save ourselves time and just dunk our heads in the nearest toilet?"

His frown deepens. "You have a problem with pools?"

"Not pools. My problem is with cryptosporidium, giardiasis, norovirus, shigellosis, legionella, E—"

"I get the picture," he says, and I have to give him

credit. He looks utterly serious, whereas usually people seem mocking after I (quite reasonably) explain such dangers to them. "How about if the pool were private?"

I shrug. "Provided it had fresh water and proper chlorination, I think I'd be comfortable letting *you* in it."

His smirk reappears. "So you're worried about *my* well-being?"

"Don't let it go to your head. I need to keep you alive until I get paid."

"Yeah. Sure. And it sounds like you're not going into the water with me?"

Is it possible to both want and dread the exact same scenario? A part of me pictures myself skinny-dipping with him, and that part is seconds away from touching herself under the table. Another, much more sane part pictures myself catching every pool-dwelling bacteria and virus known to science and shudders.

"Not a chance," I say. "You'd have to fill a pool with sterile water for me to consider getting inside. As soon as anyone—no matter how royal their blood—enters the same water, it's no longer sterile."

He nods. "I'll talk to my brother about this."

My brows furrow. "What does your brother have to do with anything?"

"I'm staying at Kaz's hotel. There's a penthouse next to mine with a small pool. I'm sure he'll let me move in there, and he'll refresh the water for us as needed."

A penthouse in a hotel? But of course, he's a fucking prince.

My financial prospects are looking better and better.

"What do you say?" he asks, hazel eyes gleaming. "Should we do this?"

Chapter Seven

Great question.

Should we?

Should I?

For one thing, I desperately need the money. Also, training him sounds kind of hot. It'd be like taming a tiger, so I'd basically be like Siegfried & Roy. Well, hopefully not *exactly* like them. Things didn't go too well for Roy at the end.

Unfortunately, there's also that bit about me not knowing what the hell I'm doing. What if I teach him wrong and he ends up drowning?

"I get it," he says. "You can't commit without talking about compensation."

To give myself some more time to think, I take a big sip of my latte.

"How about this?" He takes out a business card and writes something on it.

When I see the amount, I do a spit-take—not one of the best negotiation techniques.

With a grin, he wipes away the droplets of latte I managed to get on his cheek. "I get it. It was an insulting number. How about I double it?"

Thank goodness I don't have any more latte to choke on. Money aside, I can't believe how cool he's being about those droplets on his face. Had our roles been reversed, I'd probably be guilty of murder by now. Or is it voluntary manslaughter when it's a crime of passion?

"Was that in American dollars?" I manage to ask.

He nods.

I resist the urge to fan myself.

"Okay," he says. "I'll triple it."

My eyes widen.

"Fine, quadruple, but that's my final offer," he says, completely deadpan.

Alrighty then. My earlier moral quandary seems as distant as a divorced couple after a bitter custody battle. Most people would punch their grandmother for this kind of money, have anal with their enemy, and maybe even lick handrails in the NYC subway.

He frowns. "I mean it. Quadruple is as high as I'll go, but since you're playing hard ball, how about a bonus upon completion of the training? Completely at my discretion, of course."

"Fine," I say with a confidence I don't feel. "I'll do it."

"Great." There goes another feline-eating-a-canary expression/smirk (or FECES for short). "Any training you can impart here and now?"

Crap. I'll actually have to figure out some sort of curriculum for him.

But what?

I'll deal with that later. For now, I decide to bluff by teaching him the calming breathing I do during the desensitization exercises—a pretty useful skill.

I launch into it, explaining how he should inhale with his nose and let the air go into his belly instead of his chest. Midway into it, he raises a hand, like a dutiful student.

Paradoxically, my own breathing grows shallower. "Yes?"

"Sorry to interrupt," he says, and sounds like he means it. "I already know everything there is to know about diaphragmatic breathing."

"You do?"

It's odd to picture him using an exercise to battle stress and anxiety. He doesn't seem like the type to be fazed by much.

"Yep," he says. "Learned as part of scuba diving training."

Oh. I didn't know it could help with scuba diving. But hey, at least I accidentally sound like I know what I'm talking about. Yay.

This just might be my greatest illusion to date.

"Anything else you can teach me right now?" he asks.

Crap. I'm out of tricks. I guess I'll have to fake it before I make it.

"Let me see your belly breathing first and foremost," I say with all the air of someone who knows what she's talking about.

"Sure." He leans back in his chair, closes his eyes, and begins to breathe slowly and deliberately.

I fan myself and resist various creepy urges, like getting close to his neck and taking a good sniff.

A deliciously serene expression settles on Tigger's features, one that Buddha would be proud of… unless Buddha was aroused by it instead, like I am.

Hmm.

When I learned this technique myself, one important tip was to put a hand on my chest and belly, and then make sure only the one on the belly moves.

I figure if I'd learned with a trainer, she would've done that with *her* hands.

Yep. This isn't a creepy urge to touch him. Not at all.

"I'm going to put my hands on you," I whisper. "Okay?"

His jaw tenses and his breathing catches as he nods.

"Busted," I say sternly. "You were just chest breathing. Stay with the belly breath no matter what happens."

I can see him battling to get the serene expression back, which is when I put my left hand on his chest, and the right one on his belly.

Holy fucking muscles.

His pecs are rock hard under my left palm, and there's a sixpack under my right.

I'm not ashamed to admit that this moment will feature prominently when I play with Prince Regent tonight.

Crap.

Must focus.

He's breathing through his chest again—as in, shallowly—and I revel in the knowledge that my touch has impacted him.

"I should be feeling *this* rise," I say as I basically fondle his abs.

He gulps in a few forced breaths, and his earlier serenity returns.

"Try counting to two on the inhale, then to four on the exhale."

He does this expertly.

I have him do a different ratio—mostly because I don't want to pull my hands away.

He does every version of different counts like a champ, and much better than I can.

I let him just breathe for a few more minutes. Then, reluctantly, I remove my hands. "You're pretty good at that."

He opens his eyes and sits more upright. "Thanks."

"Still," I say. "I want you to practice this every day for forty minutes."

It can't hurt, can it?

"Will do," he says. "Anything else?"

"No," I say. "Don't want to overwhelm you on your first day."

And I have no clue what else to teach him, so there's that.

"I don't want you to go soft on me," he says.

I glance at his crotch, and my eyes bulge at the bulge I spot there. "If I said that to you, you'd be insulted."

His eyes gleam. "Oh, don't worry, myodik, we'd never go soft on you."

Was that the royal "we," or "Tigger and His Royal Hardness" kind of "we?" Instead of asking that, I go for, "Is honey a masculine noun in Ruskovian?"

"Nope. You're thinking of Russian." He grimaces. "It's a barbaric language."

"Good," I say. "For a second there, I thought you were implying I look mannish."

He drags his gaze along my every curve, and his voice turns husky. "Mannish is one thing you aren't."

I'm getting suicidally horny—on the verge of jumping his bones right here and now, germs be damned.

Can lust conquer all?

Nope. Even if it can—and that's an "if" the size of His Royal Hardness—I shouldn't act on it, and not just because we're in a public place. I'm about to make some much needed dough, and introducing sex into that equation could ruin everything.

"Hey." He makes magnetic eye contact with me,

further chipping away at my resolve. "I didn't mean to make you uncomfortable."

I shake my head in the hopes of clearing it of stupid hormones. "Don't worry. You didn't."

His lips curve into that wicked smirk. "Good. Now, I've been thinking a lot about how you stole my belt, and I think I have it figured out."

I raise an eyebrow. "Enlighten me."

"Misdirection," he says in a self-satisfied tone.

I scoff. "That's your genius answer? That's like saying 'you did it by being sneaky.'"

"Yeah. That too. Sneaky. Exactly."

"That's not an explanation."

"Then what is?" he asks really fast.

I grin mischievously. "Nice try."

He readjusts his belt. "I bet you can't do it again."

"Another nice try. Doing a trick once is entertainment, doing it twice is education."

Having said that, I resolve here and now that I'll steal his belt again anyway—just at a more opportune moment for me.

"That's convenient," he says.

I shrug.

"I bet you can't fool me again—with another trick, that is."

I resist the urge to ask him to marry me. A challenge like that is what I live for. "What happens when I do fool you?"

He leans in. "I'll do anything you want."

If the idea was to make it harder for me to concentrate on magic—or breathing—mission accomplished. I'm picturing him doing all sorts of pleasantly naughty things to me, the tamest of which are a foot massage (he can wear gloves), a video of him jerking off for my viewing pleasure, me using him as my sexy assistant—

No. He's a client.

It has to be something professional.

"How about you wear a shirt that says 'I want to be a mermaid?'" I rub my hands together like a supervillain. "And jeans and underwear embroidered with pictures of mermaids."

"Deal," he says and rakes his gaze over me again. "What will you do for me if I guess how this trick works?"

Fuck me. Now I'm blushing like a maiden.

Well, strictly speaking, I *am* a maiden.

Is he smirking again?

Grr.

If I were really magic, I'd use my power to make my cheeks normal again.

No. Scratch that. If I were really magic, I'd poof all the germs out of existence and have my way with Tigger right here and now.

Would it be consensual if I used magic to make him into it?

"Cat got your tongue?" he asks.

"No," I say. "Another feline. Big. Stripy. Rhymes with Geiger."

"Are you saying that a tiger got your tongue? Or Tigger? As in me? Also, what's a Geiger?"

I look down my nose at him. "A Geiger counter measures radiation. Read a book once in a while."

He tsk-tsks. "You never answered. What do I get if I see through your trick?"

"Same thing as if you don't—free entertainment. Take it or leave it."

"Fine," he says. "Trick me."

What should I do?

I have a few things on me. All magicians do. But I want to do something bigger, something to really blow his brain.

Hmm, did that sound vaguely sexual?

In any case, I envy some of my roomies. Clarice would pull out a deck of cards right about now, and Harry always has enough rope for a trick or a spontaneous BDSM scene, whereas I have to improvise.

Could I make one of the cups disappear? Change coffee to some other drink? Vanish a coin, then have it reappear in a sugar packet?

Nah. Not good enough.

A sugar packet inside his pants?

No, that's too similar to stealing the belt.

Then it hits me.

A classic.

Letting my stage persona settle over my features, I speak with as much gravitas as I can muster. "Go into the coffee shop and grab a spoon. A metal one, not plastic."

Looking intrigued, he does as I say and comes back with a spoon in hand.

"Here." He hands it to me.

I banish the images of us spooning and grab the utensil.

Putting the spoon at my eye level, I instruct him to watch.

He stares unblinkingly, like he's trying to see my soul through my eyes. That, or he might be channeling another Dos Equis commercial, the one where he *"once won a staring contest with his own reflection."*

When I feel like I've built enough mysterious tension, I let the illusion unfold—and he sees the spoon bend.

"Wow," he mutters as a look of absolute and utter awe appears on his face, giving him an almost boyish appearance.

Pride swells within me. It took me a while to make this illusion look exactly like that scene in *The Matrix*.

"How did you do that?" he asks, his eyes hypnotizing the now-crooked spoon.

I hand him the spoon to examine. "Does that mean I win?"

"Yeah," he says. "You win. Now tell me."

"It's very simple." I lean in closer. "There is no spoon."

He blows out a breath. "Fine. You got me twice. I feel like the mermaid clothes aren't enough anymore. You have to let me buy you lunch today."

"I'm meeting my sister for lunch," I say, almost on autopilot.

"Oh," he says. "Of course."

Is that disappointment on his face?

I clear my throat. "Speaking of that lunch, I should head out soon."

"I understand," he says, and this time, his face is expressionless. "Can we exchange numbers before you go?"

I pick up the business card he wrote his first offer on. "Is this your cell?"

He nods.

I input his digits and save him into my contacts as "His Royal Heinie," then text him so he has my number.

His phone dings.

As usual in this situation, I pay close attention to his hands. Being a magician, I make it a point to notice and commit to memory the pin codes of everyone I know. This way, if I get the chance to steal their phone at some point, I can show off my "power" to unlock it "magically." It also lets me do mentalism tricks such as "think of a person you spoke to recently" and then announcing the name of the person I saw in their recent call history. That last one almost gave Waldo an aneurism when I did it for him a few weeks ago.

Tigger types in the numbers pretty fast, but I think I got them anyway.

He then swipes across the screen, making my clit

jealous. "Got you. Thanks. I'll let you know when I'm available for the next lesson."

"Take your time," I say and mean it. If he procrastinates, it'll give me time to work out some sort of a lesson plan.

He stands up.

I do as well.

He looks on the verge of saying something.

I debate if I should get closer as if to hug him and then steal his belt again, but he doesn't give me the opportunity. With a courtly bow, he turns and leaves.

As I jump into a cab, I can't help but wonder if he left a bit too abruptly.

If so, why? Was he upset I couldn't do lunch?

Wait a second. Was that him asking me on a date?

No. Can't be. He's a hot prince and I'm a broke mess. Why would he want to date me?

Not that it matters. If, by some miracle, he did ask me out, it's a good thing I—however accidentally—refused.

He's a client, and I need the money.

Even if he weren't, I've been avoiding relationships in order to focus on my career. Which, if all goes well, will involve traveling for my shows, and travel isn't conducive to a relationship. Neither is my dislike of germs, and he's a manwhore who's probably teeming with them.

Also, he's a prince. That means he is—as my twin's favorite *Downton Abbey* characters would put it—above my station. He might not even be able to date a commoner apart from a short fling due to his royal duties. And he's probably in the public spotlight, hounded by the paparazzi and all that.

Wait, actually, that last one would be fine with me. The publicity might be helpful for my magic career.

But no. Dating is a bad idea for me in general, and with Tigger, it would almost certainly be a disaster. All the reasons I just listed aside, I have a sneaky suspicion that if I did go down this path, I might catch one of the scariest diseases I can think of.

Feelings.

The cab stops and I sprint to the restaurant Blue has picked out.

Oh, hell no.

The sign next to the door chills my blood.

Jerking my phone from my purse, I type out a message to my sister:

Where are you? There is no way I'm eating at—or even entering—this restaurant.

Chapter Eight

Almost there, Blue replies. *What's the problem?*

I stare at the sign again, fighting nausea before furiously texting: *Are you fucking kidding me? If I wanted to kill myself, I'd overdose on sleeping pills.*

A yellow cab pulls up to the curb and my sister leaps out of it, an exasperated expression on her face.

Since my sextuplet sisters are monozygotic, they look as identical to each other as Holly and I do, which is to say same faces but different hairdos, body fat distributions, and the like. There's also quite a bit of resemblance between my twin and I and the sextuplets. By the luck of genetic dice, we look more alike than most sisters. Which might explain why Blue also reminds me of Cate Blanchett, only in her role in *Heaven*, where she sports a buzzcut.

"What's wrong with this place?" Blue asks.

I point at the sign. "That."

She sighs. "Yeah. That's a 'B.'"

The New York Health Department inspects restaurants and gives them a grade between "A" and "C." "A" means the place received between zero and thirteen points for sanitary violations, while "B" means fourteen to twenty-seven violations. In real terms, a "B" translates into rats choking on cockroaches, and monkeys from the zoo showing up to throw feces at the customers. A "C" grade means twenty-eight violations or more, so I picture the inside of those restaurants as a post-apocalyptic landscape with plague-infested, mutated rats eating the staff, the customers cannibalizing each other, and food that comes back to zombie-like life.

I narrow my eyes at her. "How would *you* feel if I dragged you to Chick-fil-a?"

She shudders.

"What about KFC?"

She pales.

"Popeyes. Church's Chicken. Zax—"

"Enough," she says. "Let's find you a restaurant with an 'A.'"

Yep. Blue's fear of birds extends to the fried variety.

I pull up my phone. "Give me a moment."

I don't trust even 'A'-graded places, which is why I begged Blue to write an app for me that parses the raw inspection data that the city of New York provides to everyone for free. I give the app my location, and it gives me a nearby restaurant with a zero score.

Aha. A place called Planet of the Crepes.

Promising.

I check to make sure they don't serve any bird stuff and find that they don't. They even make the crepes without eggs.

"What do you think?" I show my sister the menu.

She sighs theatrically. "Let's go."

A quick cab ride later, we walk into Planet of the Crepes and I look around approvingly. The crepes are made in front of everyone, and the guy who makes them washes the crepe maker between each round and wears new gloves.

This might be the safest lunch I've had out in a while.

Blue orders first, choosing a savory crepe with everything.

I inwardly cringe. Whenever I watch the news, I keep an ear out for foods that give people foodborne illnesses, so I can strike them from my diet. And at least a couple of the fillings in Blue's crepe are on this "never eat" list. I don't tell her that, though, because she has explicitly forbidden me from doing so.

Which I understand. It was bad enough that I told my siblings Santa doesn't exist—magicians are skeptics by nature, so I sleuthed out that jolly conspiracy theory very early in life. I also ruined the tooth fairy for them. Speaking of which, what kind of a twisted mind came up with that story? A supernatural flying being interested in teeth? Sorry, the teeth of *children*, because that makes it so much better. Does she keep them in a nightmarish pile somewhere, or does she eat them? And if it's the latter, how hard are the tooth fairy's teeth?

Anyway, I worry that if I ruin ham and other comfort foods for my sisters, they might finally lynch me—as they almost did after Santa-gate.

When it's my turn to order, I get the sweet crepe with fillings that come straight out of a jar, like Nutella and honey.

"Do you want vanilla sugar?" the guy asks.

I almost shout, "Fuck no!" before managing a more moderate, "No, thanks."

There's a type of vanilla flavoring that comes from the anal excretions of beavers. It's the reason I'm very diligent when it comes to researching vanilla-flavored products before I put them anywhere near my mouth. And why I never drink Swedish schnapps.

When our food is ready, Blue insists on paying for us both. Carrying our crepes, we grab a table in the corner.

I cut into my crepe and look at her expectantly.

"What?" she says, sounding defensive.

"You know." I fork the bite of crepe into my mouth and resist moaning as the rich, sweet flavor explodes on my tastebuds.

"Know what?"

I put down my fork. "You paid." I fold one finger. "You wanted to share a meal instead of going for the usual video call." I fold a second finger. "Either you're about to share a big secret or you need a favor."

"Fine." She stabs her crepe with a fork. "I need your help."

I can't help a villainous grin. "With what?"

She slices the crepe in half. "I want to learn how to play—and cheat in—poker."

Wow. That's not exactly asking me to teach her how to pick locks or bend spoons, but close.

"That's a big ask," I say. "You know how I feel about breaking the magicians' code."

She sighs. "I figured you'd say that."

"I demand to know why."

She sighs more theatrically. "I figured you'd say that too." She pulls out her fancy phone, brings up an image, and shows it to me.

I wolf-whistle as I stare at the screen.

The picture looks like a setup for some sort of porn. A rare, made-exclusively-for-women kind of porn.

A group of very attractive men sit around a table in some kind of sauna, wearing only towels and—in the case of one—aviator sunglasses. Sweat is beading on their chiseled faces and their firm muscles are flexing, clearly tense from concentration.

The testosterone levels in that room would kill a horse.

Perhaps the oddest part of the tableau is that they're holding playing cards. That, combined with the chips on the table and my sister's desire to learn about poker, suggests to me that's the game they're playing.

I wonder what Clarice would think of this image? Could the sight of so many gorgeous men holding playing cards be a gateway out of her card-sexualness?

Maybe. Or it could go the other way. If a woman stares at this image long enough, she might want to buy a deck of cards. It might even be happening to me already. Why else do I so desperately wish to see Tigger naked and holding cards in that room?

My sister pulls the phone back.

I look up. "I've heard of hot yoga, but never of Bikram poker."

She smiles. "It's funny you say that. That's known as the Hot Poker Club."

I chuckle. "The dudes *are* hot. I'd let any one of them poke me." This is obviously a lie, but I've been keeping up the pretense ever since I made myself sound like a sex goddess to my sisters back in high school. "In fact, the only way this image could be any hotter is if their *pokers* weren't hidden by those lucky towels."

She frowns. "One of those pokers is off limits."

"Got it," I say. "The first rule of Hot Poker Club is 'keep your grubby hands off your sister's boytoy.'"

That also happens to be a family motto of sorts among the eight of us.

Her frown disappears. "And the second rule is—"

In unison we say, "Keep your grubby hands off your sister's boytoy.'"

I grin at her. "Which one?"

She points at the guy in sunglasses.

"Not bad at all," I say, peering at the premium man candy. He vaguely reminds me of Ryan Reynolds, but with some Slavic features. "So, what's the plan? You learn to cheat and then beat him in a steamy game of strip poker?"

She rolls her eyes. "Will you help me?"

I bite my lip. "I can, but not in the way you think."

The frown is back. "Explain."

I do jazz hands to showcase my gloves. "Card manipulation is difficult when you wear these all the time. To make matters worse, people always want to touch the magician's cards, so—and I'm ashamed to admit this—I'm not so great at that branch of magic."

"What?" She looks at me like the Ace of Spades has just appeared on my forehead. "What about those millions of card tricks you've made me watch?"

I shrug. "A famous magician once said 'card tricks are the poetry of magic.' I obviously know some. We all do, but I'm not an expert—and especially not when it comes to card cheating."

She narrows her eyes. "You made it sound like you'd help."

"And I will." It's my turn to pull out my phone. "I know someone who might be one of the best in the world at what you need." I pull up a video of Clarice doing one of her poker cheating demonstrations. "See?"

As my sister watches, her gaze turns calculating.

"Put me in touch with her," she says when the video is over.

"I'll need a favor in return," I say.

She scoffs. "A favor for just putting me in touch with someone?"

"Does a realtor not deserve her fee for connecting a buyer and a seller? Does a travel agent not deserve—"

"You know I could find her on my own if I wanted, right? I've seen her face and I know she's in your inner circle."

That's true. My sister works for the government agency that likes to listen to everyone's cell phone conversations—or as she says, No Such Agency—so she can locate someone with even less data, and probably listen to all their phone calls after that.

"Trust me," I say with as much confidence as I can muster. "You'll want me to put in a good word."

In truth, though, she'd have Clarice as soon as she said the word "poker."

"Fine." Blue forks a piece of her crepe into her mouth. "What do you want?"

I give her my most devious grin. "I want you to write me another app."

Another eyeroll. "I can't believe you need my help with that. You have the highest IQ in the family. Why don't you just learn how to code?"

Yeah, that's another trick I've pulled on them. Scientists have been studying my sextuplet sisters since they were born, looking for similarities and differences in all sorts of metrics, and my twin and I have occasionally been included in that research, which has involved IQ tests and such. So I cheated on one of those tests. Well, not cheated exactly—I just studied for the test, while my sisters didn't. So I scored way higher than I would've otherwise. Though everyone thinks these tests measure only aptitude, it's not true.

"You might not even need coding for this one," I say placatingly. "I want to mess with people's autocorrect."

Her grin makes us look even more alike. "By 'people,' you mean creatures with the last name of Hyman."

"Yep. And my roommates."

She scratches her chin.

"Can't you hack into their phones and create some shortcuts?" I ask. "Turn *coke* into *cock*, *conference* into *cunnilingus*, and so on?"

"Fine," she says. "It's a deal. But only because I might enjoy this particular project."

"Great. I hope that means you'll help me with one more thing."

She lifts an eyebrow. "Two favors now?"

"This one is trivial for someone with your resources," I say. "I want to learn all there is to know about a guy."

Her eyebrows rise. "A guy?"

"Yeah, and no questions about him either." Tigger

is my property, and I'm not ready to share him with anyone yet, verbally or otherwise.

"Fine. Text me his name, and I'll see what I can dig up on my way back." She takes a giant bite of her crepe, and I follow her example.

"So," I say when I swallow. "Are there any women in the Hot Poker Club?"

She shrugs. "Not that I know of."

"Not allowed? Or are they rare?"

This is a bit of a sensitive topic for me. Magic is a male-dominated field, and I'd felt both lonely and unwelcome until I met my wonderful roommates.

Blue is either very thoughtful or is carefully chewing her food. "I think guys are just more into poker."

"That sucks. A woman in that steam room is exactly what the suffrage movement was fighting for. Time to break the steam ceiling."

She lifts her fork like a shot glass. "Hear, hear. I gladly offer myself as tribute."

It would be more customary to use a virgin—say, me—as tribute, but I don't mention this. Instead, I steer the conversation into gossiping about the rest of our family.

Eventually, we get to the topic of Octoparents being in town and demanding a get-together.

"I'd bring some guy if I were you," Blue says sagely. "Even if he's your gay friend. It'll make things so much easier. That's what I hope to do."

She's right. My twin took her new boyfriend to

her (actually my) lunch and claims it helped greatly, even though she ended up throwing *me* under the bus in the process.

Whom can I bring?

Waldo?

Would they even believe us as a couple?

I know whom I *want* to bring… to the get-together with parents and everywhere else, even a gynecologist appointment.

Tigger.

Hmm. Is it too late to tack on a favor as an extra fee for my tutoring services?

Nah. Bringing him is a bad idea. Octomom is not a young woman anymore, and exposure to such undiluted male hotness might just make her poor heart give out.

Blue nods knowingly. "You're thinking of the guy you asked me to look up?"

"Yep."

She finishes her food, wipes her hands, and takes her laptop out of her shoulder bag. "What's his name? I'll do a quick search for you right now."

"Anatolio Cezaroff," I say.

She types that in, and her eyebrows furrow.

Oh, crap. I really hope she's not about to tell me that she's hacked him and learned that he has a venereal disease.

Or worse… a wife.

Chapter Nine

She looks up from her screen, eyes wide. "He's a prince."

Whew. Is that what's gotten her riled up?

"Well, yeah."

"A real prince?" She runs her hand over her buzzcut.

"No. Not real. He's actually a non-violent version of the Terminator, sent back in time to sneak crushed birth control pills into Sarah Connor's food."

With a huff, she looks back at her screen and begins typing away. After a few minutes, she looks back up. "Did you google him?"

"A little."

She gestures at the screen. "I'm not sure I should get you anything beyond that, especially since there's so much public info available. His more private data looks to be protected by his government, and I don't want to create an international incident by poking around. Now if Ruskovia ever harbors a terrorist group, *then* we can talk."

"Sure. Great plan. Let's hope the terrorists infiltrate his country, just so you can stalk him."

She closes her laptop and shoves it back into her bag. "You're the one who wants to stalk him."

I slice my crepe a little too forcefully. "At least I don't carry a naked picture of him in my phone."

She stabs what's left of her food even more forcefully but doesn't say anything.

"Can we change the subject?" I ask.

She gladly agrees, and we get back to gossiping about the family. With eight sisters, we've got this almost to an art form.

When the lunch is over, I take a cab home and google Tigger on the way back.

Mostly, the articles just add to the ever-growing list of his adventures, of which I find his climb of Mount Everest most impressive. I've never climbed a mountain in my life, but it's on my bucket list—along with climbing Tigger's Royal Hardness.

Some of the links are to videos of him doing his stunts, so I watch those greedily.

Interesting. A lot of the time there's an expression of awe on his face, the very same one I saw during the spoon bend trick.

I read more articles until I stumble upon one that makes my heart squeeze painfully in my chest.

Tigger got injured during a base jump not long

ago. He was actually in a coma, and it took weeks for him to come out of it.

Worry and guilt twist my stomach.

The poor man nearly died, and now I'm going to be part of another one of his stunts—and provide fake training at that.

If he drowns, I'll never forgive myself.

Then again, who says my training has to be fake? I could learn all there is to know about holding one's breath and train him the best I can. Also, I could always say that it's my professional opinion that he shouldn't free dive.

Yeah, that's it.

The guilt is lessened now, and easy to suppress. In general, guilt is a common occurrence for me, at least a specific type we call "magician's guilt" in my industry. That's what we feel when we say things like "I'll have you pick a card from this completely *ordinary* deck of cards," but the deck in question secretly consists of only aces.

Guilt quelled, I resume my stalking and come across some unwelcome images, including a picture in which Tigger is with some model type on a red carpet and one where he's kissing the hand of a famous female athlete.

Then again, what did I expect?

He's a manwhore after all.

Masochistically, I seek out more images of that sort until I notice something interesting.

Waldo's magazine has published a lot of stories on the Ruskovian royal family.

Before I get a chance to call Waldo and ask about this, the cab stops. I pay, dash into the apartment, and warn Clarice that she might hear from my sister.

"Thanks for thinking of me," she says. "I'd love to get a gig."

I wink at her. "I hope you're still grateful after you deal with Blue. She can be a handful."

Clarice tips her pirate hat. "Like you?"

Not dignifying that with a reply, I make my way to my room, behead Manny, and stick my phone in his neck.

Time to video conference Waldo.

As the call chimes, I prepare to leave a video voicemail along the lines of, "Hmm. Where is Waldo?" but I don't get the chance because he picks up.

"Hey, what's up?"

"Hey." I squint as I try to make sense of his shifting background. "Where is Waldo today?"

He rolls his eyes. "Har har. That's Central Park behind me." He turns the phone so I can see the truth of his statement. "I was just eating lunch with a chum from work and am about to head over to interview a famous hotel owner."

"Gotcha. I have a work-related question for you, if you have a second?"

"I've got a couple of minutes. Shoot."

"How much do you know about Ruskovian royalty?"

"Ah," he says. "Sounds like you also figured out who that rude asshole from the other day was."

"Anatolio Cezaroff."

"That's right," he says. "I've asked some of my colleagues at the magazine about him. A truly unpleasant fellow."

I frown. "Unpleasant?"

He nods. "A total playboy. They say he's got a different hookup every night—and never calls them after. Also, he does these crazy stunts and doesn't care if he injures himself or anyone else in the process." He looks pointedly into his phone's camera. "If *I* were a woman, I'd steer clear of him."

Fuck. I don't want him to see the impact his words are having, so I add levity to my voice. "If you were a woman, your name would be Wenda. Or Wilma."

Waldo puffs up, entering his mansplain-mode. "Wenda and Wilma are the twin friends of the fictional character in question."

"You don't say?" I decide to pretend he hasn't gone on this rant many times before.

"His real name is Wally," he continues with a decent dose of bitterness in his voice. "For some unfathomable reason, he goes by Waldo in North America. Not Charlie as in France, or Willy as in Norway, or Walter as in Germany—"

"Or Wang as in China," I say, matching his tone. "Or Weiner, as in Israel. Or Wacko, as in—"

"You know what, I'm pretty busy, so I'm going to skedaddle."

With that, he hangs up, and I feel like a crappy friend all of a sudden.

It's possible I was teasing him more than normal as a way of shooting the messenger. I didn't enjoy hearing him say those things about Tigger, even though his words support my own suspicions.

My phone dings with a text.

Speak of the devil. It's Tigger.

Do you have any more training that doesn't require a pool? he asks. *My brother says he can make a room with the pool available to me, but it'll take two days to get it clean and fill up the pool with new water.*

Yes, I reply.

The truth is that I *hope* I will, after I do some research.

Great, he says. *How about tomorrow?*

Tomorrow? That doesn't give me much time to prep. Also, my earlier guilt resurfaces.

Then an idea occurs to me, one that should buy me more time and assuage the guilt.

I need a doctor to clear you for free diving.

There. If a medical professional tells him that he can safely hold his breath for extended periods, then at least I don't risk drowning him during our training.

Speaking of, here's a fun idea: I could waterboard him. This way, he gets all the fun parts of drowning but with fairly minimal risk.

But no. It's possible I just feel like doing that to him in light of the conversation with Waldo.

Of course, he replies. *I should have that ready by 3pm. Would that work for you?*

So much for extra time.

Yes, I reply. Remembering the rent, I add, *Can I get some of the payment upfront? I need to cover a few expenses.*

No problem, he replies, and we work out how to get me the money.

I wait a few minutes before I check my account.

Yep.

This month's rent is no longer a concern.

I send the money to Clarice and ponder an issue that dwarfs that of the rent: in light of everything I now know about my client, I will have to stay extra vigilant not to catch any feelings for him.

Can I do that?

I had better. The kind of money I stand to make will get me closer to my greatest desire: my own magic show.

Thus properly motivated, I dive into research on free diving.

I start with David Blaine's TED Talk about holding his breath on TV, allegedly for real.

It's interesting. He says he'd considered hiding a breathing device inside his body, a modus operandi I find appealing. It's a rare case where, as a woman, I'd actually have an edge—an extra place to hide stuff.

I grin as I picture ordering a specialized magic

dildo from my twin's new friend. Given my brief interaction with her, she'd love such a project.

Blaine also mentions perflubron, a liquid you can actually breathe.

Nope. Not useful for free diving, not unless you can drain the body of water you plan to dive into and refill it with this cool substance. Even a prince isn't *that* rich.

Finally, Blaine goes into free diving, explaining that moving depletes oxygen. But the biggest problem with holding one's breath is the CO2 buildup in the blood.

I make a note to research that more.

He goes on to mention an important skill, a breathing type called purging—which isn't as gross as it sounds and might just come in handy if I'm ever brave enough to attempt to do an underwater stunt for real, or a blowjob.

Next, he says that losing weight can help with holding one's breath.

Yay. I have an excuse to examine Tigger's body. A part of me was a little bummed out that the pool—and therefore pool-related lack of clothing—won't be on the agenda tomorrow.

Wait, what am I talking about? I'm trying not to catch feelings.

I watch the rest of the TED Talk. Then I text Tigger to ask him if he happens to own something Blaine mentioned—a hypoxic tent.

No, but I used one when preparing for Everest, he replies.

Great, I write back. *Once you're ready, I might have you sleep in it to build up your red blood cells.*

Boom. I totally sound like I know what I'm talking about.

Will do, he says. *Can't wait to see you.*

I don't reply.

He's not eager to see me. He's eager to start his training. There's a difference—though I shouldn't care in any case.

I continue my research for the rest of the day and the next morning.

By the time lunch comes around, I have a lesson plan ready. I'll teach Tigger ways to slow down his heart rate as he holds his breath, then something called "lung packing"—a way to shove the maximum possible volume of air into the lungs.

In the hour before I have to leave, I do my makeup, going heavier than usual on the smoky eye, and flat-iron my hair until it streams down my back like black silk. Then I wriggle into a tight black dress, slip my feet into my favorite killer heels, and pull on my fanciest black gloves before surveying myself in the mirror.

Not bad. My twin would still probably say I look like a vampire, but nobody can deny that dressed-up vampires are sexy.

Not that I'm trying to be sexy. At least not with the goal of seducing him. It's just that I'm going to a ritzy hotel and don't want to look like a plebe.

That's my story, and I'm sticking to it.

My phone notifies me that my ride is downstairs. I look at myself in the mirror for the last time before departure.

Remember, Gia:

Do.

Not.

Catch.

Feelings.

Chapter Ten

When the cab drops me off, I stare at my destination in disbelief.

The Palace Hotel looks exactly how you'd expect—like a palace. A mixture of different European architecture styles has clearly influenced its design, with a little bit of everything from the Kremlin to Buckingham Palace. Inside, the giant lobby is consistent with the "hybrid of all palaces" motif: Russian icons share space with Italian frescos, and the people—probably porters—are dressed in capes, bicorns, and garish pantaloons.

Clarice would love this, especially all the colorful parrots hanging out in decorative cages. If it weren't for Hannibal, her cat, Clarice would probably own a parrot and train him to sit on her shoulder.

My sister Blue, on the other hand, would have a panic attack if she ended up here. Parrots to her are what Stephen King's clowns are to the rest of us. Oh, and if Blue could somehow survive seeing the parrots, the peacocks roaming the lobby would finish her off.

Aren't peacocks a rich people cliché?

When I was little, I mistakenly thought they were called pee-cocks, which isn't all that dumb if you think about it: pee comes from cocks, while peas and cocks have nothing in common. When I got older, I found it ironic that these birds (like all birds) don't pee. Instead, they expel a hybrid of urine and poo from an organ called a cloaca. They don't have cocks either—again, only the aforementioned cloaca.

My etymological/ornithological musings are interrupted by Tigger, who steps out of the elevator and comes my way.

Huh.

He's actually doing it.

He's wearing a shirt that proudly states "I want to be a mermaid," and his jeans are embroidered with pictures of Ariel before she grew legs. How did he get that done so fast? I can't imagine adult jeans for men are sold this way. Unless they are, and I'm just uninformed?

Is he wearing mermaid underwear too?

Nah, doubt it. Because how would I know it if he were? Also, he was commando last time.

What's mind-boggling is that despite this outfit, he looks sexy as sin. It reminds me of another ad: *"When he holds a lady's purse, he looks manly."*

It helps that the shirt is tight, and the pants showcase his muscular legs.

"Hi," he says, dragging a heated gaze over me.

I guess he appreciates the dressed-up vampire look. As anyone would.

I execute a curtsy. "Your Royal Heinie-ness. I bask in your majestic light."

He responds with a courtly bow that wouldn't be out of place in one of my twin's favorite Masterpiece Theater shows. "You honor me, Your Honey-ness."

"No, the honor is mine… Your Heinous-ness." I grin. "Nice mermaids, by the way."

He smirks. "I never welsh on a bet."

I clutch my nonexistent pearls. "Isn't that expression offensive to the Welsh?"

"Now you sound like my parents." He gestures at the elevator. "My penthouse is just a ride away."

He leads the way, allowing me to enjoy his jean-clad heinie.

Once we get into the elevator, despite it being roomy, I can't help feeling like he's taking up all the space.

It doesn't help that he smells as delicious as the last time: notes of ocean surf mixed with something very lickable.

Stop it, Gia. That way lies catching feelings… and syphilis.

Thankfully, the ride up is blissfully short.

We step out into a spacious hallway and take a sharp right.

A pantalooned porter comes toward us, holding

leashes attached to two familiar dogs: codenames Panda and Koala.

Seeing us, the beasts get excited.

I take a step back. "Please don't let them slobber all over my face."

The porter pulls on the leashes, and the dogs simply wag their tails with great enthusiasm.

"Afraid of dogs?" Tigger asks.

"I don't let anyone lick my face, but especially creatures who are happy to eat poop."

Tigger's eyes roam over my face with great interest. Is he sad that licking it is now off the table?

The dogs pass by with great ruckus and once they're gone, Tigger slides a room key through the reader on a nearby door. "In here."

I step into his not-so-humble abode and do my best not to gawk.

It's an entire suite, complete with its own full-sized kitchen. The view of Central Park from the nearby wall-to-ceiling window is spectacular, and the furniture is surprisingly modern considering the theme of the hotel. The strangest thing, though, is the assortment of flower arrangements scattered all over the living room.

Did a dozen of his female conquests leave their Valentine's bouquets behind?

"You like?" Tigger asks, following my gaze.

"They're beautiful." I walk up to the nearest arrangement and smell one of the daisies. "Is this how your brother decorates every room?"

"Of course not." He expertly rejiggles the bouquet that I've just sniffed, his hands moving in a practiced pattern that reminds me of a dance. "I make these myself."

I gape at the readjusted arrangement. It looks even prettier than before, and it was already professional level.

I scan all the bouquets again. "You made these flower arrangements?"

He nods. "I practice a Ruskovian art form called *kandelabr*. It was inspired by *ikebana*."

I hate his damn poker face. I have no clue if he's messing with me. Ikebana is a Japanese art of flower arrangement—something I can easily picture a geisha doing, not this manly, daredevil prince.

Then again, why not? How is it all that different from something like gardening? And that's unisex.

"It must be a soothing art to practice," I say, examining the symmetrical patterns and blends of colors with renewed interest.

He grins. "That's it exactly. My nanny taught this to me. The proverb 'idle hands are the devil's workshop' was particularly true in my case, so *kandelabr* was a godsend to everyone around me."

I picture the adorable image of little Tigger playing with flowers, and a goofy grin twists my lips.

He clears his throat. "So… what lessons have you got for me today?"

Right. This isn't a social visit.

I explain the breathing techniques I want him to

work on, and he doesn't seem the least bit surprised by any of them. In general, he's taking this seriously, so much so he's prepared some medical gizmos to measure his body's responses to the training. I only recognize two of them—an oxygen monitor that goes on his finger and a wristband to measure his heartbeat.

At my suggestion, he lies down on a nearby couch and practices each technique as I explain it.

I'm not an expert, but I think he makes a great student. I don't have to explain anything more than once, and he excels in each technique straightaway.

Too bad all of it turns me on. When he exhales through pursed lips, I picture how they would feel on my clit. When he slides his finger into the oxygen monitor, I wish he were sliding it into me, and so on for the rest of the exercises.

"Great job," I say when I run out of items to teach and feel like I'm on the verge of a libido explosion. "Now there's just one more thing. Please stand up."

He leaps to his feet and stretches, like a cat. Or a tiger.

As I approach him, his eyes widen, but he doesn't say or do anything, just watches me… probably for a chance to pounce.

Acting as blasé as I can, I unbutton the top of his shirt.

For the first time today, his heartrate monitor starts beeping.

As I work on the next button, my inner magician can't help herself. Furtively, I reach for his family-crest belt buckle with my other hand.

His eyes turn slitted and distinctly feline.

I unbutton the last shirt button. "Take it off."

As he peels off the shirt, I decide he's distracted enough to miss me stealing the belt, so that's what I do while trying not to look at the smooth, hard-muscled male flesh revealed to my gaze.

By the time the belt is hidden behind my back, his shirt drops to the floor.

I gulp hard, stepping back.

If I had a heartrate monitor on me, it would short-circuit.

I can no longer not look, and what I see sends heat streaking straight to my clit.

Tigger has the lean, powerful, sharply defined muscles of a Greek god. I bet he can bench-press me—and if he did, I wouldn't hold it against him… though I can think of other things, like body parts, that I do want to hold against him.

Is it even healthy to have so little body fat? At least for women, less than ten percent is dangerous, and he's probably in the low single digits.

Well, good for his health or not, it looks amazing, so much so my ovaries go into overdrive. Or rather, ovarydrive.

A cocky smirk lifts the corners of his lips. "Like what you see?"

My cheeks burn as I flash back to the other time

when he said that exact phrase: on the first day we met, after His Royal Hardness made an appearance.

Before I can make my mouth move, Tigger pounces.

Stepping closer, he dips his head.

Shocked, I stagger back. "What—what are you doing?"

The cocky smile disappears, replaced by confusion. "I'm sorry. I thought there was a vibe."

"You were going to kiss me?" The question comes out in a squeal.

"Sorry." He grabs his shirt and yanks it on. "I should've asked before going for it. It just seemed—never mind. My bad."

He was going to kiss me?

Kiss *me*.

Him.

I shake my head to clear the fog in my brain. "No, I'm sorry. I didn't mean to send you mixed signals."

He buttons his shirt, sending my ovaries into mourning. "I take full responsibility."

"No, it's my fault." I bite my lip. "I should've warned you why I asked you to take your shirt off."

He lifts an eyebrow. "And why is that?"

I swallow the drool left over from earlier. "According to my research, losing weight could help you hold your breath longer. More bang per your lung-capacity buck."

"And?" The smirk is back.

"You don't have much to lose. Here." I pull his

belt from behind my back without any flourish. I wish I hadn't stolen it in the first place. "Remember how you wanted to see this trick once again? Now you have."

He looks impressed as he takes the belt. Then a devious expression settles on his face. "Since the belt is already out, do you want to see if my legs have some fat I can shed? I'm sure that's why you stole the belt in the first place—and not because you hoped things would go just like the last time."

Heat creeps up my cheeks. "Are you commando again?"

His smirk widens. "I don't renege on bets. I owed you mermaid underwear, remember?"

Oh yeah. Thanks to the hormone overload, I almost forgot.

"I guess I have to check now." I wish I felt as confident as I sound. "But no kissing."

He looks amused as he drops his pants.

Houdini's cock!

A distant part of me acknowledges that his briefs are indeed decorated with mermaids, but the rest of me is focused on how much His Royal Hardness is tenting said briefs. One of the mermaids looks like she's lounging on a battle cannon.

I drag my eyes away and scan his legs.

Bad idea—assuming the goal was to tone down my horniness, that is.

His legs are as sexy and muscular as his upper

body and almost make me want to put kissing back on the table.

"Penny for your thoughts?" he drawls.

"Nice mermaids," I manage to say, returning my gaze back to his face. "No fat, though. Seems like losing weight won't be a part of your curriculum. Please put your pants back on."

As he dresses, his expression is darkly amused.

"So," I say, doing my best to hide any disappointment from my voice. "See you next time?"

"No," he says with the imperiousness befitting his station. "You must let me take you to dinner."

Chapter Eleven

I blink at him. "Dinner? As in a date?"

His eyes gleam. "Just a small token of my appreciation for a job well done."

I take a step back. "I'm not sure..."

He cocks his head. "I thought you believed a man and a woman could be just friends. Or has Waldo already burst that bubble for you?"

I put my hands on my hips. "We *can* be friends."

"Then there should be no problem if we have dinner," he says smoothly. "Now, tell me, do you want me to wear the mermaid getup at the restaurant?"

I give in. "Not if I'm going to be seen with you."

He nods and heads into an adjoining room, probably the bedroom.

The temptation to sneak after him and watch him change is strong, but that would be downright creepy, all things considered.

Grrr. Why didn't I just let him keep wearing the

clothes he had on? If he's all dapper, it'll make it more like a date.

Also, why am I so relieved that I'm dressed to the nines?

Before I can take that logic further, he comes back wearing a bespoke suit.

I inwardly sigh. If I wanted to soothe my lust, asking him to change was definitely a miscalculation. "How did you get dressed so quickly?"

He shrugs. "I attended a few years of military school in Ruskovia. Back then, I could've dressed and made my bed in the time it took me to put on this suit."

"A military school?"

He nods curtly. "My parents consigned me to it. Today's equivalent would probably be putting me on Ritalin."

I shift from foot to foot. Seeing him upset is strangely uncomfortable. "I wish I could change my clothes that fast," I say to distract him. "One of the stage illusions I want to do for my future show will involve a dress that changes style and color in an eyeblink."

His frown smooths out. Score for my feminine wiles. "Your show? Tell me about it."

"Not much to tell." I smile ruefully. "It's just something I'd like to do one day."

"I'd love to see that."

I wish I could kiss him for saying that, but I settle for batting my eyelashes. "If my dream ever becomes reality, I'll invite you."

He looks thoughtful. "You should meet my brother."

I arch an eyebrow. "The great and mighty destroyer of peace?"

He snorts. "Yep. It's His Majesty's hotel, so it would only be polite."

As he unlocks his phone, I verify that I got his pin correctly before. Yep, sure did. He sends a text, then walks over to a mini fridge and rummages inside.

"What's that?" I point at the clear plastic box in his hand.

He comes over and shows it to me.

"What is it?" I examine the strange white thing in the box with distaste.

"Cheese." Tigger brings the box closer to my face, and I step back.

He pulls the box away. "My brother is a cheese fanatic."

"Ah," I say noncommittally.

Some people like golden showers, and some eat cheese. Who am I to judge?

"My brother has been very accommodating when it comes to the room with a pool," he says. "I figured I'd give him a little gift."

I can't help myself. "Let's hope the cheese is pasteurized to kill salmonella, or else this gift might turn into a trip to the hospital."

He shrugs. "Considering how much it cost, I imagine it should be safe."

"Let's also hope the cheese hasn't developed any molds with mycotoxins. That can be deadly."

His phone vibrates with a text, and he glances at it. "If anyone knows how to safely consume cheese, it's Kaz."

Since I'm used to people's lax views on food safety, I mentally agree to disagree.

He walks over to the door and holds it open for me. "He's in the suite I'm moving to."

We cross the hallway and enter the suite in question.

Wow.

This penthouse is even fancier than the one we left, but that's not what I find most interesting.

A man is waiting for us inside, and he looks even more like the product of a *Brokeback Mountain* romance than Tigger does, perhaps due to his broody expression.

I wonder if that's because it's been far too long since his last cheese fix. Cheese contains casomorphins, morphine-like compounds that attach to the brain's opiate receptors. After I read the news article that made me quit the stuff cold turkey, I had cravings for a year. Incidentally, when I quit turkey itself—cold or otherwise—I only got cravings for one day that year, on Thanksgiving.

Oh, and did I mention there's a grizzly bear next to Mr. Dark and Broody?

Yep. A surprisingly well-behaved bear that might just be a dog.

So now I've seen a panda dog, a koala dog, and a maybe-grizzly dog. Where is the polar bear dog to complete the set?

"Brother," Kaz says, his voice emotionless.

"Brother," Tigger replies, matching Kaz's tone. "Is the room clean and orderly enough for you?"

The expression on Kaz's face seems to say, "We are not amused," with a royal "we." "No," he says out loud. "But it might be by tomorrow."

I look around. Even my twin, who could give Marie Kondo a run for her money, would consider *this* room tidy.

"This is for you." Tigger hands the box to his bro.

Kaz opens the box, and a strangely familiar—and quite unpleasant—smell permeates the room.

As Kaz sniffs the air, a warm emotion flits across his taciturn face, though maybe I'm imagining it.

"Pule?" he asks, closing the box.

Are we playing Word of the Day? I *think* that's how I first learned that "pule" means to cry querulously, or weakly.

"Indeed," Tigger says proudly. "I had it flown in from Serbia for you."

"Thank you so much," Kaz says, closing the box.

I clear my throat. "A cheese from Serbia?"

"Where are my manners?" Tigger says. "Kazimir, please meet Gia. Gia, this is my brother Kaz."

"A pleasure," Kaz says with so much haughtiness that I'm tempted to do a sarcastic curtsy. "Have you never heard of Pule cheese?"

Great. A cheese that makes you cry querulously, or weakly.

What's next—hysterics cheese?

"It's sixty percent Balkan donkey's milk and forty percent goat's," Kaz continues.

Okay, that explains the smell. My parents have donkeys and goats on their farm, and now that I have the context, the cheese does smell like what it is.

Yum. Sign me up. Maybe toss some skunk's milk in there too? And a few dung beetles.

Whose idea was it to milk a donkey, a creature also known as an ass? Or a goat? For that matter, who came up with the idea of milking a cow, a bovine creature with horns? What do the cows think when that happens? No doubt the same thing I would think if I were lactating and an elephant waltzed up to me and used his trunk to milk *me*. Also, did the person who came up with the milking idea also think, "Yay, now that I've finished that weird act, how about I drink this white bodily fluid." What was the inspiration there? Bukkake? Speaking of, do any cultures consume semen from a bull or any other animal? I know some eat the testicles—which is in the same ballpark, no pun intended.

Note to self: conduct some anthropological research.

"Gia is not just a breath trainer," Tigger says. "She's an illusionist."

"Oh?" Kaz looks at me with fresh interest. "Where do you perform?"

"She's looking for a venue," Tigger says. "She's amazing. You should see what she does with a spoon."

Kaz raises an eyebrow. "There are utensils in the kitchen."

"Get one," Tigger tells him. "You won't regret it."

Kaz heads into the suite's kitchen, and his dog keeps sitting there like a statue.

I give Tigger a narrow-eyed stare. "You think you're so sneaky? I know you just want to see me repeat a trick."

He winks. "Are you going to be able to resist showing off in front of a new spectator?"

Damn. How does he already know me so well?

Kaz returns holding a fork and looking broodier than before. "They didn't prepare any spoons in the kitchen." This is said with the same tone I'd expect someone to utter something like, "The surgeon left his scalpel inside you before he stitched you up."

"A fork will work even better," I say.

With a dubious look, Kaz hands me the fork, and I hold it dramatically before I begin. Then I watch their expressions as they witness the middle tine bend in front of their eyes.

As before, an awed expression is on Tigger's face. In contrast, Kaz is completely unreadable.

"Wow," Tigger mutters as the next tine bends.

Kaz is still keeping a poker face.

When the fork stem bends in half, however, Kaz's eyes widen and Tigger gasps.

I hand them the twisted fork. "They used CGI to do something like this in *The Matrix*."

Tigger examines it carefully, and then Kaz does the same.

"Thank you," Kaz says, pocketing the fork. "Between the cheese and the entertainment, I can almost forgive my brother for switching rooms yet again."

"This is only my third time," Tigger says.

"Exactly," Kaz retorts.

"Can I see the pool?" I ask to diffuse any potential hostilities. If these two are anything like my sisters, this could escalate to hair-pulling in a heartbeat.

"This way," Kaz says and leads us to a balcony with another breathtaking view. The pool is there, with the water dribbling into it slowly.

"I'm having it filtered via reverse osmosis," Kaz says at my questioning look. "Tigger said it needs to be clean enough to drink."

I look at the water with envy. I'm too chicken to go into most pools, but this is a rare case when I would swim—and I haven't done that since I was a kid.

"Would you like to take a dip before my training tomorrow?" Tigger asks.

Are Ruskovian royals telepathic? I desperately want to say yes, but I can't. After my swim, the water will be contaminated for him.

"In fact, I insist that you do," he says. "Whatever

techniques you want me to perform, I want to see you do them first."

I bite my lip. "Well, if you insist…"

"I do." Tigger crosses his arms over his chest, his stern expression making him look like Kaz's twin.

I take a deep breath. "I'll shower extremely thoroughly tomorrow. And I have a clean bill of health."

Kaz throws his brother a questioning glance, and Tigger makes a "don't ask" gesture.

I guess he already understands a lot about my attitude toward germs.

Tigger's phone vibrates once more, and he glances down at it. "Ah. Our dinner reservations came through. We'd better head out."

My stomach rumbles treacherously.

I suppose I could eat.

"It was nice to meet you, Kazimir." I wave at him. "Your hotel is impeccable."

Is that a hint of a smile touching Kaz's eyes?

"It was a pleasure to meet you as well. You have real talent." He pats the pocket with the bent fork.

Glowing from the praise, I let Tigger lead me out.

The bear is still sitting where Kaz left it. It must have an honorary PhD from Harvard in "who's a good dog?"

When we get into the elevator, however, the glow fades and worry creeps in. Despite what Tigger said about dining in friendship, this outing is going to feel like a date. Any meal with a prince as gorgeous as this one would, even a fast-food drive-through.

Am I strong enough not to catch a feelings infection tonight?

Maybe.

Hopefully.

When it comes to Tigger, my flesh isn't the only part of me that's treacherously weak.

Chapter Twelve

A black Lamborghini is waiting for us by the hotel entrance.

Huh. I wonder if, like in the ad, *"When he drives a car off the lot, its price increases in value."*

Tigger beats the valet to open my door.

Crap. He's a gentleman too? My poor ovaries.

As I buckle my seatbelt, I feel a tinge of a different sort of concern. The seatbelt is in the style of a race car, reminding me that Tigger is famous for breaking speed records.

He slides behind the wheel and buckles himself in as well.

"You're not going to go fast, are you?" I ask warily.

He flashes me a grin. "This is Manhattan. There are speed limits."

I let out a sigh of relief, but the air gets stuck in my windpipe when Tigger floors the gas pedal.

The tires screech and the smell of rubber hits my nostrils as the Lamborghini roars onto the road at ten times the speed limit.

Does he think those beer commercials are true?

"Cars look both ways for him before driving down a street."

"He once got pulled over for speeding, and the cop got the ticket."

"Is this okay, or should I slow down?" Tigger asks. In the time the sound takes to reach my eardrums, we zoom through at least five city blocks.

Fuck. What is wrong with him? I once read about Urbach-Wiethe disease, an unusual genetic disorder that causes a person to lose all sense of fear. Could Tigger have it? Maybe it runs in the Ruskovian royal family, a bit like hemophilia in Queen Victoria's descendants?

"Gia?" he says. "Are you okay?"

I grunt something in the negative.

He darts me a worried glance—and if I thought his driving was scary when he was looking at the road, now we're reaching terror levels equivalent to visiting a public bathroom. In Staten Island. In that landfill-turned-park.

My face must be paler than its usual hue because Tigger looks back at the road and slows the car to about double the speed limit. "Sorry. How's this?"

My words come out on a gasp. "Still too fast."

He slows the car until we're no longer leaving the other vehicles in the dust.

I finally catch my breath. "Thank you. Is the place far?"

"We're here actually." He smoothly pulls up next to a storefront that has something written in Cyrillic.

Whew. Made it in one piece. Also, much to my relief, the health inspection grade beside the window is a proud "A." Otherwise, we'd have to have an awkward conversation.

"Is that Russian?" I ask, nodding at the sign.

"No. Ruskovian. But the name would mean the same thing if you read it in Russian."

"They're similar languages, right?" I ask after he opens the door for me.

He rubs his chin. "I'd say about as similar as French and Spanish."

"I have no clue how similar that is." I look at the sign again as if it could help me.

"You don't speak Spanish? I thought most Americans knew some."

I shake my head. "I took it in school, but I remember very little. And I never studied French. How about you? What languages do you speak?"

"Russian, French, and Spanish, obviously," he says and proceeds to list half the languages spoken in Europe. "Some I'm less fluent in than others. All depends on how long I spent in that country."

Yet again he reminds me of that Dos Equis guy who can *"speak Russian… in French."* Maybe also, *"He is considered a national treasure in countries he's never visited."*

Two burly dudes stand outside the restaurant, holding the doors for us. They're dressed in the pantaloon outfits of the porters in Kaz's hotel.

Must be some Ruskovian thing.

When we're halfway to the entrance, a strange man in a tweed jacket blinds me with a flash of his professional-looking camera.

What the hell?

With an angry scowl, Tigger shouts something at the bouncer dudes.

They rush the picture-taking stranger like a pair of linebackers.

"Hey," the man yells when the bigger of the dudes grabs his camera. "You can't take that."

The pantalooned bruiser doesn't even reply. He simply walks into the restaurant, camera in hand. The other one returns to his door post as if nothing has happened.

"What was that?" I ask Tigger when we step inside.

"Paparazzi." Tigger says the word with as much distaste as I'd say, "E. coli."

"Ah." I glance back. "That makes sense. For a second there, I forgot how important your Royal Heinie is."

He leads me to a cozy, candlelit table and pulls out a chair for me. "Sorry about that. I'm usually good at dodging those vultures, but that one was smart enough to stalk this place. Must've figured it was just a matter of time before me or one of my brothers would crave Ruskovian cuisine."

"Nothing to be sorry about." For the first time, I look around the place. There are pictures of mushrooms everywhere. The theme here must have something to do with *Alice in Wonderland* or, relatedly, psychedelics.

Tigger's brows furrow. "No. I really am sorry. Anyone seen with me inevitably gets their picture in the tabloids, usually in an article filled with lies."

"Like those women you were chummy with?" is what I don't have the balls—or ovaries—to ask. Instead, I go with, "I'm not concerned in the slightest."

"No?" He bites the inside of his lip, a distracting move.

I do my best to focus. "Any publicity would be great for my career as an illusionist—no matter how scandalous."

He gives me a warm smile and picks up his menu. "That's a relief."

I pick up the menu as well, but it's in Ruskovian.

"What kind of restaurant is this?" I ask.

"It's called Crispy Mushroom. They specialize in all manner of mushroom dishes, which are very popular in Ruskovia. Do you like mushrooms?"

I shrug. "They're on my safe food list, but I've always thought of them as a side dish."

"You're in for a treat then," he says and waves at a pantalooned waiter.

As they begin to converse in Ruskovian, I sneak my phone out and check the exact sanitary violation score for this place.

They scored a zero, which is awesome.

The waiter stops speaking, and Tigger turns my way. "Of the two specials, you might like the Lion's Mane steak."

"Lion, not tiger?" I ask with a grin.

He grins back. "Lion's Mane mushrooms are famous for their health benefits. They help memory and cognition and have been used by Buddhist monks for thousands of years to help them focus during meditation."

I look at the waiter. "Is this man working with you guys on a commission basis?"

The waiter takes a step back. "This restaurant belongs to His Royal Highness, Andrej Cezaroff."

I move to the edge of my seat and return my attention to Tigger. "Your father?"

He shakes his head. "Brother."

I regard him curiously. "How big is your family?"

"I have nine brothers," Tigger says without batting an eye. "So, what say you to the Lion's Mane steak?"

Nine? Sounds like our families are quite similar—though I bet having all boy siblings is very different from growing up with a bunch of girls, not to mention living in a castle rather than on a crazy animal farm.

I turn to the waiter. "Is the mushroom cooked well?"

"Yes, mistress," he says.

Mistress? And I'm not even wearing my leather pants today. "Okay. I'll try it."

The waiter bows and rushes away.

"What are you getting?" I ask Tigger.

He says a word that sounds like Paganini, but I'm sure he's not eating a famous dead violinist—though you never know with royalty. They could've always pickled some.

"Great. That explains it," I say.

He laughs. "It's a mushroom. I believe in English it's called fly agaric, or maybe amanita."

I frown. "Red cap, white spots?"

He nods.

"The one the caterpillar sat on in *Alice in Wonderland*?"

He puts a napkin on his lap. "Not that exact one, but yeah."

"Aren't they poisonous?"

"Not if you boil them twice and change the water each time."

I gape at him. "That sounds dangerous."

He spreads his hands. "I've eaten worse. Fugu, Ackee fruit, Sannakji, Hákarl—you name it, I've tried it."

I pointedly raise my phone to my face and look up the dishes just mentioned.

Yep. As I thought, he must have the Urbach-Wiethe disease.

Fugu is doubly crazy: it's sashimi, so raw meat, plus it's made from a lethally poisonous puffer fish. Ackee, the fruit, is not as deadly, but can still lead to coma and death if you eat it improperly ripened. Sannakji is live octopus tentacles, which are a choking hazard, and Hákarl is cured Greenland shark, a fish that uses a toxic compound in its body as a natural antifreeze and, if uncured, can lead to all sorts of deadly fun.

Worried now, I look up Lion's Mane mushroom.

Nope. Not toxic, and the brain benefits seem to be true.

I put my phone away and give Tigger a disapproving glare.

"Don't worry, amanita is very safe cooked," he says, apparently discerning my thoughts.

"What if the chef makes a mistake?"

He waves dismissively. "I've actually eaten amanita raw once—under a shaman's supervision. You just have to throw up at the right time, and then you go on a nice hallucinogenic trip."

I narrow my eyes at him. "When you say, 'at the right time,' what you mean is 'before it kills you,' right?"

He grins. "If you're that worried, I won't eat it raw ever again. Mushrooms that contain psilocybin are much better."

Before I can reply, the food arrives.

His doesn't have the recognizable red caps, and

mine looks like some kind of meat from a small animal. What are the chances that Lion's Mane steak is really made from kittens or lion cubs?

I cut off a small slice and put it in my mouth.

By Houdini's tastebuds, this is the yummiest thing I've ever had. It's sweet, rich, earthy, and meaty, with a texture similar to a lobster tail.

Tigger is looking at me hungrily. I must've moaned from the culinary pleasure.

I do my best to be more discreet with the next bite, and he digs into his food as well.

"So," I say, trying not to watch him eat his poisonous choice. "What are so many Ruskovian royals doing in New York City?"

He swallows the bite he was chewing. "The answer lies within your question. There are so many of us that we don't all have the royal responsibilities you're thinking of. Speaking for myself, I'm here for physical therapy."

My next piece of mushroom is flavorless. "I read about your coma. Something about a base-jumping accident?"

He nods. "It was the highest skyscraper in Moscow. Everything was amazing at first, then… I woke up in a hospital in Ruskovia."

The dark expression on his face tugs at something in my chest. I'm not a hugger, but I desperately want to hold him until that uncharacteristic-for-him somberness is gone.

"Your family must've been devastated," I say softly.

He picks up his fork. "My brothers were very supportive. My parents had more of a 'told you so' attitude."

I frown. "Seriously?"

He laughs, but there's definitely an edge to it. "My parents disinherited me long before that event. 'Unbecoming behavior' is what they think of what I've chosen to do with my life."

I put my gloved hand over his. "I know it's not the same, but few in my family take my magic career seriously. They think if you don't have a college degree, you'll never make any money."

His gaze homes in on me, and the intensity in his hazel eyes makes me feel like a doe in the sights of a tiger. "You're a more talented magician than any who've entertained at our castle. I'm confident you have an amazing career ahead of you."

I grin like a doofus. If his evil plan is to use flattery to get into my pants, it's working.

Hello? No catching feelings, remember?

My euphoria fading, I pull back my hand. To make it less awkward, I grab the salt shaker and sprinkle some onto my plate. "Speaking of careers, do you monetize your adventures somehow, or do you make a living doing something else?"

Crap. Why did I just remind him that he's cut off from his family's wealth?

"Both," he says, and to my relief, he doesn't seem

upset. "I have sponsorships from countless brands, but my most substantial income comes from my theme park."

My eyebrows shoot up. "A theme park?"

His eyes are bright as he nods. "Before my parents cut me off, I leveraged my family's connections to put together a coalition of investors to build a Ruskovia-themed adventure park in my homeland. It has everything from rollercoasters and 3D thrill rides to the 'be royal for a day' type of experiences."

"Oh, wow. What made you decide to do that?"

"I wanted the general public to experience the adrenaline rush and the sense of awe that I get from my various pursuits." He smiles. "I would've been happy to break even, but the venture has succeeded beyond all expectations. People come to Ruskovia to visit it, a bit like tourists going to Orlando for Disney World."

Huh. So he's a successful entrepreneur, not just a thrill-seeking playboy. I guess it makes sense. How else would he be able to pay me so well when he's been disinherited?

Also, I was right when I thought I saw awe on his face during his stunts.

The interesting part is that I noticed that same expression when he watched my magic. He wasn't just blowing smoke up my ass when he complimented my deception skills.

Unable to help myself, I fish for another compliment. "I also try to give people a sense of awe with my magic. Less so an adrenaline rush."

"And you do," he says earnestly. "I think your magic will do the world a lot of good. People tend to lose the sense of awe as they grow up, and that's a shame."

Wow. I never thought of magic arts as doing something more than providing entertainment. He's right, though. If done correctly, magic *can* give an adult the wonderment of a child, if only for a moment.

He spears a piece of I-don't-want-to-think-what with his fork. "Is that why you decided to become a magician?"

I cut off another piece of my mushroom steak as I ponder this. "I got interested in it after seeing a magic performance. When I tried performing a trick myself, I found that I enjoyed the attention. Later, it became all about making people feel awe, wonder, astonishment, and amazement. It's also important to me to become a famous *female* magician."

He arches an eyebrow. "Why?"

"To best understand it, I usually ask people to do a little thought experiment. Want to try it?"

He nods.

"Step one, picture yourself as a little girl," I say with a grin.

He closes his eyes, and a look of deep concentration comes over his face. In a high-pitched voice, he says, "Done."

I suppress a laugh. Is he picturing having pigtails? Jumping rope? Pickpocketing the next-door bully?

"Now answer my questions quickly, without thinking too hard," I say. "Start by naming a male scientist."

"Einstein," he says, still in that little-girl voice.

"Now name a female scientist."

"Madam Curie," he replies, staying in character.

"A male magician."

"David Blaine," he replies without hesitation.

"A female magician."

He opens his mouth, then closes it. His eyebrows furrow. Finally, he opens his eyes and looks at me in frustration.

"Rasputina," I say, figuring he'd know her as someone who resides in his homeland.

He slaps himself on the forehead. "You're right," he says in his normal voice.

"The difficulty you had is my point," I say. "There are no household names yet."

"I see. And you want to be that household name to inspire girls to become magicians?"

"Exactly. Just like Rasputina and the other trailblazers who inspired *me*. It's time to break through the rabbit-hat ceiling."

He nods approvingly. "I bet anything that you'll succeed in your noble goal."

"I sure hope so." A swarm of butterflies rummages around in my belly, though I should probably say "a dule of doves" since magicians are known for making doves appear out of thin air.

Personally, I wouldn't do dove—or rabbit—tricks for reasons of hygiene. If spoons could poop, I wouldn't bend them either. Then again, even if someone genetically engineered poo-less doves, I wouldn't be able to use them. Blue would never visit me, plus it would only be a matter of time before Clarice's cat, Hannibal, would have my poor helpers for dinner… with a nice Chianti.

Tigger's expression turns sly. "Speaking of your skills, can you perform another trick this evening?" He eyes a nearby fork.

"No repeats and no props during a meal," I say.

He looks like a kid who was denied dessert.

"I *can* do some mentalism for you. That's a type of magic that deals with the mind."

His eyes gleam with excitement. "Please."

"Okay. Think of two simple shapes—one inside the other, like a heart inside a square." I draw the example in the air.

"Done," he says.

"Now picture any playing card inside the inner shape."

"Got it," he says, looking uneasy—a common reaction for a spectator at this point.

I extend one hand forward dramatically and put the other to my temple, channeling Professor X. Being a magician (or a mentalist) is a lot like being an actor who's taken on the role of a magician or a mentalist, or so said the famous Robert-Houdin.

Acting like I've snared Tigger's thought, I solemnly announce, "You're thinking of the Queen of Hearts inside of a triangle inside of a circle."

Tigger drops his fork.

My grin is evil.

"How?" he whispers.

"Quite well," I say.

He picks up his fork again. "You're a dangerous woman."

"And don't you forget it."

Before he can beg me to tell him my secrets, I change the topic by asking about his brothers.

He eagerly shares anecdotes from his past, such as the time when his bros and a cousin formed a soccer team together.

"What about you?" he asks. "Any siblings besides Holly?"

I tell him about the sextuplets and how crazy things would sometimes get with eight girls on a farm full of all sorts of exotic rescue animals.

We go back and forth sharing stories—which are surprisingly similar despite growing up in different countries and with different socioeconomic backgrounds.

"I guess a herd of siblings can provide the same kind of chaos, no matter the gender," he says.

"Is a herd the right collective noun in that case?" I ask him as I eat the last morsel off my plate.

"Maybe it's a mischief?" He waves at the waiter.

"That's rats and brothers." I grin. "With sisters, it's a murder—like with crows."

The waiter hurries over and converses with Tigger in Ruskovian.

"Dessert?" Tigger asks me.

I nod, mostly because I'm curious if it will have mushrooms in it. The only stranger ingredient would be garlic.

Yep. The dessert is a caramel porcini mushroom brûlée with green tea ice cream. To my surprise, it's creamy, toasty, and makes me feel warm and cozy.

It could be worse. My Anglophile twin once served me a pudding called Spotted Dick, and it wasn't even shaped like a dildo.

The coffee-like drink served here is, not surprisingly, also mushroom based—and I like it. If I spoke Ruskovian, I might even come back to this place, assuming I could afford it.

As we enjoy the dessert and the mushroom brew, Tigger tells me stories about Ruskovian traditions. Turns out, they have a holiday reminiscent of La Tomatina in Spain, but instead of tomatoes, they throw ripe grapes at each other.

"Why?" I ask.

He shrugs. "Why do we have a bear festival?"

"Let me guess. People dress like bears?"

He smirks. "And eat bear food, such as *myodik*."

The devouring look he gives me almost makes me choke on a piece of porcini mushroom—though as I picture him lapping at my honeypot, he's more feline than bearlike.

I clear my throat. "Is that why your dogs look like bears?"

He eats the last bite of his dessert. "I never thought about it, but maybe. Kaz's dog has the typical look of a Ruskovian breed called *Misha*—originally bred for the royal family."

"Then how did you end up with a panda and a koala?" I ask.

He grins. "Caradog is the name of the one that has to wear corrective goggles, and he's a regular Misha. Just happens to have an unusual coloring. Mephistopheles, on the other hand, looks the way he does because he isn't purebred."

"You named a dog Mephistopheles? Isn't that just asking him to be a troublemaker?"

He chuckles. "He doesn't need encouragement in that department. Being my fur baby, he was destined to be trouble."

Did I just ovulate? Must be the unwelcome images of a half-Gia, half-Tigger troublemaker running around, causing all manner of mischief.

This is ridiculous. There should be some sort of vaccine against feelings.

Determined to keep myself together, I push my empty plate away and slurp the last of my mushroom "coffee" pointedly.

"Ready to head home?" he asks, catching my drift.

I fake a yawn. "Yeah. I'm pretty tired."

Tired of swooning over him.

I give him my address as we get the check. He rejects my offer to split the bill and has me back in his suicide car in a blink.

To my shock, he keeps to the speed limit from the start. Despite that, my heart rate is as high as it was when Tigger drove like an extra in *The Fast and the Furious*.

What's happening? Have I been conditioned to fear his car from that single ride?

It doesn't take me long to understand what's really going on.

Though my mind is firmly on the whole "our dinner was not a date" mantra, my heart—and other vital and not-so-vital organs—clearly didn't get the memo. In my heart's defense, the dinner was pretty date-like. More date-like than most real dates I've been on. The crux of my adrenaline overload is simple to puzzle out now.

We're nearing the part of a date where things would always go horribly wrong for me in the past.

The goodbye kiss. Or lack of one.

This is the point when all of my dates realized I wasn't worth the trouble and dumped/ghosted my ass.

I swallow and perform a breathing technique I recently taught to my oh-so-hot student.

Nope. Not working. Nor does reminding my heart—and other organs—that this wasn't a date.

"You okay?" Tigger asks.

Fuck. We're not driving anymore.

I glance at the window.

Yep. Home sweet home. Did we teleport here?

"Peachy," I say belatedly.

Unbuckling the high-end seatbelt, I catch his feline gaze, and the dule of doves throws a prison riot in my belly.

He unbuckles his seatbelt without looking away. "I had a great time."

Curse him. That's the most typical post-date, pre-kiss line.

"Me too," I say—an understatement of my life.

He presses a button, and the car locks pop.

Neither of us moves.

Leave.

Open the door.

Stop staring.

I stay welded to my seat, as if hypnotized—and I'd know what that feels like since one of my roommates is a hypnotist.

Slowly, ever so slowly, a gravity-like force pulls me toward him.

What the fuck?

He leans my way also. He's not immune to whatever physics, chemistry, or mass insanity is at play here.

Is this finally going to happen? For a second, I let myself have hope.

If there were ever a time when lust could conquer

my fears, it would be now. Ever since I've seen his naked everything, I've been a walking, talking, hormone-producing machine that is ready to blow at any provocation—in more ways than one.

Our lips are now an inch apart.

By Houdini's balls… are we actually going to kiss?

Chapter Thirteen

Two things happen at the same time.

He begins to murmur something, but I don't hear what because my germ-avoiding instinct kicks in and I jerk away—and smash my head into the side window.

The look on his face is one I haven't seen in this situation before.

It's not annoyance, or betrayal, or rejection.

It's worry. Maybe pity too—and I hate that.

"My head is okay." Contradicting my words, I rub the back of my throbbing skull.

"I swear I was about to ask you if you wanted to kiss me," he says earnestly. "I wasn't going to just go for it this time. I'm sorry if—"

"I was the one who was going for it," I say bitterly.

He cocks his head. "Then why—"

"There's a risk of herpes, hepatitis B, syphilis, and HPV," I blurt. "In general, a single kiss can deposit eighty million bacteria from one tongue to another, and after a kiss, our microbiomes—"

"I get it," he says softly.

I blink dumbly. "You do?"

He shrugs. "That's not inconsistent with the gloves and the pool water concerns."

Right.

How could I forget?

I chew on my lip. "You must think I'm crazy."

"Never." His eyes drill into mine. "Believe it or not, I always run a risk assessment analysis before doing my stunts. Sometimes, I don't take the chance because the risk feels too great, but usually, I go for it. Most people think I'm crazy because my risk tolerance is higher than theirs. It would be hypocritical of me to call *you* crazy for having a risk tolerance that skews in the other direction."

I sigh. "Why can't you be an asshole about this? You make me want to kiss you even more."

His gaze darkens. "So you do want this? It's just a matter of health concerns?"

I look down. "I think so. Maybe. I had a traumatic event in my childhood that started this whole business."

"What happened?" The expression on his face is frightening when I look up. "Did someone do something to you?"

The question carries so much menace my blood chills—and that's despite the fact that the rational side of me knows he's furious with the hypothetical culprit of an event that never happened to me.

"No one hurt me," I say quickly. "It was something else, something kind of silly."

I tell him about The Zombie Tit Massacre, and as I do, the frightening expression turns into a compassionate one.

"Have you seen a therapist?" he asks.

I shake my head. "I did some research on my own. I don't want a medical solution—which would be something like Zoloft—and the therapy would be the cognitive behavioral type, which is something I've been doing on my own."

"Oh?"

He looks impressed, so I tell him about using porn as exposure therapy, and as I go on, a thoughtful and rather Machiavellian expression settles on his face.

I narrow my eyes. "What?"

"I was just thinking about the many things we can do without any fluid exchange."

My breath catches. "What do you mean?"

A sexy smirk tilts his lips. "You can use me for some real-world exposure therapy."

My ovarydrive kicks into high gear. "Use you?"

"If you don't like how that sounds, you can think of it as me training you. You've done it for me, and I'd be glad to return the favor."

I don't know which is hotter—the idea of using him sexually or the idea of naughty training.

"When?" I gasp.

His nostrils flare. "Now?"

I moisten my suddenly dry lips. "How?"

"Any way you want to," he murmurs. "I'm yours this evening."

I have no words. A kaleidoscope of dirty images flits through my brain, and it's a wonder I don't have an orgasm here and now.

"Let me set up my room," I say faintly.

He nods. "I await your instructions."

Mind foggy, I climb out of the car and rush into my apartment.

No roommates cross my path. Good. I hope it stays this way when I bring Tigger in here. I don't want to waste any time on introductions.

I don't even know what I plan to do with him, but whatever it is, safety must come first, so I rummage in the hallway closet and locate some items we used when we repainted the walls in the living room.

Nearly tripping over the furniture in excitement, I run to my room and set everything up.

Is this really about to happen?

Worried that Tigger has changed his mind, I sprint back and find him waiting by the front door. He must've followed me.

I swallow hard and crook my finger seductively. "Come in."

He steps in with feline grace.

As we head down the corridor, I notice that he's stopped walking.

Oh, no. Is he getting cold feet?

I turn to find him staring uneasily at something near the door to Clarice's room.

Fully expecting a giant spider, I follow his gaze.

A flat, furry face looks up at me.

This is Hannibal, the cat—a fluffy white Persian with blue eyes, and therefore not a creature you'd look at the way Tigger is doing.

"What's up?" I mouth at Tigger.

"Nothing," he says but stays put, eyes on the furball in his path.

"Are you allergic to cats?" I ask.

He shakes his head.

"Then what?"

He rolls up his sleeve and shows me a faded scar on his forearm. "My cousin's grandmother, the dowager duchess, was what you'd call a cat lady. I got this from one of her charges. Since then, I'm more of a dog person."

I look from Tigger to Hannibal and back. "You're afraid of cats?"

Could this mountain of muscles actually fear a ball of white fur?

What would he do if he knew the cat's sinister-sounding name? Or if he met my sister Blue's Machete—a truly scary cat that even normal people might want to stay away from?

A hint of color stains his high cheekbones. "Not afraid. This is purely a risk-assessment situation. I was in the hospital with an infection for a week the last time I got close to one of these." He gives Hannibal a glare, and the cat glares back at him, tail twitching warningly.

I could swear Tigger pales slightly before breaking the staring contest.

Usually, it's the princess who needs saving from a monster. Today, it's the prince. I walk over to Clarice's door and very softly open it. "Shoo."

Pretending like this is what he wanted all along, Hannibal whooshes into the door crack, tail held high.

I close the door just as softly and look at Tigger. "Ready to go?"

"I'm *not* afraid of cats," he mutters and follows me.

I pat his sleeve sympathetically. "One thing you might want to try is handling cat poop."

"Why?" As he narrows his eyes at me, he reminds me of a beautiful cat—oh, the irony. Speaking of irony, was the nickname Tigger part of some ironic ribbing by his siblings?

"Cats carry a parasite that supposedly makes people like cats more. So, in your case, you might just feel neutral about them."

"No, thanks," he says.

"Yeah, maybe that's for the best. A cat parasite is also said to lead to risky behavior, and you do enough of that."

He sighs. "Can we please drop the cat subject?"

I feel like an ass. "I'll never mention it again," I

say solemnly, and mean it. Given how understanding he is about my issues, it's the least I can do.

Besides, I'm actually relieved that there's something he fears. It means he doesn't have Urbach-Wiethe and thus can't pass it on to our hypothetical children.

Wait, children? Maybe start by kissing him first?

I open the door to my bedroom and gesture for him to get inside. He steps into the room, and his eyes widen.

"Sit here." I point at the chair I prepared.

As he sits down, the thick plastic drop cloth on the chair makes a crinkly sound.

"Give me a second." I pull on the suit I bought a while back in case I ever have to visit a hospital—which fortunately hasn't happened yet.

It's a full-body biohazard jumpsuit with a heavy-duty face mask, and it came in very handy during the painting project. Thanks to the mask, I was the only one of my roommates who wasn't high on fumes.

Tigger surveys my suited-up self from head to toe, amusement glimmering in his eyes. "Am I about to get murdered?"

What is he talking about?

I examine myself in the mirror, then scan the room covered in heavy plastic, the duct tape I used to attach it all, and finally the mannequin in the corner.

Oh, crap.

He's right.

My room looks like a serial killer's lair.

Chapter Fourteen

I wince. "I'm sorry. It's probably not the sexiest décor. I just want to be safe."

"So you go *Dexter* on me?"

My face burns underneath the mask. "I figured whatever we do, you'll come…"

The amusement in his eyes deepens. "My cum shouldn't be radioactive."

Depends on one's definition. "I've seen enough porn," I say defensively. "That stuff can shoot all over."

He grins. "Do you think I go off like a firehose? I guess I'm flattered—but wouldn't a condom do the trick?"

A condom. Great idea. I walk over to my nightstand and toss him the little silver packet.

He frowns at it. "Why do you even have this? I thought you didn't have sex."

"True, but I'm not a nun." Blushing, I open my nightstand drawer and take out my two dildos—Prince Regent and the small one.

You think he can tell I'm his stand-in? Prince Regent seems tall and proud as I wave him in the air.

My old dildo, on the other hand, looks like it has shriveled. *I'm simply "the small one?" Why don't you just melt me and make a vagina?*

Tigger's jaw flexes, and I wonder if he's picturing me playing with the toys.

My blush spreads down to my chest. "Do you think we'll need these? One can be controlled via an app so that—"

"No, myodik." His voice is hoarser than usual. "For now, I just want you to touch yourself for me."

And just like that, my breathing turns ragged and my nipples stiffen into bullets. Swallowing, I pull my arm from the sleeve of the suit and slide it down my body until I reach my sex.

"Like this?" I move my hand in an exaggerated motion so he understands what's happening.

He nods, eyes burning. "Just like that."

Wait. Hold on. This is supposed to be *my* porn therapy.

"Take your clothes off," I say.

A dark smile curves the edges of his lips, and he begins to strip.

By Houdini's sixpack… He only has the shirt off so far, but the sight of those hard pecks and abs doubles my already-racing heartbeat.

By the time his pants drop, I'm hyperventilating.

"Is your pussy wet?" he murmurs.

"Like water," I blurt.

"Keep touching yourself." He takes off his underwear, unleashing His Royal Hardness.

Fuck. Me. Sideways.

How did he get so hard with me looking like an extra in *Contagion?* Also, how is His Royal Hardness even bigger than I remember? It effortlessly dwarfs Prince Regent.

Hey. That doesn't feel very nice. Prince Regent seems to shrink like his smaller brother.

Not my brother—and it serves him right for making me feel like a clit.

Speaking of clits, mine is swollen and throbbing, with a coiling tension building behind it, but there's an emptiness too, one that only His Royal Hardness can fill up.

"Stroke it," I manage to squeeze out.

With an approving grunt, Tigger rips the condom packet open with his teeth and sheathes himself.

Fuck, that's hot.

Maybe the condom was overkill, though? I prefer an unobstructed view. Also, would it be awkward to put music on at this juncture? I usually do this sort of thing to "The Final Countdown."

"Slide a finger inside," he orders, and begins to move his fist up and down his length.

I do as I'm told, and my inner muscles squeeze the finger greedily. The sensation is unsatisfying. A finger is a poor approximation of what I'm looking at.

He speeds up the movement of his fist. "Squeeze your nipple."

I get my other hand inside the suit, slide it under the bra, and make his words reality.

Fuck, that feels good. A bolt of pleasure shoots down my body, turning my clit into a beacon of bliss.

"Faster," he groans, pumping his cock almost viciously.

Moans escape my lips as I match him swipe for stroke.

His muscles tense.

My toes begin to curl.

A distant sound threatens to penetrate the fog of pleasure, but I tune it out.

"Gia," he groans.

That does it. With a scream muffled by the mask, I come.

He grunts in pleasure and shoots his load into the condom.

Wow.

That looks like a lot of liquid.

The extra protection might not have been overkill.

"Whew." I work my arms back into the sleeves of my suit.

He grins at me. "That was unbelievable." Carefully, he removes the condom from his massive cock.

The sound from earlier recurs, and my brain recognizes it as a knock on the door.

Crap.

I'm about to ask "who is it?" when the door flings open.

Chapter Fifteen

I hear Clarice's voice before I see her. "Hey. Were you the one who let Hannibal into my—"

She stops short, eyes bugging out.

I follow her gaze, and a fresh wave of heat assaults my face.

His Royal Hardness is still at full mast. I guess it takes a few seconds for things to come down.

I'm also acutely cognizant of the hazmat-style suit I'm wearing and the plastic-shield-covered room.

I can't even imagine what kind of kink Clarice thinks she's just walked into. Is there such a thing as serial killer roleplay? Or maybe she thinks we're playing doctor… during the outbreak from *The Andromeda Strain*?

"I'm so sorry," she mutters, backing away. "I thought I overheard your porn, not—"

I don't hear the rest because at that moment, Hannibal streaks into the room.

Seeing his nemesis, Tigger drops the condom he's been holding and instinctively grabs his pants.

I half expect Hannibal to get scared by His Royal Hardness, or Prince Regent for that matter. When one of my roommates put a cucumber behind him once, he freaked the fuck out.

But no, he's heading right for Tigger. I guess the phallic object has to be green to be a problem.

"Stop," I yell at the cat.

"Hannibal!" Clarice says sternly.

The cat actually speeds up. In an eyeblink, he's at Tigger's feet.

Oh, no. His Royal Hardness is still out and proud. Is that what the cat is going for? Is he thinking of finally living up to his name and—

Nope.

The cat isn't yearning for a taste of man meat. His real goal turns out to be—to quote his movie namesake—"a thousand times more savage and more terrifying."

I gape in horror as Hannibal snatches the condom with his teeth and dashes toward me.

My mask muffles my scream as a terrible scenario plays out in front of my eyes: the cat claws holes in my suit, then forces the man juices in there… somehow.

The scream must upset Hannibal. He veers off his course—by running up the plastic-covered wall as though he's been bitten by a radioactive spider.

The duct tape I used to keep the plastic in place doesn't like this and gives up, but Hannibal leaps to the next piece before he can be smothered, and then he lands on the floor behind me and Clarice and streaks out of my room.

"Hannibal!" Clarice shouts and gives chase.

I dash after them, only to learn that my getup isn't meant for running.

Panting as I waddle, I watch Clarice disappear into the kitchen.

I follow, and when I arrive, she's standing there confused.

"Where is he?" I ask breathlessly.

She shakes her head. "I thought I saw him run in here."

A motion behind me gives me a start, but it's just Harry.

"I Tawt I Taw a Puddy Tat," she says in her best Tweety impersonation. In a normal voice, she adds, "He was carrying a condom. What's up with that?"

"Where is he?" Clarice and I shout in unison.

Harry looks me up and down. "What the hell are you wearing?"

"Where is the cat?" I growl.

Harry takes a step back. "Chill. He's in my room. I locked him in there before I came over."

With a sigh of relief, Clarice steps over to a drawer, takes out a pair of tongs, and shoves it into my hands.

I narrow my eyes at the thing. "What's that for?"

"To get the condom," Clarice says with an eyeroll.

"Why me?"

She looks me up and down. "You're wearing a hazmat suit, plus it's your boyfriend's condom."

Harry looks intrigued. "A boyfriend?"

"He's not my—"

Before I can finish the sentence, my not-boyfriend waltzes in.

Harry looks impressed, as does Clarice—despite the fact that she just saw him pants-less.

"Let me," he says, reaching for the tongs. He doesn't seem the least bit embarrassed.

"No." I bravely grip the tongs. "I got this." The last thing I want is Tigger losing one of those beautiful eyes to the cat.

We creep over to Harry's room, and she opens the door.

Hannibal is there, in the middle of the floor, rolled up into a contented ball, ignoring us as only a cat can.

The condom is next to him.

Eeek.

I steel myself.

You're wearing a suit. You can do this.

Bravely, I waddle over and pick up the biohazard with the tongs… and goggle at it, turning it this way and that.

"What's the matter?" Clarice asks.

"It's empty." I keep examining the latex as though I can conjure the cum back—which hey, might be a neat magic trick.

"Empty?" Tigger asks, incredulous.

"What was in there?" Harry asks, and gets a funny look from Clarice.

As one, we look down at Hannibal—who was clearly waiting just for that moment to very pointedly lick his chops.

There may even be a slurping sound.

"Eww!" Harry shouts. "He ate it?"

Chapter Sixteen

Tigger levels an insulted look at Harry.

Clarice looks constipated. "I believe 'swallowed' is the correct nomenclature," she says in a choked voice.

I don't know if I should be jealous of Hannibal, grossed out, or worried about half-tiger, half-Persian kittens.

This does set a bad precedent. Next thing you know, the cat will crave human milk. Or blood. Also, bodily fluids might be the perfect gateway to flesh, especially for a creature that shares 95.6 percent of his DNA with lions and tigers. Clarice already jokes that she needs to feed Hannibal well, or else he will feast on our eyeballs.

Tigger's spine straightens, like he's about to lead troops in a parade. "Allow me." He reaches for the tongs.

I hand them over, careful not to release the condom.

"I'll go dispose of it," he says, then looks at my roomies. In an imperial tone, he adds, "I'm Tigger. And you are?"

They look like they're straining to hold in laughter as they introduce themselves.

"It was nice to meet you, Harry and Clarice," Tigger says with a courtly bow, the tongs clamped firmly around the condom.

"Likewise," Harry says bashfully.

"Come again," Clarice says with a giggle.

I make sure Clarice can see my eyeroll before I turn to Tigger and say, "Let me walk you to the door."

My friends hang back, though I know they're hanging on to every word.

When we get to the door, I unlock it for him.

Tigger shakes the tongs, making the empty condom flap like a flag in a breeze. "That was memorable."

I try not to look at it as heat spreads from my face down to the recently stimulated regions. Instead, I latch on to the most neutral topic I can think of. "Are you up for your training tomorrow?"

A smirk dances on his lips. "You up for yours?"

The blush covering me spreads down to my toes. "Sure," I say in a strained voice.

"Good." He opens the door. "I'll text you."

He heads for his Lamborghini, his posture all

dignity despite the burden he's carrying, and I watch him rocket away at the speed of sound.

"Nice car," Harry says from behind me.

"Nice everything." Clarice gives me a mock pout. "You've been holding out on us."

"Oh, yeah." Harry puts her hands on her hips. "Spill."

I heave a sigh. "Wait in the living room. I need to change first."

By the time I'm hazmat suit-free, all my roommates are waiting in the living room, not just Clarice and Harry.

With another sigh, I launch into the story, which is made easier because, unlike my blood sisters, my sisters in magic know all about my issues with intimacy.

When I'm done, everyone starts talking at once, and all I can make out is, "Can't you kiss him through some plastic wrap?" and "Can't you do it with a condom?"

"Thanks, but I'll figure out what to do," I say sternly.

Clarice shushes everyone and gives me a pitying smile. "You poor thing. You must feel like a diabetic at Charlie's chocolate factory."

"You have no idea," I say, then bid them all good night and head to my room.

As I put my room back in order and go through my nightly routine, a dozen questions coo frantically in my head, like a dule of doves at a feeding.

Why did he offer to train me? What did it mean to him? Will I be able to face him tomorrow? Train him? Let him train me? I tremble feverishly at the thought.

Speaking of his training, did it work? Am I any closer to being able to be intimate with a guy?

It's hard to say, but the idea of being intimate with some hypothetical rando doesn't appeal to me anymore. I have someone specific in mind, someone who reminds me of beer commercials such as: *"He once brought a knife to a gunfight… just to even the odds."* Or *"When in Rome, they do as HE does."*

No. That's crazy. He's a client. And a playboy prince.

That brings me back to the question of why he even offered his services. What's his goal?

Clearly, the end game of the training is for us to sleep together—unless that is wishful thinking on my part. But why would a guy who can have any woman bother with me? Is the difficulty piquing his interest… for the moment? Am I some sexual Everest he's decided to conquer? Going where no man has gone before by fucking the unfuckable?

Unable to come up with satisfying answers to any of it, I get into bed and toss and turn for hours before falling into a restless sleep.

I wake up very late and check my phone.

Nothing from Tigger.

I hope he hasn't changed his mind about further training.

Pulling out my laptop, I research what I can teach Tigger if he does turn up. When I get hungry, I grab a coconut yogurt for breakfast—another minor type of exposure therapy, in a way. Yogurt is teeming with bacteria, but since it's the beneficial kind, I let it into my body… with only a minor reluctance. It really helps that since its founding in the eighties, this brand of yogurt has never been the cause of a foodborne illness.

I just wish I didn't have a strange fuzzy sensation on my tongue with each spoonful, one that feels eerily like the tiny tails of millions of Lactobacillus shaking as they dance to "The Final Countdown."

Just as I finish up, I finally hear from Tigger:

I'm going to see a doctor this morning. Can we meet later today? Maybe 4 p.m.?

Ah, so he *is* seeing a doctor to make sure he's allowed to free dive. I'm glad. This way, I'll be less concerned about him drowning.

I'll see you at the hotel, I reply, and the stupid doves flutter in my belly in anticipation.

I return to my free-diving research, but a text distracts me just a few minutes in.

It's from Blue.

Your card expert friend didn't make it to the brunch we

scheduled. I called and texted her but never heard back. Is everything okay?

Hmm. It's so not like Clarice to flake on a business opportunity.

I walk over to her room and knock.

No answer.

When I open the door, all I see is Hannibal with his eyes closed—no doubt sleeping off the heavy meal from last night.

I'm careful not to wake him as I close the door. I have an unspoken agreement with the cat. I don't bother him, and he doesn't smother me in my sleep, eat my face, or rub himself against me.

Where is Clarice?

I call and text her.

She doesn't reply.

I start knocking on the doors of my other roommates, but they're all out.

Just as I prepare to call everyone at random, I get a group text from Harry.

Clarice is in the hospital.

Chapter Seventeen

I read the rest of Harry's message in a panicked daze.

She explains that she got a slurred call from Clarice that only lasted a couple of seconds, and that she has no idea what is wrong with our friend, only knows the name of the hospital.

Heart pounding, I summon a car and hurry to my room to prepare.

To avoid a trip to a hospital, I'd consider licking a subway handrail, using a public bathroom, and maybe even eating at a restaurant with a C rating.

But Clarice is my friend and I must go visit her.

Somehow.

Stomach tight, I locate last night's biohazard suit. Going to the hospital is the reason I bought it in the first place—not to arouse a prince. I pull it on but don't yet put the mask on since the cab driver just might flee at the sight.

I also grab a gorgeous deck of cards I bought for Clarice's birthday. Nothing cheers her up more than cards.

Waddling outside, I locate the car.

No mask was a good call. The lady driver gives my outfit an uneasy look as is.

"I'm going to the hospital," I say.

The lady acts as all New Yorkers do when faced with someone who clearly belongs in an institution—no eye contact, and not even a hint that she heard me.

I text Blue and update her on the situation.

Which hospital? she asks.

I tell her and return to pondering what could've happened.

All sorts of scenarios play out in my masochistic imagination. Was Clarice in a car accident? Did she get mugged? Is she sick from a foodborne illness?

She's too young for a heart attack or stroke, but you never know.

The car stops.

I climb out as fast as the suit allows, put on my mask, and wobble over to the hospital entrance.

The automatic doors slide open for me, yet my feet aren't moving.

Shit.

Clarice is inside. She might be fighting for her life. The least I can do is go in there and be with her.

My feet still don't move.

Even with the suit, I'm too afraid to enter.

Fuck.

I'm the worst friend in the world.

I take a small step toward the door.

Nope. My feet take me right back.

A text ding from my phone startles me out of my stupor.

It's Blue.

I just checked with the hospital. Clarice had an allergic reaction.

Oh, no. I feel cold all over. Allergies are extremely dangerous. What is she allergic to? She never said.

I gather all my willpower to step inside the doors in front of me, but before I can muster the courage, another text from Blue arrives.

She's fine. She's just checked out.

A wave of relief washes away my anxiety, and it occurs to me that the info Blue has been getting sounds pretty private.

Would the folks at the hospital tell her all this over the phone?

Hopefully, she didn't hack into the hospital database—or if she did, she won't get caught.

"Gia?" a familiar voice says from behind me.

It's Harry, her eyes wild and her short blond hair more disheveled than usual. "Have you seen her?"

Shaking my head, I tell her what I've just learned from Blue.

"Let's go get her," Harry says.

I'm about to explain my trouble with that, but the doors open and Clarice steps out, her face only slightly swollen.

As I take off my mask, the relief I feel is tinged with guilt. As happy as I am to see my friend alive and well, a part of me is nearly as relieved about not having to go inside the hospital.

"Are you okay?" Harry and I ask in unison.

"I'll get us a ride to take you home," I say, taking out my phone.

Clarice nods. "Fucking ants."

Done summoning the ride, I exchange a worried glance with Harry.

"Did your aunts visit you?" Harry asks carefully.

"I'm pretty sure she's talking about the insects," I say. "Not that it makes anything clearer."

But wait. I think I get it now. The—

"The fucker crawled into my shoe," Clarice says indignantly. "As I was trying to let him out, he bit me."

"They're all female," Harry says.

I give Harry a disapproving look.

"Fine." Clarice readjusts her pirate hat. "*She* bit me. That bitch."

"And you're allergic to ants?" I ask.

"As it turns out," Clarice says. "I swelled up right away." She nods at the hospital. "They told me that if I hadn't called 911 right away, I'd be dead."

"Fucking ants," I say in horror. Should I add ants to my list of tiny creatures to avoid?

"We should get a black widow spider for the house," Harry says.

This time, it's Clarice and I who stare like she's lost her marbles.

"Black widow spiders eat ants," Harry says, as if it's obvious.

"They're also venomous," I say. "And, though it's not pertinent to us, they eat their mates."

Clarice shudders. "I'll take my chances with an EpiPen."

"Hannibal should be more useful than a spider anyway," I say. "Cats actually like eating ants."

Our car arrives and we all get inside. I notify our other roommates and Blue that Clarice is okay and heading home with us. Then I fish out the deck of cards I brought with me and hand them to Clarice.

As I hoped, her spirits lift considerably as she examines the fancy deck. Throughout the entire ride home, she shows card tricks to me and Harry, and continues doing so as we all eat lunch together at our place. Since nothing cheers up a magician faster than performing, I ooh-and-ahh long after I tire of the card magic, and I suspect the same is the case for Harry.

"Crap," I say as we're cleaning up after lunch. "I almost forgot. I have a meeting with Tigger."

Clarice grins. "Don't forget to bring a condom to the 'meeting.'"

"And your hazmat suit," Harry adds.

I snort as I head to my room. "I'll do no such thing."

In reality, I'm glad she mentioned the suit. It reminds me that I need to bring my swimwear.

It takes me a while to locate the bathing suit I bought a long time ago, during those happy days before I learned that ocean water can have flesh-eating bacteria, and that lakes are teeming with brain-eating amoeba.

Hmm. The bathing suit is tight. I hope my girls don't fall out.

Packing the suit and an extra pair of panties, I put on a dress designed to kill and choose a magic trick to perform in case Tigger asks for one—a twist on a classic.

My roommates wolf-whistle as I head out, and the male driver seems impressed with my décolletage, so I hope Tigger will be as well.

When I'm on the way, I get a call from Blue, and I update her on Clarice's well-being.

"Where did she find an ant in this concrete jungle?" Blue asks.

I scoff. "This coming from someone who always complains about the proliferation of birds in said concrete jungle?"

"Touché. Anyway, how are things going with the Ruskovian prince?"

Eyeing the driver warily, I switch to a form of Pig Latin Blue herself developed when we were kids. The idea then was to have secret conversations in front of our parents and schoolmates, but it should also keep the cab driver in the dark. "We did things," I say, "but

I'm not sure what base it would be in the baseball sex metaphor."

"What did you do?" she asks, needlessly speaking in Pig Latin as well.

I flush. "Masturbated in front of each other."

"Wow. Why?"

Should I tell her about my intimacy issues? Unlike my twin, Blue *can* keep a secret. State secrets, even.

But no. I don't want to be pitied.

"I'm taking things slow," I say, and it's not untrue. "I'm worried I'm his sexual Everest."

She rightfully asks me to explain that last bit, so I tell her that I think he views me as a challenge.

"If he leaves you after sex, you let me know," Blue says menacingly. "I just might risk an international incident."

Yeah, okay. Note to self: no telling Blue anything of the sort. The last thing I want is for her to get kicked out of the No Such Agency, or worse, to end up in a Ruskovian equivalent of Guantánamo Bay.

"I'm not even sure what *could* happen between us," I say, thinking out loud.

"Dating," Blue says. "You know, that thing people do when they eat meals together in nice restaurants."

I roll my eyes. "I'm not sure I'm even allowed to date a royal. Maybe I have to go to etiquette school. Learn to walk with a book on my head. Borrow corsets from Clarice. Hold forks with my left hand. Keep my vagina temperature a ladylike 99.5 degrees."

I can hear her evil smile as she says, "I'd start by taking him to your get-together with our parents."

"Great idea. That way, he'll run straight back to Ruskovia and never look back."

Before she can reply, another call flashes on my screen, so I apologize and switch over to it. It's my twin—and the Tigger conversation repeats with her, right down to "you should take him to your get-together with our parents."

Before I can tell her what I think of that idea, the cab stops and I hurry into the hotel.

Tigger is already waiting for me in the lobby—and if his hungry gaze is anything to go by, he does appreciate my décolletage.

Good.

Let's see what he thinks when I'm in my bathing suit.

I flush as I realize the other side of that coin.

He will be swimming as part of his training. That means I'll see his body again. Slick with water. Back muscles flexing as he torpedoes through the water…

Houdini have mercy on my ovaries. I'm glad I have a spare pair of panties.

Chapter Eighteen

As we make our way through the lobby—me a bundle of hormones, him with a graceful stride—a pantalooned dude walks up to us with a glass bottle filled with white liquid. Reverently, he hands it to Tigger and says something in Ruskovian.

With a curt nod, Tigger dismisses him, then uncorks the bottle and takes a gulp of whatever it is. A blissed-out expression appears on his face, and he extends the bottle toward me.

"Want some?"

I hide my hands behind my back. "What is it?"

"Matilda's milk." He looks completely nonchalant as he summons the elevator, as though his statement doesn't need any explanation.

"Who's Matilda?" Does my voice sound a bit green? "Please don't say she's your dutiful girlfriend who caters to your lactation fetish."

He laughs. "I don't have a girlfriend. What about you?"

The elevator opens and I step in. "I don't have a girlfriend either, but if I did, her name wouldn't be Matilda. She sounds underage."

He presses the button for the top floor. "Matilda is a cow."

My eyes widen, and I back away as far as the elevator car will allow—and not because he's on a first-name basis with a cow.

He frowns. "She's one of the few of her kind here in the US, a breed originally developed for the table of Ruskovian royalty."

My face must show my distress because he sounds defensive as he adds, "She has a good life. She roams free on an upstate farm. Gets massages that even Kobe cows would be jealous of." He takes another swig from the bottle. "This milk is like a taste of home."

My eyes bulge. "It's fresh?"

He frowns. "Yes."

"As in not pasteurized?" The elevator doors open and I quickly escape proximity to that bottle. Because what if he trips, the bottle flies into my mouth, and I accidentally swallow?

As he follows me, a realization seems to dawn on him. "You're worried this milk will make me sick?"

I vigorously bob my head. "Drinking unpasteurized milk is more dangerous than anything you've ever done. Sky diving, cliff diving, free diving—all other divings combined. It should be called hospital diving. Or Ruskovian roulette."

He caps the bottle. "It wouldn't taste the same if you boiled it."

"But you'd get to go on tasting other things… like poisonous mushrooms."

With a shrug, he leaves the bottle by the door leading to his new penthouse and I sigh in relief.

Hopefully, whoever milked Matilda did it the way my parents do on their farm: washed the udders and teats and then dipped them in an iodine solution.

Is it weird that I'm still a little jealous of Matilda? He consumes her bodily fluids, but not mine. That means she's further along with him in baseball metaphors—maybe halfway to first base?

Thankfully, Tigger is unaware of my musings as he swipes his card to let me in.

Wow. The suite now looks lived-in, and the flower arrangements appear brand-new.

One in particular catches my attention. There are a lot of a lupines and peonies in it, a pretty combo that makes me think of werewolf cocks. The arrangement also has bent spoons and his belt integrated into it.

"That one is for you to take home," he says, following my gaze.

He got me flowers? And not merely flowers, a freaking arrangement?

I suppress the swoony feeling blooming in my chest. This is our training time, so I need to keep things professional. "Thank you," I manage in a casual tone.

"The pool is ready for you," he says, his voice slightly husky. "You can change in there." He points at a nearby door.

I gulp at the heat in his eyes. So much for keeping things professional. I'm a puddle of need, and we still have our clothes on.

Stepping through the door into the bathroom, I swiftly undress, only to pause.

The last time I got naked outside of my room was when I was shopping for underwear. I feel more naked now than then. Probably because I've taken off my gloves this time around.

Also, unlike that time, I'm turned on and the temptation to stroll out naked is strong. So is the urge to masturbate. Even with a wall between us, Tigger's proximity is like lady Viagra.

But no. I'm a magician, not a nymphomaniac.

I put on my bathing suit, grab my dress and purse, and return to the living room.

Tigger is missing.

I put my stuff on the couch, and before I can call his name, Tigger comes back, wearing only a tight blue Speedo.

By Houdini's bulge. Why didn't I masturbate when I had the chance?

My nipples salute the sight, and it's an effort to keep the drool inside my mouth.

On his end, when Tigger takes in my outfit, the bulge in his Speedo grows tenfold.

Some of my drool escapes.

His Royal Hardness stretches that polyester-and-spandex blend, making the walls of my vagina sweat with envy.

"I'm ready for that swim," I choke out.

If the water is cold, maybe it'll provide that cold shower effect I desperately need.

He growls something unintelligible and points in the direction of the pool. Fighting the urge to sway my hips, I prance over there.

Yep. The thing is filled up.

"My brother told me it was sterilized before the water was refilled," Tigger says from behind me. His voice is still rough. "You're going to be the first to dive in."

I'm so horny even that hoarseness in his voice is driving me mad.

Taking in a deep breath in the way I'm going to teach him later, I dive in.

Whoosh.

The water isn't cold. It's perfect.

The feeling of weightlessness reminds me of childhood.

I hold my breath and swim until my lungs begin to scream, and then I swim some more.

"You were under a while," Tigger says when I resurface.

I wave it off, my inner magician activating. "I can do ten times that, you know that."

Lies, but I'm stuck with them if I want to keep this gig.

Deciding not to dive any more for fear of revealing my inability to hold my breath for as long as I claim, I do simple laps around the pool—and it's beautiful. Once I'm a famous magician and can afford it, I'll have my own personal pool that gets filled with clean water like this on a regular basis.

Eventually, I get tired and cold, so I swim over to the steps and climb out. I feel vulnerable being so naked and wet—that is, until Tigger walks over with a giant towel in his hands.

When he envelops me in the towel, I feel like I'm getting a hug for the first time in decades, and I warm up almost instantly.

First swim in forever, first hug, first sexual experience—Tigger is a source of a lot of firsts. Would it be so bad if I let that trend continue and had him be the first inside me?

He steps away, leaving me wrapped in a towel. A mixture of relief and disappointment floods me, but the disappointment evaporates as I enjoy watching him walk to the jumping platform of the pool.

"What exercise am I doing?" he asks.

"It's called a blind swim," I say. "You close your eyes and swim underwater, guiding yourself with just touch."

He nods approvingly, then turns and dives in.

I watch him do the exercise with his characteristic fearlessness. The idea behind the blind swim is for him to learn how to deal with the stress of the unknown, but I think I'm more scared on his behalf than he is.

When he resurfaces, I tell him to do some laps, mainly because I want to enjoy the view.

Oh, and what a view it is. The dudes from *Magic Mike* have nothing on this. Watching him turns me on so much I have to sit down and switch exercises.

We go on like that for a while, and the entire time, I'm aware of one simple fact: when his training is over, he just might offer to train me again.

What will that be like? How many orgasms will it entail?

Just thinking about it sends my heart for a loop. To forestall dealing with that possibility, I force Tigger to exercise until my bathing suit dries, then an hour after that—until I see his lips turn blue.

"You can come out," I say. "Don't want you to get hypothermia."

"Can you get me a towel?" He points at a table with a pile of them.

I do as he asks while he comes out, giving me the view from my wet dreams.

Since I'm unable to envelop him in a towel the way he did for me, I simply hand it over—and drool as I watch him dry himself.

By Houdini's clit, I'm so turned on I'd probably come at the touch of a feather.

"I have a surprise for you," he says. "Let's go inside."

I follow on unsteady legs.

He tosses the towel on the couch, sits down, and grabs a thick stack of papers.

"Can you sit here?" He pats a spot within kissing distance of him.

Can I? Sure. Should I? Probably not.

I do it anyway.

"This is for you." He hands me the stack.

I examine the pages with my mouth open.

It's his medical results, and they have nothing to do with free diving.

I look up from the papers. "Is this—"

"Test results," he says. "I went to the doctor and got myself checked for any and all communicable diseases known to medical science."

I greedily return to the pages.

He's not lying. It's test after test—and some of the diseases sound made up, while others seem like overkill, such as malaria, which is spread through the bite of a mosquito.

I guess if we're ever locked in a room with a mosquito, I'll feel safer now. Though, if he's like the Dos Equis man, *"mosquitos refuse to bite him purely out of respect."*

Another thing I'll do as a rich magician is get a hold of Tigger's doctor and have him run this panel of tests on me.

All the results I look at are negative.

When I get to the page labeled "STDs," I study it closer.

Gonorrhea—negative. Chlamydia—negative. HIV—negative. The list goes on and on.

"To sum up, I'm clean," Tigger says when I look up again. "I figured that maybe this will save you from having to wear that suit in my proximity."

Again, the ads pop into my head.

"He once tried to acquire a cold just to see what it felt like, but it didn't take."

"His sweat is the cure for the common cold."

"Some STDs have a long incubation period," I blurt.

He smirks. "I haven't been with anyone for the last four months. Does that help?"

I blink at him. "You haven't?"

Does he want to lose his manwhore badge?

He sighs. "Despite what the tabloids say, I don't sleep with everything that moves. In fact, I usually only have sex when I'm in a relationship, and my constant travels aren't exactly conducive to that."

Wow. His thrill-seeking sounds as bad for relationships as my magic career will be once it takes off.

More importantly, he's not actually a manwhore?

And he's clean?

This is hard to wrap my twisted mind around.

If this is true, I can kiss him and not die. It would not be very different from eating yogurt… in that his mouth is teeming with bacteria, but none of them are a threat.

I can also lick him.

And fuck him.

Except all these options sound frightening still, despite the papers.

I take in a breath and slowly let it out. "Can you please put your hand like this?" I raise my hand as though I'm about to swear on a bible—or Houdini's biography.

Bicep flexing, he does as I say.

"Can I touch your palm?" I ask.

He nods, his hazel eyes curious.

I reach toward him, as if I'm giving him a high five in slow motion.

When our palms are just a hair width apart, I stop.

Our skin is so close I can feel the heat radiating from his palm.

Another couple of millimeters, and I could experience my first human touch in a long time.

Only my palm doesn't move farther.

Closing my eyes, I even out my breathing to calm myself, but when I open them again, my stubborn palm doesn't budge.

I drop my hand in frustration.

Is that a pitying look on his face?

"Why can't I do this now?" I ask, more myself than him. "Germs aren't in the picture."

He lowers his hand. "It's okay, myodik. I didn't get those tests to rush you into anything, only to give you peace of mind."

"You don't understand," I mutter. "This is just like what happened at the hospital."

Worry lines cross his forehead. "What hospital?"

I explain what happened with Clarice, ending with, "And I was wearing a suit, so I was safe, but I couldn't walk in."

He brushes his fingers over the faded scar the asshole cat gave him. "I know my cat thing isn't the same, but I can sympathize. When I meet one, rationally I know that the little creature isn't more dangerous than something like surfing, but that doesn't help."

I flatten my hair with my palms. "That's just it. I've been telling myself I was simply being careful. That I was avoiding germs." Lowering my hands, I look at him wearily. "You must think I'm hopeless."

"No," he says gently. "I think you're stronger than you think."

I stand up and turn away. He's wrong. I'm about to fall apart.

He doesn't get it. This is a paradigm shift for me. I thought I was simply smarter than everyone else, but it turns out I'm no different from my sister Blue with her bird phobia. Worse maybe.

She's not afraid of birds that aren't there.

On some level, maybe I've always known I had a problem. Instead of wearing gloves all the time, I could just wash my hands after touching people, but I don't. I don't feel comfortable touching anyone, no matter what the science says.

Without my gloves, I feel naked.

Wait a second.

I'm gloveless now, but I don't feel that way.

That counts for something, right?

"Would you like me to distract you from whatever is going on in your head?" Tigger murmurs, and I turn to find him standing next to me.

I swallow at the look in his feline eyes. "How?"

A hint of a smirk curves his sexy lips. "I think it's time for your exposure therapy lesson."

Chapter Nineteen

Yep.

I'm distracted all right. So overstimulated by hormones, in fact, that I go into ovarydrive in an eyeblink.

"What kind of a lesson did you have in mind?" I whisper.

He crooks his finger. "Follow me."

Heart in my throat, I comply.

Not surprisingly, he leads me into his bedroom.

"One second." He takes two bulky bundles out of his closet and sets them down on the giant bed, then unrolls them.

I frown at the gloves and headgear attached to the jumpsuit-like things. "What are those?"

"VR suits," he says. "I thought you'd be familiar with them. They're the result of a project your twin was working on."

I blink in surprise. I know exactly what he's talking

about. The suits were designed by Holly's new bestie —she of the box of dildos.

The moment I heard about these, I loved the idea. The suits let you have realistic sexual experiences without touching anyone. It's like they were made with me in mind. Getting one has been on my wish list for when I have money to spare, especially since VR is one of the best ways to do exposure therapy.

Except, how does he have them?

"These aren't available to the general public yet," I say. "I asked my sister to tell me when they go on sale."

Tigger nods. "These are prototypes. My brother's venture capital firm funded the project, so he was able to pull a few strings and get these for me. I figured it could've been a good backup in case my bill of health wasn't one hundred percent… or if I was clean but you didn't feel ready to jump into bed with me."

Jump into bed with him.

That's the next phase of the training?

If it weren't for my Everest concerns—and my inability to touch him—I'd say "yes, please."

As is, I unseal the VR suit and watch him do the same.

"It's sterile," he says. "I checked."

Well, that's good. According to the instructions, you wear this thing in the nude.

My heart beats faster, and a hot flush spreads over my face.

Will he make me look away when he takes his

Speedo off?

Should I make him turn away when I strip off my swimsuit?

"I'll give you a moment," he says and opens the bedroom door.

"You don't have to leave," I blurt. "You've shown me yours. It's only fair I show you mine."

His eyes take on a predatory gleam. "You sure?"

Instead of wasting time answering, I take off my bikini top, ignoring the burning of my face.

His nostrils flare, and the spandex in the Speedo looks like it's about to rip. Before that can happen, he pushes the Speedo down, freeing His Royal Hardness.

With a loud gulp, I peel off my bikini bottoms.

We stand there for a few beats, drinking each other in. His body is all gleaming muscles and smooth, tan skin, every inch of him gloriously masculine.

"Gorgeous," he growls, his eyes devouring me.

I will my vocal cords to function. "Thanks." Grabbing the VR suit, I awkwardly adjust its straps.

"Lie down," he orders. "It's safer to put it on that way."

I comply and swiftly wriggle into the suit. When I put on the VR headset, I feel the bed dip. He must be lying on the other side now, only a short crawl away.

I hear the material rustling as it glides over his body, and I feel jealous of the suit.

I want to be the one covering his hard, delicious body.

"Ready?" he asks.

"Yeah."

"Turn it on."

I do that. Now the suit and I are both turned on.

A virtual reality dashboard appears in the air in front of me. It only has one app, represented by a golden sphere.

"There should only be one icon there," Tigger says. "Touch it, and I'll do the same on my end."

I poke the sphere.

Wow. My sister told me these gloves are good at faking tactile sensations, but I didn't expect the sphere to feel so smooth and round. It's only a silly icon, after all.

The suit comes to life and squeezes my body all over, providing a hug-like sensation. The view changes as well. I'm in a white room with two more spheres, with text hovering above them: "Design partner" and "Use defaults."

"Is it okay if I design my partner to look like you?" Tigger murmurs.

I nod, then realize he can't see me. "Sure. What about you?"

"I'd be honored if you made your virtual partner look like me." His voice is low and seductive.

I jab at "Design partner," then choose "Male."

The white room fills up with disembodied male heads.

Is this meant to be creepy?

"I think you just wave your hands to move the

heads around," Tigger says.

Yep. The heads fly back and forth at my command until I locate one with a face that most closely resembles Tigger.

"Change chin?" the app asks.

I do, and then I keep changing features until a slightly computerized version of Tigger's face is staring at me.

"Bodies are next," Tigger says. "I guess it's a good thing we've seen each other. No need to use imagination there."

Sure enough, "Upper body type" is the next choice. I recreate his torso in every mouthwatering detail, and when I'm done, the head attaches to his midsection.

Is the next step going to be what I think?

Yep. Every inch of the virtual space gets filled with cocks.

Large. Micro. Thick. Thin. Different colors. Different species. It's like that box with dildos from the other day, but on major steroids.

I go for the largest of the bunch, though it's a pale approximation of His Royal Hardness—a bit like how that CGI face is a crude copy of Tigger's real face.

Oh, well. VR beggars can't be choosers.

The next choice is legs, then butts.

"Hey," I say. "I didn't get a good look at your ass."

"I didn't see yours in enough detail either," he says. "We'll have to use our imaginations for this."

"Okay." I scan all the choices. "In case you're

wondering, mine has a butthole."

For whatever reason, some of the choices on display lack that anatomical detail, and some have it, but with a bejeweled CGI butt plug inserted—shameless product placement, no doubt.

"Does your butt have dimples?" he asks.

"Nope. Yours?"

"I think so."

Yum.

There. Finally finished.

As if to celebrate, virtual Tigger does a stripper dance for me.

This ovarydrive might just end in exploding ovaries.

Tigger's breath hitches. The virtual version of me must be doing this kind of dance for him.

Silicon hussy.

Two new spheres show up: "Multiplayer" and "Standalone."

"I assume we're doing Multiplayer," I say.

"Yep. Choose that and then 'Connect to the local network.'"

After I do that, everything goes white for a moment. When my vision returns, virtual Tigger is a few inches away from me, his bearing reminding me of the real prince's predatory grace.

In terms of the way he looks, though, he's still the same pale approximation of the real deal—from head to cock to toes.

Actually, the CGI toes look surprisingly real.

"Put your hand out the way you did before," I say breathlessly.

His avatar nods approvingly and does as I ask.

I reach out and touch his virtual palm the way I was too chicken to do earlier.

Again, the technology of the gloves amazes me. It feels as if I were doing this wearing my normal gloves.

How realistic is this suit?

To get an idea—and because I've dreamed of this for so long—I take his hand and put it on my virtual breast.

Virtual Tigger's face is impassive, but I know he likes this because I can hear him inhale deeply in the real world. He cups my breast, kneads it, and gently squeezes my nipple.

By Houdini's binary code, how did they make this feel so fucking real?

A zing of pleasure arcs down to my nether regions.

Unable to stop myself, I run my hand down his pecs and washboard abs until I reach virtual Royal Hardness.

The nice thing about VR is he can't see me blush like the maiden that I am. The textures of everything feel amazing. I'm beyond turned on now. If this suit isn't waterproof in the crotch area, it might short-circuit at any moment.

"Can you feel that?" I ask hoarsely as I stroke him up and down.

"Oh, yeah."

That response breaks the VR illusion because the words aren't coming from the avatar's mouth, but I don't care. I'm at Charlie's chocolate factory again, only my diabetes is cured.

"Can you touch me?" I ask.

"Fuck, yes." Without letting go of my breast, he slides his other hand down my belly.

Wow. I feel it. Maybe not as intensely as on my breast, but I definitely feel the motion.

How much is this suit? It's the best invention since the wheel.

His hand continues its wonderful journey farther down until it reaches my virtual folds.

"Damn," I gasp as the pleasurable tactile sensations reach my clit. "Are you touching me over the suit?"

"No." His voice is rough. "This technology is genius."

Oh, it is. His clever virtual fingers are stroking my clit, applying just the right amount of pressure.

An orgasm builds in my core.

A moan escapes my lips, and I stroke His Royal Hardness faster.

Tigger's groan is my reward.

I'm so close to the release I can taste it.

I move my hand faster.

He speeds up his strokes on my clit.

Yes. Yes!

"Please don't stop," I pant, squeezing him harder.

And at that moment, the fucking barking begins.

Chapter Twenty

Are there such things as pre-orgasm hallucinations? If so, why would I hallucinate dog barks? My kinks don't swing that way.

The barking grows louder, and I discern that there are at least two dogs making the sound.

Tigger pulls his hand away. His tone is filled with frustration. "We'd better get out of the suits."

Shit. Not a hallucination then.

I sit up and rip the headset off my head, then lie back to peel off the VR suit.

He's already wearing his trunks and holding my bathing suit out for me. Those military school drills at work.

Flushing again at his heated stare, I pull on the bikini and follow him out into the living room.

Not surprisingly, the barking is coming from two unleashed dogs: the panda and the koala, a.k.a. Caradog and Mephistopheles. They each have a piece of cloth in their maws and are tugging it in opposite directions.

Impressive. I bet I wouldn't be able to bark with fabric in my mouth.

What is surprising is the pantalooned dude sprawled on the floor, his feet tangled in leashes.

Did the dogs tie him up so they could play this canine tug of war?

Wait a second.

I narrow my eyes at the cloth they're pulling—just as it rips into two jagged halves. "That's my dress!"

Tigger shouts something in Ruskovian.

Caradog sits his butt down instantly, and a ragged piece of my dress covered in drool falls out of his maw.

Mephistopheles continues to shred his half of the dress.

Tigger repeats the command with more edge in his voice.

Mephistopheles looks up with puppy eyes. His gaze seems to say, "I'm innocent. I've been framed."

Caradog's goggles point right at the smaller dog, and he produces the scary growl I heard when Waldo held the knife.

Looking sheepish, Mephistopheles sits down with a whine but doesn't let go of the small piece of dress that's still in his mouth.

Tigger walks over and locks eyes with the dog. "Don't you dare swallow that."

Bossy. If I had something in my mouth and he

didn't want me to swallow it, I'd spit it out immediately. Or swallow it if that's what he wanted.

Mephistopheles whines more pitifully and finally spits out the cloth.

I'm reminded of the beer ads once again:

"He has taught old dogs a variety of new tricks."

"He once taught a German shepherd how to bark in Spanish."

"Good boy," Tigger says and helps the pantalooned guy get to his feet.

The guy darts a glance at me. Noticing that, Tigger says something sharp in Ruskovian. It doesn't take a lot of imagination to guess the translation: "Don't gawk at the almost naked magician."

The guy replies in Ruskovian.

"Speak English," Tigger growls.

"I'm so sorry," the guy says with a thick Eastern European accent, his gaze as far away from my naked flesh as possible. "The vet appointment must've gotten them overexcited."

Vet appointment?

"Watch them," Tigger says to the guy imperiously. Turning to me, he gentles his tone. "Let's get you something to wear."

Seriously, why do I like this bossy side of Tigger? All my life I've been told I have problems with authority.

I wink at Mephistopheles to show him I don't hold a grudge, then follow his master into the bedroom and watch as he pulls out a tank top and a pair of ripped jeans.

"Try this on." He thrusts the clothes into my hands and leaves for the living room.

I put on the tank. It's too long and my bikini top is visible from the side, but after I tuck the bottom of the tank into the jeans and roll up the pant cuffs, I look semi-presentable. Boyfriend jeans are totally a thing—if you can call them that when the guy is not your boyfriend. All I need now is—

Tigger walks back in, carrying a belt. "I had to take this out of your flower arrangement."

I loop the belt into my jeans. "Well, that was crazy."

He grimaces. "I take full responsibility. They're my dogs."

I waggle my eyebrows. "Sounds like you owe me."

He nods earnestly. "Anything you want, just let me know—aside from a new dress, of course. That's a given."

I don't know what possesses me to say the next words. If I didn't know any better, I'd accuse my sisters of hypnotizing me when we talked earlier. "I want you to join me and my parents for dinner."

No. Idiot. Sleep with him first. Once he meets the Octo-parental units, it's game over.

He cocks his head. "You make it sound like a big favor. I'd love to meet your parents."

Why am I sabotaging this non-relationship?

"When you meet my parents, you'll see how big of a favor this is."

He doesn't look intimidated. "When?"

I pull out my phone. I have ten unread texts from Octomom suggesting we meet "tomorrow."

I've now ignored at least five tomorrows.

Guilt bites at me. I'm such a bad daughter. I should've replied earlier, but I couldn't bring myself to do so.

My twin doesn't realize this, but there was a good reason why I asked her to pretend to be me, allowing me to skip this cursed lunch, and it wasn't the reason I gave her: that I didn't want our parents to bug me about my love life. Well, it's in part that. Mostly, though, I'm fed up with the lie I've been living in front of my family, the lie of being a daughter/sibling *without* intimacy problems.

The lie that keeps getting deeper each time I talk to my parents, thanks to their obsession with everything sex.

"Are you free tomorrow?" I ask cautiously.

"Sure," Tigger replies.

I text Octomom back and see if a dinner tomorrow will work.

The reply is instant:

Finally. How does 7pm sound? Where?

After a quick check with Tigger, I give her the location—the cleanest restaurant I've ever been in: Magia Pan Tumaca.

When we return to the living room, the dogs are

eating food out of their bowls, and the shreds of my dress have been cleaned up.

I rush to the couch to make sure my purse and gloves have survived.

Whew.

I put on the gloves and hang the purse over my shoulder. "I should go."

"One second, please." Tigger walks over to his dog sitter and takes a pile of papers the man has prepared. He then examines the papers approvingly before handing them to me.

I scan them.

They look to be test results.

Has he forgotten that I already saw his bill of health?

Wait. The names on the papers are Caradog and Mephistopheles Cezaroff—not Anatolio.

It's the dogs' health results.

I flip the pages. Damn. Even his canines are free of STDs. Why did he have them tested for that?

Should I tell him my kinks don't swing that way?

"I had the vet test them for everything known to science," he says, as though reading my mind. "I don't want you to worry about my fur babies when you visit."

"Wow. Thanks." Overwhelmed, I hand the papers back.

He drops the documents on top of his own. "I can also train them not to lick you, or rub against you, whatever you need."

The doggies must know he's talking about them because they look at him, then at me.

"They can rub against me if I'm dressed," I say. "In fact, can I pet them?"

Nodding, Tigger repeats the command from earlier.

Caradog is again the first to sit, but eventually, Mephistopheles does as well.

Readjusting my gloves, I walk over to the larger dog and gently stroke his fur.

Caradog's tail begins to wag, and the eyes behind the goggles close in pleasure.

Even through the gloves, his fur feels rougher than I'd expect. It reminds me of a donkey instead of a panda. Not that I've ever petted a panda.

A goofy grin spreads across my face. This is the second time today that I've channeled my childhood. At my parents' farm, we had a whole petting zoo of exotic and mundane animals to play with. Nowadays, I only have access to a cat—Hannibal—but he only lets Clarice pet him, and even then only when *he* feels like it.

Mephistopheles whines.

"You're jealous, huh?" I croon, then walk over and pet the little rascal.

This one's fur meets my expectations, in that this is how I've always imagined a koala might feel.

I look up to see Tigger gazing at me with a strange expression on his face.

I clear my throat. "Do you have round-shaped

treats by any chance?"

Tigger looks pointedly at the dog sitter.

The guy turns out to have pockets in his pantaloons, and he rummages in there to the point where one might suspect him of playing with himself. Eventually, he pulls out two cookie-like objects.

I take the first cookie and kneel in front of Caradog.

The panda looks excited about the prospect of the treat, but feeding isn't what I have in mind.

I recently heard that you can fool dogs with sleight-of-hand magic, but I haven't had the chance to try it.

I take the cookie in a finger grip so the doggie can be sure I have it, and then I perform a beginner trick featured in every book on coin magic—make it disappear right in front of my spectator's large, wet nose.

When I show my hands empty of the treat, Caradog's eyes widen comically behind his goggles.

I think if he were human, he'd rub those eyes with his furry paws.

He sniffs the air and his confusion deepens. No doubt he can still smell the cookie nearby.

To my delight, Tigger and the sitter also look amazed. I must not be as bad at coin magic as I thought.

"Now watch," I tell the panda-like dog and execute the most classic magic trick in history: making a coin—or in this case, a cookie—appear from the ear of a child… or a dog in this case.

Tigger and his minion clap. On his end, Caradog doesn't waste time. Minding my fingers, he snatches the treat from my hands before it can vanish again.

Mephistopheles whines again.

"I didn't forget about you." I take the second cookie and repeat the show.

Mephistopheles doesn't look as surprised as Caradog when the cookie vanishes, but he's extra ecstatic when it appears from his ear.

"That's not fair," Tigger says when I stand back up. "I want a trick too."

I was ready for this.

Opening my purse, I take out the props I brought just for this eventuality—three metal rings.

"Check these out." I hand two rings to Tigger and one to the dog sitter.

Tigger examines the rings carefully, no doubt looking for secret holes.

Is it wrong that I want him checking *my* holes, secret and otherwise?

When the rings are back in my possession, I perform another classic routine: first the two rings "magically" link together, then all three.

This time, it's only my human spectators who are amazed. The dogs act like metal penetrating metal is possible, and maybe it is in the canine version of the laws of physics.

I think they hope for a game of Frisbee with the rings.

Tigger exchanges a confused glance with the dog sitter. "That's just impossible."

"Check it again." I hand Tigger the three-ring arrangement so he can be sure they're now all linked together. "Keep that as a souvenir," I say with a cocky grin. "Maybe you can figure it out after I leave."

He shakes his head and walks over to the flower arrangement. "Speaking of keepsakes, don't forget this."

After I take my flowers, Tigger calls someone on his phone.

"A limo will take you home," he says a moment later. "This is also for you." He hands me a box.

When I see what's inside it, I chuckle.

It's brand-new tongs. I resist the urge to ask what he did with the ones they're replacing.

"Bye." I wave at the dogs and their sitter.

Tigger opens the door for me and walks me to the elevator. "Training tomorrow?"

The dule of doves resumes its fluttering in my belly. "Sure. When are you free?"

"Afternoon, before the dinner?"

I bob my head, not knowing what else to do. I'm becoming increasingly uneasy when it comes to the stupid free-diving training, but I don't know how to get out of it.

The elevator opens.

"Later," he says.

I step in and press the lobby floor button with an unsteady finger.

Chapter Twenty-One

As soon as the elevator doors close, I wonder why I left in the first place. Couldn't the dog sitter have watched the two bears while Tigger and I headed back into the bedroom?

Too late now.

The worst part is I miss him already.

What is wrong with me? Am I delusional enough to believe he likes me?

He doesn't. He can't. I'm just a challenge, nothing more.

Besides, he's a prince, and I'm a nobody. I still have no clue if he can date a commoner apart from a short fling. Also, he's a client—and one I'm lying to about my breath-holding expertise.

The only thing that's changed today is that he's not teeming with germs as I feared when I thought him a manwhore. Not that knowing that has helped my intimacy issues.

By the time the elevator opens, I'm almost glad I left when I did. I was at risk of catching those sneaky feelings I've been trying to avoid.

My step is more confident as I stride through the lobby, at least until I almost trip over a peacock.

Blue really would have a panic attack at this place.

The limo is already waiting for me when I come out, and as we depart, I realize something interesting.

I've been wearing Tigger's clothes and feeling zero skeevyness about it. I'm not usually so cavalier, not even with my twin. If I give her my clothes, I never ask for them back, and I certainly never borrow anything from her or any of my other sisters.

Speaking of the devils, I have texts from my twin and from Blue. I text them back, updating them on what's happened. They reply right away, each psyched that I'm taking Tigger to dinner with our parents.

In the middle of my exchanges, a text from Waldo arrives. He wants to hang out the day after tomorrow. I tell him to meet me at the coffee shop at eleven, since Tigger doesn't seem to be a morning person when it comes to training.

At home, my roommates make fun of my change of clothes.

"It's the famous disappearing dress trick," Harry says with a grin.

"I'm actually jealous." Clarice tips her pirate hat

to me. "I've always wanted someone to rip my bodice in the throes of wild passion."

I tell them all to shove their jokes up their hoohas, grab some dinner, and take it to my room.

As I eat, I research ideas for Tigger's training tomorrow, and my sense of unease about my lies and his eventual free dive deepens. What am I doing? I look over website after website, searching for some way to appease my guilty conscience, and then I come across a concept that really piques my interest. So much so, in fact, that I text Tigger and ask if he has a moment to talk via video or on the phone.

Can we do it in an hour? he replies. *Playing with the dogs in the park.*

I agree, smiling at the mental image.

As I put my phone aside, my smile turns upside down. One thing I haven't let myself think about so far is the other side of this coin.

His training of me.

We didn't make plans for that, which is good. If I want to stay safe, feelings-wise, we probably should stop that altogether. But if we do stop, what will I do for exposure therapy? I'm not willing to join the nunnery just yet.

I guess one thing I can do is get back to the usual: porn. In fact, that might be a good way to kill the hour as I wait for the chat with Tigger.

Locking my door, I fire up the porn and seek out something I haven't tried before.

Interesting. There's a whole genre I've never seen: double penetration or DP.

I let one video roll.

Wow. As the term implies, the woman takes two cocks, one in the butt and one in the vagina.

Hmm. I'm not as freaked out as I'd usually be. Am I getting better at this sex stuff, or is there something about this act that I actually like?

Have I just found my kink—getting stuffed like a turkey?

No clue, but I do have two dildos in case I want to find out. As a bonus, I could burn off a whole day's worth of sexual energy generated by looking at mostly naked Tigger, not to mention our encounter in VR.

Taking the toys out, I spot a few of my cherry-flavored condoms that would be appropriate for this occasion. I bought the first batch of these on the fateful day when I popped my own cherry, and kept buying them afterward on a lark. It would be symbolic if I used one of these to pop my butt-cherry—and DP cherry too, assuming I go through with this.

I examine the dildos.

Well. If this is to have any chance at all, Prince Regent would have to go into the front.

The big question is, can the smaller guy fit into the back?

Has it really come to this? A glorified butt plug? I bet you won't bother taking me out of your ass once I'm in.

Hmm. A butt plug. That might be a better idea. Too bad I don't have one.

The more I look at the smaller dildo, the less I think it will fit by itself, let alone allow me to DP myself.

Too big? It's too late for flattery at this point.

I get an idea. Something I probably should've tried a long time ago.

I go to my desk, grab a pair of latex gloves and a bottle of lube, then head over to the bathroom and lock the door.

My finger is pretty small. Smaller than even a butt plug.

Also, going where I'm about to go with my finger is probably the ultimate exposure therapy.

Before I chicken out or a roommate knocks on my door, I put on the glove, lube up a finger, and gently insert the tip where the sun doesn't shine and where no person has gone before.

Nope. The burning feeling isn't fun at all.

I might just be "exit only" when it comes to that hole—no DP for me, it would seem.

But hey, I'm proud I was able to do this.

I dispose of the glove and take a shower.

Returning to my room, I put DP out of my head. A regular go at Prince Regent is the ticket.

Yes, baby. Use me. Maybe get some of that yogurt from the fridge so you can dribble it all over yourself afterward.

Hmm. The yogurt idea isn't all that bad.

I pick up the eager dildo and start the phone app that controls it.

As I go to press the "vibrate" button, my screen

lights up with a video call from Tigger—and I accidentally click "accept."

Chapter Twenty-Two

I'm holding a dildo.

On a video call.

A huge dildo—though I'm not sure if that makes a difference.

Yeah baby, when it comes to Prince Regent, size matters bigly.

I'm tempted to drop the dildo, but the magician in me knows that would only bring *more* attention to it.

Too late anyway.

Tigger's eyes lock on to the dildo and his lips curve in a smirk. "Nice, myodik. Love your initiative."

I do drop Prince Regent then, and he smacks my foot painfully.

What did you expect? Prince Regent is massive.

Doing my best not to wince, I say, "That wasn't what I wanted to talk to you about."

He arches an eyebrow. "You sure?"

I fight the urge to fan my burning face. Business.

This is about business. "How much of a purist are you when it comes to free diving?" I ask in a business-like tone. *Good job, Gia.*

He runs a hand through his dark hair. "What do you mean by that?"

"What's your motivation for free diving? You said you wanted to explore an underground lake where scuba gear is prohibited. But do you have to have regular air in your lungs when you do that?"

He shrugs.

"What if instead of gulping air before the dive, you breathe nitrox—an oxygen and nitrogen mixture of the kind they use during a scuba dive? This should reduce problems if you go too deep, allow you to stay underwater longer and in greater comfort, and make the whole thing safer."

He scratches his chin. "I guess. It feels a little bit like cheating."

"They call it technical freediving," I say. "To me, it feels more like a magic trick."

There. That's as close as I've been to telling him my underwater illusion was just that—an illusion.

He smiles, his hazel eyes crinkling in the corners. "Well, you're my trainer, so if you think that's what I should do, I will."

I put on a serious expression. "I order you to use nitrox."

He gives me a military salute. "Yes, ma'am. I'll get gas."

I laugh. "In that case, here's a way you *can* cheat

the system: pump your butt with oxygen, learn to fart it in small doses, and capture the bubbles with your nose. Now *that* would be proper cheating."

He grins. "How about we focus on pre-breathing the gas mixture for the time being? I'll get a few different proportions, and we can experiment with them in the pool. It'll take me a couple of days, though. What do we do in the meantime?"

"Why don't you sleep in a hypoxic tent until then," I say. "We can resume pool training once you've got gas."

He gives me a mock frown. "So no training tomorrow?"

I wink. "You'll see me at the dinner."

And, hopefully, I'll think of a way to tell him that I don't want him to train me in the sexual arts any longer. More time should help with that.

"Is that all?" he asks.

"As far as your training goes, yes," I say, not liking how heated his gaze is turning.

"Great. Now it's my turn to train you," he says. "Pick up the dildo and wash it."

Well, so much for flaking on Tigger's training. There's no way I'm backing out of it now. My pussy would disown me.

I dash over to Manny, twist his head off, and prop my phone in his neck.

"Hold on," I tell Tigger as I snatch Prince Regent off the floor and sprint to the bathroom to clean him up.

The royal treatment. As befitting a figure of Prince Regent's stature.

When I come back to my room, I double-check that the door is locked, roll a condom onto Prince Regent, and smear lube on it before returning to the camera's view.

"What's the app that controls the toy?" Tigger asks.

"Search for Belka," I say and walk him through the process of installing it and syncing his phone with Prince Regent.

"Now," Tigger says when everything is ready. "I want you to strip and get on the bed in my view."

Not sure why I even bothered with that lube earlier. His commanding tone sends a surge of natural lubrication down south.

Blushing profusely but making sure I'm in view of the camera, I undress seductively, then lie on the bed, legs spread even though he didn't order for me to do that.

"Good girl," he murmurs. "Now place the tip on your clit."

I do as he says, and he gets Prince Regent vibrating—one-handedly at that.

Fuuuck. Why does this feel so much better than when I was playing with myself? A soft moan escapes my throat as I feel the orgasm creeping up on me. Except I shouldn't be the only one to come. That's selfish, right?

"Get naked too," I mutter, my voice hoarse.

Without slowing the vibration, he puts the phone aside so I only see his ceiling, then rips—or at least that's what it sounds like—his clothes off.

Before I can blink, the phone is back in his hand and he's mouthwateringly nude, with His Royal Hardness held tightly in his fist.

That was fast. Did he practice *that* at the military academy?

He ups my vibration speed, which, combined with the view, takes me over the edge.

Toes curling, I come with a choked cry.

"Now slide it inside," Tigger growls. "Slowly, just the tip for now."

As I obey, I fantasize that this is His Royal Hardness stretching me, not a silicone impostor.

He speeds up his fist and ups my vibrations another notch.

By Houdini's dildo, this really, really feels better than when I play with myself. Masturbation must be like tickling: doing it to yourself is meh, but if your evil sisters gang up on you, you just might pee yourself from giggles.

Tigger squeezes His Royal Hardness and grunts in pleasure. "Slide that deeper now."

I do, and a massive orgasm coils inside me from all the vibration.

While I can still talk, I manage to get out, "When you shoot your load, do it into the camera. Pretend you're coming on my face."

His pupils dilate to the size of nickels.

There. Two can play the dirty-talk game.

He increases the vibration further and speeds up his strokes.

A moan of pleasure is wrenched from my lips.

Then another one.

And another.

With a scream, I come all over Prince Regent.

Breathing audibly, Tigger repositions the camera so it's inches away from His Royal Hardness.

Sploosh. His cum gushes out like a fountain.

Eat your hearts out, bukkake videos. This is way hotter.

Suddenly, my view goes topsy-turvy and Tigger shouts an obscenity.

It takes my orgasm-addled brain a moment to understand what's happened: he's either dropped his phone in the heat of passion, or the cum has made it slip out of his grasp.

A crashing sound confirms my suspicions, and then all I can see is the ceiling.

The force of the impact must do something to the app because it cranks up my vibrations beyond anything I've ever felt. Before I can remove Prince Regent from inside me, I come one more time.

Great. If we keep this up, I might develop a new kink—a type of BDSM but with phones. I'll dress up in all leather, smash an iPhone, kick a Nokia in the screen, blend a Motorola in a blender, and water-board a Blackberry with toilet water.

Tigger is lucky he doesn't live with Hannibal, or

else the phone would have cat cooties from getting licked right about now. He does have the dogs, but I guess they missed their chance for a meal.

Breathing unevenly, I pull out Prince Regent and manually shut him off.

By the time I look back at the screen, the phone has been picked up, and Tigger's face is staring at me hungrily—though with the camera splashed with man-juice, he looks like the star of a bukkake video.

"That was fun," he murmurs.

"Yeah." I sigh. I can't bring myself to tell him that this was the opposite of what I had in mind when I decided to stop his version of training. My brain is flooded with oxytocin and his face is no less gorgeous with the cum obstructing my view.

I bite my lip. "I'd better go."

He gives me a tender smile. "Sweet dreams."

Sweet? No.

Wet? Definitely.

My X-rated dreams feature Tigger all night, and sometimes a gang bang of Tiggers.

"Which hole do I get?" asks one of the naked Tiggers.

I hungrily lick my lips and go for the method my sisters and I used to select which of us would be the victim of a tickle assault. "Eeny, meeny, miny, moe. Catch a Tigger by his cock."

When my holes are thusly assigned, we do everything from DP to bukkake, and my slutty dream-self loves every second and every droplet.

Chapter Twenty-Three

I wake up with a start and throw off my blanket.

Oh.

I'm just sweaty. For a second there, I thought I was covered in jizz. The wet dreams were *that* real.

I eye the drawer with Prince Regent. The "training" with Tigger burned off some of my sexual energy last night, but the dreams brought it all back with a vengeance.

My stomach rumbles.

Fine. Maybe I'll eat first.

I head over to the bathroom and then the kitchen.

"Hey," Clarice says when I enter.

I grin. "Are you munching on Captain Crunch?"

She grins back. "Are you about to gobble Frosted Flakes?"

Nodding, I grab the box with its Tigger-like tiger

and pour the cereal into a bowl before drowning it in oat milk.

"I think I heard your porn last night," Clarice says conspiratorially. "Hope you didn't dislocate anything."

I roll my eyes. "A lady doesn't kiss—or masturbate—and tell."

She chuckles. "That means *you* can kiss and masturbate, then shout it from the rooftops."

I stick my tongue out. "I'm totally a lady."

She nods in that "sure, sure" way, then says, "So, completely unrelated to anything, do you know how to dispose of used sex toys?"

I nearly choke on my cereal. "Why?"

"I'm just speaking hypothetically."

Sure. Hypothetically. Someone clearly doesn't like the gift from the box my twin's bestie brought.

"Hypothetically, can't you just toss them in the garbage?"

She shakes her head. "Stuff with batteries shouldn't go to a landfill. That's bad for the environment."

I purse my lips. "Recycle?"

"Nope. At least not in the trash version. I guess I could take it to The Salvation Army… hypothetically."

I eat a few spoonfuls in thoughtful contemplation. "What if you just take out the batteries and then trash it?"

"What if you can't?" she says. "Hypothetically."

She's got a point. I don't know where Prince Regent's batteries reside. "Burn it?"

She gives me an exasperated look. "Burn silicone? Do you recall what our muffin mold is made from?"

"Hopefully not recycled dildos."

"Silicone," she says. "And it only burns inside stars, so if you wanted to melt it, you'd need a bit more power than our oven provides."

"What if you bury it?"

Her eyes widen. "And have some neighborhood dog dig it out and then play fetch with a kid?"

"How about you turn it into arts and crafts?" I pour myself more milk. "Or use it to massage some *other* part of your body?"

She scoffs. "I'm serious."

"Can't you just leave it in the back of your nightstand drawer, like a normal person?"

"What if I have a heart attack?" she says. "My family will come to claim my stuff, and there it will be. Hypothetically."

I shrug. "My mother would be happy in that scenario and would probably keep it as a family heirloom."

As I speak, my food loses all flavor. I can already picture Octomom in the same room as Tigger. The dreadful event is just hours away.

"You're no help." Clarice takes off her pirate hat and scratches the top of her head. "On a different topic, I talked to your sister yesterday."

I dip my spoon into the cereal. "Oh?"

"Yep, but I can't tell you much about it. It's a private matter between me and Blue. I'm sure you understand."

Evil. She's making me curious on purpose. Probably wants to know about the porn sounds, after all. Or, more likely, she might be angling to trade the info for a secret behind one of my illusions.

My guess is that she likes one of the guys in that Hot Poker Club picture. That or she's fallen in love with the deck of cards they're using. After all, it must be water- and sweat-proof for that environment.

Yeah. She must be thinking of replacing her dildo with waterproof cards. That's why she's planning on tossing it.

"Nice try," I say. "I'm sure I could get Blue to tell me whatever it is if I tried."

She shrugs. "Good luck with that."

"Uh-huh, thanks." Since I'm done with my breakfast, I put my bowl into the dishwasher and bid Clarice good day.

Returning to my room, I decide to keep busy to prevent myself from panicking about the dinner. The best distraction, as usual, is magic, so I work on the routines for the show of my dreams.

This work is bittersweet. On the one hand, I love the fantasy of my own show, and fleshing out the routines brings it closer to reality. On the other hand, I'm far, far away from achieving my dream. I'm not famous yet, so who'll give me a venue?

At least the money I'm getting from training

Tigger will let me do more visibility-gathering stunts in the future, bringing me closer to my goal.

Around lunch, I get an idea for a new illusion that I could do on a big stage, one a lot like The Transported Man in *The Prestige*. The problem is, I would need to—spoiler alert—convince my twin to help out. In a pinch, sextuplets would work too. In fact, if I convinced all of them—which would be like herding a million cats—I'd be able to "teleport myself" up to eight places around the theater.

The spectators' minds would be blown.

A text from Tigger yanks me out of my magical scheming.

Pick you up at 6:30?

Shit. I need to get dressed ASAP.

I reply in the affirmative and begin frantic primping.

When I'm presentable, I decide on a magic trick to bring with me, in case someone asks to see something. The trick I go for limits my choice of shoes, but hey, great art demands sacrifice.

My phone dings. It's Tigger again.

I'm outside.

Crap.

Did I forget the ads? *"He never wears a watch because time is always on his side."*

I hurry out, ignoring the comments and wolf-whistles from my roommates.

Tigger stands next to his Lamborghini, holding the door open for me.

Fuck me. He's wearing a tight muscle shirt that makes me want to rip it off his body and lick his abs. And pecks.

He just might give Octomom a heart attack too. She's no spring chicken anymore.

Even though I'm not a hugger, I instinctively go in for a hug, and when he envelops me in his powerful arms, I nearly swoon on the spot.

"You look amazing," he murmurs when we separate.

"You're not hideous yourself." I plop my butt on the Lambo's seat and buckle up.

He gets behind the wheel and drives at the speed limit again—clearly for my comfort.

"How was your day?" I ask.

"Took care of some theme park business," he says, eyes on the road. "What about you?"

"I worked on my magic show," I say with a measure of pride.

"Wow. Cool." He starts to turn my way, then remembers that I prefer to have him looking at the road ahead. "When can I see this show?"

I shrug. "I have no clue."

"Why? Do you not have a repertoire yet?"

"A repertoire is only part of it," I say. "I could do an hour's worth of material today if I miraculously got the chance. What I don't have is a venue to perform in, and more importantly, enough fame to pack said venue with paying spectators."

"Hmm." He comes to a complete stop at a stop

sign, like a gentleman. "I would've thought knowing the secrets to illusions was the key."

"Secrets are only a small part. If you have no creativity but a large budget, you can buy illusions from other magicians. In fact, that's largely how I've been making *my* money—by selling my secrets to bigger performers. To perform, you need showmanship."

"You have that in spades," he says confidently. "I think you've got everything you need to be a star."

I feel all warm and tingly inside. If his goal is to use flattery to get into my panties, it's working.

"What about you?" I ask. "Is running a theme park your dream job?"

He nods. "It doesn't feel like a job-job, but sure."

I scratch my head. "What about the flower arranging? Does that feel like a job?"

He chuckles. "No. That's a hobby. I do it for fun."

I smooth my palms over my pants. "I watch movies for fun."

"You're a movie buff?" He glances at me, then returns his gaze to the road.

"Yeah, I love movies," I say. "I think it goes back to magic tricks for me. A video is a set of pictures flashed quickly enough to create the illusion of movement. Using the tools of their craft, the actors create the illusion of real people on the screen—people who don't actually exist. A good soundtrack can create illusory emotions. The comparisons can go on and on."

"I've never thought of films that way." He turns the wheel and parks the car in one smooth maneuver. "We're here."

Yep. There it is.

Magia Pan Tumaca, where the Octoparents await.

Chapter Twenty-Four

The first thought that comes to mind when you enter the restaurant is "clean", which is one of the reasons it's my favorite. It's got a modern-art aesthetic, with chrome dominating all the surfaces. Hell, even the tablecloths look metallic, as they're made from some type of tinfoil that's replaced between each customer's visit—another reason I like this place.

Sitting at the bar are my folks, and though I can see their reflections in the mirrored wall, they haven't noticed me.

Octomom looks as amazingly youthful as always. She could easily pass for my older sister, and therefore looks a bit like Cate Blanchett in the later parts of *The Curious Case of Benjamin Button*. Dad looks like he should be very rich to be with a woman like her, except he isn't—he just hasn't aged as well. Octomom says he looked like Bob Dylan when he was young, but now he looks like a hybrid between Danny Devito and Jeff Bridges: a shaggy beard, a beanie hat that hides his bald spot, and last but not least, a thin silver ponytail scrounged up from the hair that's left.

"Wait here," I tell Tigger. "I'll introduce you in a second."

He nods, and I go over to the bar to clear my throat.

Mom turns, beaming, and puts her hands in a yoga greeting. "Namaste, sunshine."

"Thing 2." Dad pats my shoulder, his face lighting up with a goofy grin. "Are you tense? Uncentered? My shoulder rubs have gotten even better."

Oh, yes, I almost forgot that I'm Thing 2. Since my twin was the first to leap out of Mom's uterus, she's considered "the oldest" and Dad calls her Thing 1 (out of 8).

Octomom narrows her eyes at me. "You *are* Gia, right?"

Since I made my twin pretend to be me at the last "get-together with Gia," I can't blame her for being suspicious.

"I'm Gia," I say. "I swear."

"Prove it," Octomom says.

"*Downton Abbey* sucks," I say solemnly. They don't look convinced, so I add, "It's called a bathroom, not the loo. Elevator, not a lift… and I like the number four." They're almost convinced by the last bit since my twin abhors any numbers that aren't prime to the point where she might've looked pained to lie about it.

Before I can come up with something even more convincing, Octomom lunges at me and gives my hair a vicious tug.

"Ouch!" I yelp. "Are you crazy? It's attached."

She releases me and nods approvingly. "Not a wig. Might be Gia this time. That or she colored her hair."

I turn to Tigger and give him a "watch this" look.

"Here," I say, turning back to my parents. "Can Holly do this?"

With that, I perform the magic trick I prepared for today. It's a type of levitation where my legs are bent backward as though I'm in a sitting position, making it so my butt floats in the air, defying gravity.

When Neo was dodging bullets in *The Matrix*, he would do this in slow motion.

This trick is part of the routine I'm preparing for my eventual show. During an actual performance, I'd follow this up with the iconic forty-five-degree lean-forward à la Michael Jackson in "Smooth Criminal."

"Wow," Tigger exclaims, and it's music to my ears. "How?"

Other restaurant patrons express similar sentiments, which makes me feel more confident about adding this trick to the show.

"It's Gia all right," Octomom says.

I straighten and wink at them. "As I said. Now come, there's someone I want you to meet."

I drag them over to where Tigger is standing, mouth still agape from my awesome display of powah.

"These are my parents, Crystal and Harry Hyman," I say to Tigger. Then I gesture at Tigger as though he were a museum exhibit. "Mom, Dad, this is Anatolio Cezaroff."

"Call me Tigger," he says.

Octomom recovers first and launches herself at Tigger, enveloping him in a huge hug.

"Mom," I say sternly when the hug goes on longer than what is socially acceptable. With as much sarcasm as I can muster, I ask, "Don't you want to give Dad a chance to hug my date also?"

When Octomom reluctantly disconnects, her cheeks are flushed and her smile disturbingly coquettish—not that I can blame her.

Oblivious to my sarcasm, Octodad dives for his hug. A moment into it, he starts feeling up Tigger's back.

"Dad." My voice is even sterner. "We should get to our table."

Octodad disengages and looks worriedly at Tigger. "Your shoulders are so tense."

Tigger shrugs. "I think I'm overwhelmed by your daughter's beauty."

Boy, does this feel good. Tigger is turning me into a flattery junkie. Before I know it, I'll be turning magic tricks for a fix.

Fuck.

While I was basking in the compliment, Octodad grabbed Tigger's hand and is now dragging him to a nearby chair.

"Sit," he says. "I'm going to recharge your batteries."

Looking a little stunned, Tigger sits down, and Octodad begins massaging his princely shoulders with his hairy, sausage-like fingers.

Is this a battery recharge or an assault? Octodad works with such vigor his silver ponytail trembles like a seismograph during an earthquake.

Meanwhile, Octomom looks on with envy.

On my end, I want to scream from embarrassment—a sentiment that Tigger doesn't seem to share. If anything, he seems to be enjoying the impromptu massage. But of course. What did I expect? This is a guy who doesn't get perturbed when standing with his cock out in a coffee shop.

Why is this happening? What have I done to Octodad for him to behave like this? Did my unwillingness to let him hug me drive him to get handsy with my date?

"Dad," I plead. "Come on."

"One sec, just a quick head rub," Octodad says and begins massaging Tigger's skull. "Do you feel it? The energy?"

I'm going to need therapy. Maybe it was living with nine females that did Octodad in? Or did he witness a Zombie Tit Massacre of his own?

The other patrons are beginning to stare as well. Between my earlier trick and now this, they'll remember us forever.

"You have to stop," I growl at my father.

"Just one more thing," he says and kneels at Tigger's feet.

I'm speechless.

Is he going to offer him a reenergizing blowjob?

"Take off your shoes," Octodad says.

Nope. It's even worse. "Dad," I grit out. "What the hell?"

"I'm a master at foot massaging," Octodad says proudly. "Just ask your mother."

"Sir," a new voice says, and I pray it's a voice of reason. "This table is reserved for a party of two."

I turn and give a grateful look to the hostess, who's wearing a stoic expression.

"Are you the Hymans?" She says this as an accusation instead of a question.

My nod looks a bit like I'm hanging my head in shame.

"Come this way." She gestures to the other side of the restaurant.

Tigger leaps to his feet and helps Octodad stand up.

"What a gentleman," Octomom says approvingly.

It turns out that the hostess wants us to sit in a private alcove. She's even giving us a table that's clearly meant for a bigger group. I wonder why.

"There will be no foot massage," I hiss into Octodad's ear when Tigger takes the lead.

"Why not?" my father whispers.

"I don't know where to start," I hiss back. "How

about this: taking shoes off in a restaurant is unhygienic."

"Oh, yeah," Octodad says. "You're Gia for sure."

Upon reaching the table, Tigger pulls out a chair for Octomom, prompting her to begin drooling.

Octodad looks at me pleadingly. "Can I sit next to him?"

Okay. I have a new theory about my male parent's apparent insanity. He sees Tigger as the son he never had. After all, it's not a secret how much he's always wanted one. Both Octoparents have. After girl twins, they used assisted reproduction technology in the hopes of getting a male child. When cruel fate gave them girl sextuplets instead, Octodad lost a marble… or six.

Tigger pulls a chair for me next to Octomom. "Sure thing."

Hey, at least if I sit side by side with her, I won't be embarrassed by the lustful looks she's shooting at my fake date.

A waiter appears out of thin air. "Can I get you some drinks?"

I ask for a sealed water bottle while everyone else goes for the restaurant's signature drink: sangria with Rioja wine, peaches, nectarines, and pears.

"So," Octomom says to Tigger when the waiter is gone. "Are you *really* Gia's boyfriend?"

Shit. This is what happens when you have a trickster reputation.

"Of course," Tigger says. "Who else would I be?"

"A male friend pretending to be one," Octomom says.

Tigger smirks. "I don't believe a straight man like me and a woman as gorgeous as Gia could ever be platonic friends."

Even though he's teasing me about Waldo, all I can focus on is the "as gorgeous as" bit. I know he's just playing a role here, but it still feels amazing to hear. That addiction to compliments is imminent.

Octomom's forehead furrows. "You might be the boyfriend of one of her many sisters, who's returning a favor. My daughters are all about exchanging favors, like gangsters."

Tigger winks at me. "Your daughter has a cute birthmark under her right breast. Would the boyfriend of one of her sisters know that?"

That birthmark is tiny. How closely was he looking at me?

Also, I love that he thinks it's cute.

Mom strokes her chin. "Her twinsie knows about the birthmark, and so might the other sisters."

I heave a sigh. "This is ridiculous. Tell me honestly, if Tigger were *your* boyfriend, would you let any other woman borrow him?"

Octomom looks thoughtful. "Good point. He's not a borrow."

Our drinks arrive, and the waiter places the menus in front of us before leaving.

Eyeing Tigger speculatively, Octodad pours

sangria for everyone except me. "Maybe he's a male escort?"

I roll my eyes. "If he were an escort, I wouldn't be able to afford him."

"Not true." Tigger grins at me. "I'd give you an amazing rate."

"See," Octodad says triumphantly.

I shake my head. "Please take out your phones and google 'Anatolio Cezaroff.'"

While they do so, I unscrew my water bottle and take a sip.

My phone vibrates in my pocket.

I pull it out and sneak a peek.

It's a text from Tigger.

Your parents are sweethearts, especially compared to mine.

Well, it's a relief that he feels that way so far. I was half expecting him to run away screaming by now.

Just wait, I reply.

He grins and sips his sangria.

"Wow." Octodad looks up from his phone with a stunned expression. "You're a prince?"

Tigger shrugs. "It sounds fancier than it is."

"And you're from Ruskovia," Octomom says in awe. "Did you know her twin's boyfriend is from Russia?"

"I've met him," Tigger says. "A nice guy… for a Russian."

"Many Eastern Europeans don't like Russia, thanks to their Soviet past," Octodad says in a professorial tone.

"Tell us what Ruskovia is like." Octomom is almost bouncing in excitement. "And what it's like to grow up as a royal."

Sipping his drink, Tigger tells them some of the things I've already heard, but I learn a few new tidbits too, like that his family has an honest-to-goodness motto: "In tradition, strength."

After he tells them what he does for a living, he asks them the same, and I cringe.

"I'm a penetration tester," Octodad says proudly. "But it's not what you might think."

"He penetrates computers," I say with an eyeroll.

"No, I penetrate computer systems," Octodad says.

"And me," Octomom adds with a grin.

"Of course." Octodad looks at his wife as if she were a slice of ham. "Though that's a hobby, not a job."

Shoot me now. If they start talking about their sex lives, Tigger will run for sure—and I'll sink through the floor.

"And what do *you* do?" Tigger asks Octomom, unfazed.

"I'm a chick sexer," she answers with relish.

"Which also sounds like my hobby," Octodad says with a wink.

My eyes are tired from all the rolling. "Mom helps large commercial hatcheries separate baby chickens into male and female."

Octomom sighs. "Nowadays, I do more around

our farm since my job is slowly being replaced by in-ovo sexing."

I start typing a text to Tigger under the table:

Please do not ask what she does on the farm.

Too late. Before I can click "send," he asks that very thing.

"Do you know what you want?" the waiter asks, appearing next to me.

Everyone looks at one another.

"I know what I'm having," I say. "I've been here before."

"Why don't you order as we check the menu?" Octomom says.

Whew. The farm question is forgotten.

"I'll have the Pan Tumaca," I say to the waiter. To everyone else, I explain, "This is their signature dish. A yummy toasted bread with salty tomato and olive oil."

"I'll get the same," Octomom says.

"I'll get a Tortilla Española," Octodad says.

"That's a potato-and-egg omelet," I tell him.

"I knew that," he says, but I can tell he's lying. "I want it."

"I'm very hungry," Tigger says, his eyes roaming the menu. "I'll get a Pan Tumaca also, and a Tortilla Española, and chorizo."

All blood drains from my face. "Chorizo is sausage."

It was also not on the menu before, or else this place would've ceased to be my favorite.

Tigger closes the menu and hands it to the waiter. "Yeah. Pork sausage. I went hang gliding in Spain last year. Love that stuff."

It takes all my willpower to keep my mouth shut regarding sausage. I know from experience that my truths are not welcome at the table.

But seriously, sausage? Hang gliding is way safer. Sausage is made from all the parts of an animal that no one wants to buy. No other food item has had more media coverage, everything from foodborne illnesses down to the grossest stuff I've ever heard—like when they found human DNA even in the vegetarian versions. And the worst part? The traditional casing for sausages is intestines.

It's like some butcher's idea of a cruel joke.

On a separate note, it reminds me of the Dos Equis ad where, *"when he goes to Spain, he chases the bulls."*

"Great choices," the waiter says. "The chorizo especially—it's a new item. The chef makes it from scratch from Mangalitsa pigs."

Ugh. At least this is a fancy place, so the chef might use high-quality cuts of meat. Hopefully, that means Tigger will survive this.

"To answer your earlier question," Octomom says when the waiter leaves. "I do everything at the farm, but my favorite is husbandry."

Shit. Octomom is like a fucking elephant. If it leads to embarrassment, she won't forget.

I give Tigger my best "please don't ask" look, but

he doesn't seem to get it and raises an eyebrow, clearly intrigued.

Sure enough, Octomom tells him the story of how she brought Petunia—a piggie who was like a pet to us growing up—to orgasm during an artificial insemination session.

"It improves the chance of piglets by six percent," Octomom says proudly.

Dammit. Is she thinking of switching jobs from chick sexer to pig orgasm bringer?

Tigger just nods.

I hope that picturing Mom mounting and fisting Petunia ruins his appetite for that chorizo.

"Anyway," I say, looking from one parent to the other. "Tell us about your New York tourist adventures."

This has to be safer than farm topics, right?

Tigger sits straighter. Being more or less a tourist himself, he's clearly interested.

"So much to tell," Mom says. "Yesterday, we went to a foot party."

Is that what I think it is? Please let it not be.

Tigger arches an eyebrow. "A foot party?"

"It's a get-together for people with a foot fetish," Octomom says.

Sadly, it is what I guessed.

By Houdini's toes, what have I done to deserve this?

Before anyone can elaborate—and I know they want to—our waiter comes back with a tray.

As the plates are placed in front of everyone, I wish most reverently that they'll forget this topic of conversation, but I know they won't.

Yep, as soon as the waiter is gone and Octodad tastes his omelet, he says, "To spice things up, we've been researching all sorts of kinks."

I bite into my bread with desperation. Maybe a miracle will happen and they'll follow my example, stuffing their mouths with so much food that they'll stop talking.

"Yeah." Octomom picks up her bread. "Turns out, we both like foot play."

Nooooo. I can't unhear that. Also, with that disturbing new information in mind, was Octodad trying to get kinky with Tigger when he offered him that foot massage earlier?

Should I be jealous of my own father?

"The food is getting cold," I say and give my Pan Tumaca another huge bite.

That seems to help. Everyone attacks their meal, and there's blissful silence for a couple of minutes.

As I'm eating my second Pan Tumaca, my phone vibrates.

It's a text from Tigger.

Impressive. I didn't even see him type. Then again, I'm doing my best not to watch him eat the sausage, because yuck.

Once again, myodik. Love your initiative.

What? The last time he said that was when he

thought I intentionally took his video call with a dildo in my hand.

Was I just eating my bread seductively? Licking tomato from my lips?

I peer at him.

His lids are hooded, like I'm doing more than eating to seduce him.

What the fuck?

I sneak a glance at Octomom to see if she's noticed.

Octomom has a piece of bread in her hand, but something is off about her posture. She's slumped low in her chair, almost as if—

No. Please no.

I raise the metallic tablecloth and use my phone as a flashlight.

For a second, I refuse to believe the information my eyes are sending back to my brain, as every little detail adds to a truly disturbing whole.

Octomom's shoe is off, which is bad. Her foot is naked, which is worse. And it's clear she's taken the foot fetish to heart: she has on an impeccable purple nail polish, an ankle bracelet, and a toe ring.

Of course, what makes my brain hurt is not the adornments on her foot, but what it is doing—and where.

It's rubbing a humongous pants tent… on Tigger's crotch.

Chapter Twenty-Five

"Mom!" I yell so loudly the other patrons turn our way. "What the hell?"

Octomom looks under the table, turns beet red, and jerks her foot away from His Royal Hardness.

"I'm so sorry," she says to Tigger. "I thought it was Harry."

Once again, Tigger seems impervious to embarrassment. "It's an honest mistake," he says. "It would've been worse if Gia had mistaken Harry for me."

Great. Thanks. Now *that* mental image makes me want to commit suicide by sausage.

"No," I say sternly. "I'm sane enough to know that foot play isn't for the dinner table. A table in public. In front of someone I've just met."

"Hey," Octodad says, matching my sternness. "Don't kink-shame your mother."

"Yeah," Octomom says, her blush dissipating.

"You should be happy your parents have an amazing sex life."

I glance at Tigger.

He seems to be on their side.

Taking a few deep breaths, I say, "Sorry. I didn't mean to shame anyone. I'm happy for you guys. Just keep all your appendages away from my man going forward."

Upon hearing me call him "my man," Tigger gives me his cockiest smirk yet.

Octomom winks at her husband. "She's jealous. Definitely not a pretend boyfriend."

I stuff my mouth with tomato toast before I say something I might regret.

"Yep, he's real," Octodad says. "First one twin, now the other. It's the karmic balance at work. Isn't love grand?"

Is he on Ecstasy? Maybe both of them are? It might explain some things.

"Let us know if you ever need sex advice," Octomom says to Tigger with utter seriousness. "Between the two of us, we've got decades of experience. We believe everyone should have the most toe-curling, mind-boggling, tantric orgasms they can accomplish."

I nearly choke on my bread.

"Thanks," Tigger says, matching her tone. "I might just take you up on that."

Coughing tomato-y crumbs out of my breathing pipe, I squeeze out, "Or we'll manage on our own."

Octomom nods solemnly. "Just know that the support system is there, should you need it."

A lanky guy waltzes up to our table with rubber bands on his thin wrists. "Good evening, folks. My name is DJ. I'm your entertainment for tonight."

Ah. Right. Another reason I like this restaurant is that they hire magicians to work the tables. Though this is not my style of performing, I like supporting my fellow deception artists, plus there's always that small chance that someone will actually fool me.

"Are you a magician?" Octomom asks him.

"Yes, ma'am," he says.

"My daughter is too." She nods at me.

DJ looks me over skeptically. "That's nice."

Octodad grins at DJ. "Are you as passionate as our Gia about your art?"

DJ shifts from foot to foot. "Sure."

Octodad smiles. "I admire people who follow their passion. Magic makes people feel good. If you put out loving energy into the world—"

"Dad, let the man do his trick," I say.

DJ frowns at me. "Maybe what *you* do are tricks. I perform *effects*."

So, he's one of *those*—magicians who consider the term "trick" demeaning. Some of my roommates are in this camp, but I consider the distinction silly. When people go home and tell friends about the magic, it's always, "I saw her do this cool trick," and never, "I saw her do this cool effect." Even the term "illusion" is rarely used by lay people—and *that* word does sound better than "trick," even to me.

"DJ, was it?" Tigger says coldly. "Please watch your tone."

Wow. I'm conflicted. A part of me is giddy that Tigger is defending my honor, but a much bigger part is annoyed because I can take care of myself.

"Let's give him a chance to show the tricks," Octomom says to DJ with a smile.

"Effects," he mutters, then pulls out a red sponge ball.

So, let me get this straight. He's about to do something that involves an object resembling a clown nose, yet he wants it dignified by the term "effect?"

I don't say anything because DJ already looks pretty sullen.

Since everyone else is silent as well, he performs a few mediocre vanishes with his ball.

My parents look bored. I did this sort of thing for them when I was ten.

Hopefully, I did it better.

Tigger looks grudgingly impressed, so I make a mental note to do something magical for him that also involves balls. All kinds of balls.

"I'd like to borrow someone's hand," DJ says in a bored tone.

"Have mine." I open my gloved hand.

Reluctantly, DJ puts the "single" sponge ball into my hand and makes a magic gesture.

Feeling mischievous, I use this moment to steal the rubber bands from his wrist.

"Open your hand," DJ says triumphantly.

I open, and two balls fall out—as I expected.

Tigger's eyes widen.

Yep, I definitely see major ball action in his future.

"For my next effect, I'm going to use cards," DJ says and pulls out a deck from his back pocket. "I'll demonstrate a technique called palming." He looks snidely at me. "Maybe you'll learn something."

"Excuse me?" I narrow my eyes at him. "What's that supposed to mean?"

Hmm. Maybe that was too unfriendly? Cards *are* my weakness, so I guess I'm a bit touchy.

"Girls are bad at palming," DJ says. "Everyone knows that. Their hands are too small."

Oh no, he didn't. If Clarice were here, she would make him eat that deck. She might be the best in the world when it comes to palming—and the fact that her hands are tiny only helps it seem more impossible.

"I bet she can palm better than you," Tigger says and pulls out a crisp one-hundred-dollar bill.

"Yeah," I say. "And just to make it easier for you, I'll do it with my gloves on."

DJ scoffs and hands me the deck. "Be my guest."

I take the cards out and spread them out as I say, "Let me see if you play with a full deck."

What I'm really doing is desperately thinking up something on the spot. Then it hits me, and I sneak the four of clubs into a palm position—something no one should see since the trick hasn't officially begun.

"Name any card," I say to DJ as I put my hand with the card into my pocket and fasten his rubber bands over it.

"Four of clubs," DJ says as I get my hand out of my pocket.

"Four of clubs?" I do my best not to show my glee. As I hoped, he named the card most popular among magicians. Now for a bluff, "Do you want to change your mind?"

Please don't.

He shakes his head. "I'll keep the mind I have."

Thank goodness.

"Watch me palm it," I say and wave my empty hand over the deck. "Did you see it?"

DJ rolls his eyes. "You didn't do anything."

"Oh?" I ask. "Then what if I told you I did palm the four of clubs, snuck it into my pocket, then stole your rubber bands and wrapped them over it?"

Tigger's eyes widen, and even my magic-savvy parents look impressed.

DJ's gaze darts to his wrist, and he pales when he sees it empty.

"Want to check my pocket?" I ask.

Tigger clears his throat. "If he touches you, he'll lose his hand—and he needs it to continue palming."

I roll my eyes. "Fine. How about you fish it out for him?"

Tigger complies, holding the rubber-band-wrapped card up to DJ's face.

DJ snatches the card and backs away. "I have to go to another table."

"I accept your defeat," I call after him as he skedaddles.

"This reminds me of the bet I made with your father the other day," Octomom says. "He thought my Kegel muscles were not strong enough to crack a walnut."

And just like that, the happiness from my win is gone without a trace. All I want now is for someone to bathe my brain in bleach.

"Yeah," Octodad says wistfully. "I still owe her a sexual favor for losing."

Maybe bathe my ears in bleach also?

"Would anyone care for dessert?" the waiter asks, appearing out of nowhere and thus proving himself a better magician than DJ will ever be.

"I'm stuffed," I say, though even if I were starving, I wouldn't want to continue this conversation.

"I'm too full also," Octomom says, and the men agree.

"Here's the check then," the waiter says.

Tigger snatches it quickly. "My treat."

Octomom beams at him. "Only if you let us get it the next time."

She thinks he'd be willing to do this again?

"It's a deal," Tigger says, sounding like he means it.

Somebody give this man an Oscar. Or if it's for real, a halo.

"You'll also have to visit the farm," Octodad adds.

"Sounds good," Tigger says.

Yeah, sure. Over my dead and fully decomposed body.

As Tigger pays, a hint of anxiety spreads through me. Bidding parents farewell, I miss whatever embarrassing thing they say as a goodbye because the feeling grows.

When we start the drive back, I'm able to pinpoint the cause.

I'm worried about that moment when we get to my place. Despite knowing that this wasn't a date, my parasympathetic system is on full alert—as though it totally was a date, and it's about to end in the usual disaster.

By the time he parks next to my house, I'm ready to bounce off the walls.

Tigger turns to me. "Just to make it clear, I will not try to kiss you."

I blink at him, not sure if I'm relieved or disappointed. "You won't?"

"Not unless you want me to," he says, his hazel eyes soft and warm. "Bear in mind, we're skipping all training today. If anything happens, it should be purely out of desire, not for educational purposes."

Unbuckling my seatbelt, I process his statement.

He's not training me today, but it also sounds like if I wanted to kiss him, he'd be down.

Fuuuck. Do I want this—assuming I can do it?

Hells yeah.

It might be lust clouding my common sense, but I do want it. Badly.

And why not? Even if it's just this once, what better first kiss can I ever hope for?

He's a prince. The only way a kiss could be more epic is if he were a frog that turned *into* a prince after a little bestiality action.

Which gets me back to "Can I?" That's a million-dollar question. The answer is that it's super unlikely today, but what I do want to try again is touching him without a glove.

That should be doable, right?

Tigger watches me think silently, and I can't help but feel that he looks like a predator patiently stalking his prey.

"I want to touch hands," I say finally.

"Sure." He puts his hand out, like for a high five.

I shake my head. "I don't want to do it here. I have bad associations with cars."

He nods in understanding. "Just tell me where you'd be more comfortable, and we'll go there."

"My room," I say. "But you should know that I will most likely chicken out."

His lips quirk. "No worries. I'd be happy just to see another magic trick."

I playfully narrow my eyes at him. "Like, say, my clothes disappearing?"

His gaze grows heated. "That would be nice."

I clear my suddenly dry throat. "Just give me a moment. I need to make sure my room is presentable."

He walks me to the door. "Come get me when you're ready."

I rush into my room and hide a few unmentionables before swapping my tricked-out shoes for an exact duplicate pair that aren't enhanced. Then I set "The Final Countdown" to play on a loop to set a pleasant mood.

As I head back to get Tigger, I spot Hannibal going into the kitchen.

Oh, no. This won't do.

I knock on Clarice's door.

"Come in," she says.

I stick my head in and ask her to take her cat and keep him in her room tonight.

"Why?" she asks.

"I'm bringing Tigger to my room."

She claps excitedly.

I give her a flinty stare. "It goes without saying, but I'll say it just in case: stay away from my room. I don't think anything will happen between us, but if it's about to and you mess it up, you'll start finding laxatives and sleeping pills in your food and drinks. Sometimes separately. Sometimes together."

She grins. "I love it when you ask me nicely like that."

I leave Clarice alone then, and just in case, I

conduct a similar "stay out" conversation with all of my roommates.

Here goes nothing.

I return to the front door and open it for Tigger.

He looks me over. "No hazmat gear?"

I shrug. "What's the point? You're clean."

"And I'll be even cleaner once I wash my hands," he says, grinning.

He knows me so well. Grinning back, I wave for him to follow and point him to the bathroom. When he emerges a moment later, I lead him to my room.

"See, no serial killer getup either," I say as he steps in and looks around. "That mannequin is for pick-pocket practice, not to hang skin suits made out of ex-boyfriends."

Tigger looks Manny over disapprovingly. "So you don't attach dildos to it?"

I shake my head. That's a great idea, though. Why didn't I think of it?

Tigger's eyes are catlike as he shifts his attention back to me. "What now?"

I take in a calming breath. My palms are sweating, and my heart is hammering against my ribcage.

"Put your hand out," I say. "Like the other day."

He complies, and the sexy flexing of his biceps makes the anxiety gnawing at my stomach worth it.

"I'll touch your palm, okay?" I say.

He nods, his feline eyes hypnotizing me.

I reach toward him. This time, it looks less like a

slow-mo high five and more like I'm channeling E.T. and his glowy finger.

Just like the last time, I stop when my finger is a hair width from his hand, so close I feel the heat radiating from his palm.

Damn it.

As if it's got a mind of its own, my damned hand refuses to move any farther.

Closing my eyes, I even out my breathing.

"You can do it," he says softly. "You're stronger than you think, remember?"

As my racing heart begins to slow, I psych myself up by listening to the song.

"We're headin' for Venus."

Well, that doesn't really help. If women are from Venus, I'm *headin'* for Mars. I should've put on "Eye of the Tiger." Granted, touching the palm of an attractive prince might not be as big of an ordeal as what Rocky had to endure, but it's close.

"It's the final countdown."

Yes. It is. On three, I'll touch his palm or give up trying.

One.

I grit my teeth.

Two.

I open my eyes.

Three.

I use all my willpower… and my finger connects with his skin.

Chapter Twenty-Six

By Houdini's lightning… It's as though an arc of pure electricity shoots down my finger, zings my nipples to attention, and zooms all over my body before settling warmly in my core.

Is touching always like this?

No. This is special. Only Tigger feels like this.

"You okay?" he murmurs.

In answer, I interlace my fingers with his.

If I were to vary our music tonight, Madonna's "Like a Virgin" would be the most appropriate song right now.

Holding his hand fully feels even more amazing, but I'm greedy. I want more.

Heart hammering, I bring his hand to my mouth and lick his finger.

He inhales sharply. In his pants, His Royal Hardness is at full mast.

"Kiss me," I say breathlessly, surprising myself. "Please."

For a moment, it feels like we're about to ballroom dance. His left hand is still holding my right, and he loops his right arm behind my lower back to pull me closer.

Then he dips his head, and our lips lock.

Chapter Twenty-Seven

Un. Fucking. Believable.

His lips are soft and delicious, his breath warm and pleasantly scented with sangria. He runs his tongue over the seam of my lips, teasing and stroking, and I feel like I might explode from the pleasure of it.

How have I lived without this?

My lips part, and his tongue ventures into my mouth, warm and slick and oh-so-clever. My heartbeat spikes further, and the world around us disappears. All I can feel, all I can focus on, is him. My skin burns, my core aches with emptiness, and my belly feels like someone is hunting the dule of doves in it with fireworks.

The wait was so worth it. I can't imagine a better first kiss.

Breathing hard, he pulls me closer to his warm, hard-muscled body. His erection juts into my belly, and my nipples press into his chest. I kiss him back almost violently, my head spinning from the pleasure overload. My mouth feels like it's on the verge of coming as our tongues dance and our microbiomes merge.

It's done. There's no going back, and I don't want to. His germs are inside me, just as mine are in him, and I don't mind it one bit.

No matter what happens going forward, we'll always carry a part of each other within ourselves.

After an hour of bliss, he tears his lips away and frames my cheek with his big, warm palm. "Still okay?" he asks, his voice rough with need.

I touch my tingling lips. "More than okay." I drag in a breath and call upon my newfound courage. "Let's lose these stupid clothes."

His eyes flare with heat. Without another word, he strips with military precision.

Wow. Is His Royal Hardness winking at me?

If so, it truly is the eye of the tiger.

Meanwhile, all I manage is to get my shoes and socks off.

"Let me help," he says raggedly and peels all my layers off me. Raking his gaze over me, he takes a deep breath and his voice roughens further. "I'll say it again: fucking gorgeous."

Blushing, I run my hand down his pecs and washboard abs the way I did in VR.

By Houdini's estrogen, the way this felt then is but a pale approximation of the real thing.

My hand lands on the real Royal Hardness, and my breath hitches. I have bad news for Holly and Bella: VR sucks compared to reality. His cock feels like a steel rod encased in silk, except warm and alive and all things panty-drenching.

Grunting approvingly at my ministrations, Tigger cups my breast.

Double wow.

He kneads it.

Triple wow.

He gently squeezes my nipple.

I'm running out of wows.

A wave of pleasure shoots down to my core, and I don't bother comparing this reality to VR anymore.

"Let's get on the bed," I say, pulling him in the direction I want by His Royal Hardness.

Like a tiger who's been waiting to pounce on a delicious gazelle, Tigger blurs into motion. One second, I'm standing and holding his cock, and the next, I'm spread out on the bed, with him over me in a plank position.

Did he just manhandle me, or perform a magic trick worthy of my future show?

Before I can catch my breath, he kisses me ever more passionately, as though there's something tasty in my throat.

I melt into my mattress, my hands gripping at the sheets.

Freeing my lips, he kisses my neck. My skin tingles with the overabundance of sensations, the heat inside me growing by the second as his lips move to my shoulders, then over my clavicle and down to my right nipple.

By Houdini's erogenous zones, is it supposed to feel this good? I'm in heaven, yet there's a gnawing emptiness in my core, a need for something—and I'm pretty sure I can feel that something pressing against my thigh.

Tigger moves his attention farther down my breast, and for a second, my nipple is sad to be free.

So much for my support of the Free the Nipple movement.

He nibbles his way down my ribcage, a sensation part tickly, part delicious. When he passes my belly button, I forget about the nipple. I've seen enough porn to know his destination, and I can't believe it's about to happen to me.

And then it does.

He gently kisses my sex, his lips pliant with just a hint of tongue.

"Delicious," he murmurs against my folds.

Before I can reply, he places a kiss directly on my clit, and my words fail me. All I can manage is an incoherent moan, every muscle in my body tensing with the growing tension.

He slides his genius tongue over my clit. Once, twice, thrice, on and on with excruciatingly pleasurable relentlessness.

The tension intensifies, a powerful orgasm building inside me as his licking picks up pace, his teeth scraping gently over my folds. It feels as if he's devouring my sex, consuming every inch of it. Dazedly, I wonder if he's even breathing.

If not, the training I've given him is paying surprising dividends.

Panting, I coil my hand in his hair. I'm about to come. Should I pull him away? Would it be rude to come all over his mouth? Or selfish? I haven't had the chance to please him in any way. This isn't training, so it should be—

Too late.

With a gasping cry, I come—and nearly scalp him in the process.

He doesn't seem to mind. It's the opposite, in fact. Looking up with an expression of purely male satisfaction, he murmurs, "That's good, myodik." Then he gives my over-sensitized clit a light peck and kisses each of my inner thighs.

"Okay," I say when I catch my breath. "Now I do the same to you."

He glances at his huge erection, then back at me. "You sure?"

Biting my lip, I nod.

His eyes burn hotter. "Fine, but use a condom. I don't want you worrying about the cum."

To my surprise, I'm not worried about it in the least. I don't want to ruin the moment by getting into a debate, though. Besides, I can use one of my cherry-flavored condoms—pop my blowjob cherry to the taste of cherry.

Languidly, I crawl across the bed to get the condom from the nightstand. Not only do my muscles feel like overcooked noodles after that orgasm, but this moment is a lot like a magic trick after the initial setup. When the spectator is on the hook like this, a little delay will make the payoff that much more powerful.

Yup. Tigger's eyes are glued hungrily to my curves as I return with the condom.

My evil plan is working. Continuing to move sensuously, I turn the process of rolling the condom onto him into another teasing delay.

His flaring nostrils are my reward.

Next time, maybe I'll do this with my mouth. I've seen that trick in porn.

When the condom is on, I examine His Royal Hardness with some trepidation. It seems like this emperor looks even more intimidating in his new clothes.

I'm going for it anyway.

Wrapping my fingers around the shaft, I say, "Lie back, close your eyes, and think of Ruskovia."

His eyes are slitted as they meet mine. "Oh, no, myodik. I'm going to watch."

A fresh wave of heat streaks down my spine. I guess my showmanship skills are about to be put to the test.

Given the feline nature of this cock's owner, channeling a sexy kitten is my best bet. Maintaining eye contact, I give His Royal Hardness a languorous lick from base to head.

Yum. This is like licking a cherry Jolly Rancher… made for Godzilla.

Volcanic fire rages in Tigger's eyes.

Is it normal to feel this desirable during a blowjob? This powerful?

I give His Royal Hardness another vertical lick, and he twitches in response, a truly jolly rancher indeed.

Time for the big guns.

Once again, I wish it were "The Eye of the Tiger" playing on a loop instead of "The Final Countdown." What I'm about to do is something in the league of *Rocky*.

Rounding my back like the cat yoga pose, I then arch it for cow pose before sliding the head of His Royal Hardness into my mouth.

Wow. It feels humongous this way. If I get TMJ, I'll know why.

Ignoring the urge to gag, I slide it deeper.

Tigger's eyes widen, encouraging me to go down a smidge more. I come back up, then down again, over and over, relishing it when he starts to grunt in pleasure.

The more I do this, the more the walls of my vagina become jealous of my mouth. When I can't fight the temptation any longer, I pull away and blurt, "I want you inside me."

"Fuck, yes." The sentence sounds like a tiger's territorial challenge.

Wow. Easy there… tiger. My heart is already making cartwheels in my chest as is.

Taking in a calming breath, I scoot forward and straddle him.

He grabs my ass with his powerful hands and helps me descend as I guide His Royal Hardness into my opening.

By Houdini's silky heat.

Nothing—not Prince Regent, nor any other object I've had the pleasure of having inside me—has ever felt like this.

The stretching sensation hovers on the edge between pleasure and pain, but as I slide down further, then up again, that ratio shifts firmly into blissful territory, which makes me ride him with greater enthusiasm.

My heart feels like it's about to explode again, and blistering heat boils under my skin as an orgasm to rule them all coils inside me. With each stroke, ever-louder moans escape my lips.

Tigger's breathing grows heavier, and he squeezes my bottom hard enough to leave a handprint. "Fuck, you feel good."

That low growl pushes me over the edge, and I come with something resembling a Tarzan yell. Everything inside me simultaneously clenches and releases, bliss streaking through my nerve endings as I collapse on top of him.

As I come down to Earth, I wonder distantly if Tarzan ever had to deal with a tiger. I know Mowgli did. And Pi in *The Life of Pi*.

"Such a good myodik," Tigger says raggedly.

If the idea was to encourage me to keep riding him, it works like a charm. Pushing up to a sitting position, I slide up and down his length until another orgasm builds inside me and my leg muscles begin to burn.

As if sensing my discomfort, Tigger performs another version of his manhandling trick. One moment, I'm on top; the next, I'm pinned underneath him—and to make it more impressive, I could swear His Royal Hardness never left my sex.

Maybe we should start a whole new branch of magic together—sex magic. Or a new category of porn.

Thinking of magic reminds me of the oldest trick in history—cups and balls—so I reach over and cup his balls.

He grunts approvingly and thrusts deeper into me.

My brain is on the verge of short-circuiting.

He nibbles on my neck, driving me further into madness as he picks up the pace of his thrusts.

Moans are wrenched from my lips.

He goes faster still.

My moans turn into screams.

His balls feel tight and full in my palm. He's getting closer, which is good. My tsunami of an orgasm is about to make landfall.

Almost there.

It *is* the final countdown.

As the wave of pleasure crashes over me, my toes curl, and I only have enough rationality left to *gently* squeeze his balls.

With a hybrid between a roar and groan, he surges deeper into me, grinding against me as his climax hits, and another orgasmic wave sizzles through my oversensitive nerve endings.

In the afterglow, I feel like I'm sinking into the mattress, every bone in my body liquified from bliss.

With a tender peck on my lips, Tigger pulls out of me and takes off the condom, then ties it into a knot and puts it into his pant pocket. "I'll take this with me, so the cat doesn't get it."

"Okay," I say, my voice slightly hoarse.

I might've done another Tarzan impersonation at the end there without realizing it.

A washed-out smile curves my lips. I feel too much like a squeezed lemon to carry on any more conversation. It's a marvel I remember how to breathe.

Returning to the bed, Tigger arranges my noodle-like body into a spoon position and hugs me from behind.

"That was some serious hand touching," he whispers.

Yawning, I nod.

His words make the reality of what happened crystalize.

I did it. I finally had sex—and it was more

amazing than anything I'd imagined. Not an easy feat, as my expectations were sky high.

I wouldn't be surprised if I turned into Octomom after this, never shutting up about the benefits of orgasms. Sex might be even better than magic—and no one will believe me if I tell them that.

As sleep begins to claim me, I can't help but feel hopeful. Maybe whatever this is between us could work. Despite his being above my station and being my client, and despite the big lie I told him.

After all, the biggest obstacle was always my inability to do what we just did.

He hugs me tighter, and I yawn again.

Yeah. Maybe this *could* work.

With a blissed-out grin, I drift off.

Chapter Twenty-Eight

I wake up with my cheek on a hard-muscled chest and a yummy scent of ocean surf in my nostrils.

Hmm. What's happening?

Oh.

As I recall the prior day, any hint of drowsiness evaporates as though chased away by a large espresso.

My comfy pillow is Tigger, and he's here because we slept together, in every meaning of that phrase.

By Houdini's inappropriate behavior, I slept with a client… and a prince. I slept with him without coming clean about my breathing stunt and despite concerns that he might've seen mounting me as purely a challenge—like a mountain climber seeking that elusive peak.

"Good morning," my pillow murmurs, startling me. "How did you sleep?"

I rub my eyes. "Out like an LED lightbulb. You?"

He stretches like a tomcat. "Best night of sleep I've had in years."

I sit up.

He bounces from the bed, channeling his fictional doppelganger.

"I've got an important meeting at eight, so I have to run," he says as he begins to dress. "When I'm done, I'll get in touch."

"Okay," I say.

If I sound uncertain, it might be because his military-speed dress-up ability is disorienting first thing in the morning. In the time it takes me to place my feet on the floor, he's all ready to leave.

"Talk soon?" he says.

I nod, still a bit dazed.

He kisses me on the cheek and strides out.

Touching the cheek, I blink at the empty room.

Was he really just here?

Everything is taking on a wet-dream quality.

Pushing to my feet, I dress and hurry to the bathroom for my morning routine. Then I return to my room and sniff the sheets.

Yep. It all happened. I can still smell his yummy scent.

I go to the front door.

More proof here. It's unlocked.

Navigating to the kitchen, I get myself some Frosted Flakes and ponder the events of last night. I don't get far because my phone dings.

Is it Tigger?

Nope. It's Blue. She wants to know what's new with me.

I videocall her.

"Hey," she says, peering into the camera. Like me, she's got a bowl of something drowned in milk in front of her. "What's up, sis?"

I tell her what happened, including my concerns.

"Wow," she says. "A prince, huh? You don't do half measures, do you?"

I shrug. "Given what I said, do you think what we did was a one-night stand?"

She frowns. "He said he'd get in touch with you after his meeting. He also said, 'Talk soon.' That doesn't sound like something a one-night stand would say."

She's got a point, but my cereal is tasteless anyway. "Should I tell him my underwater illusion was merely that?"

She nods vigorously. "As soon as you can. You clearly like this guy, and people can be pretty touchy about the whole honesty thing."

Like the guy? That's an understatement.

Before I can say anything else, Machete, Blue's cat, strolls into the view of the camera.

Or more like blocks it with his patchy fur.

"Shoo," my sister says.

Did he just hiss at her?

I chuckle. Large and mangy, this rescue is my sister's perfect bodyguard against the evil that is birds. I suggested she name him as she did because he resembles Danny Trejo, the actor who plays a kickass character named Machete in a movie by the same name. Compared to Machete, Hannibal is a pussy, and it's a good thing Tigger isn't here. For him, seeing *this* cat would be like me walking into a biohazard lab without my suit.

"I'd better go feed the beast," Blue says, and we hang up.

Feeling a bit blue—no sister pun intended—I finish my breakfast.

Now what?

It's eight thirty. Too early for Tigger to be done with his meeting, right? I shouldn't expect his call so quickly, should I?

To stop my mind from wandering further down that path, I make myself busy. Luckily, I've come up with an idea for an illusion. To the audience, it will look like I've turned a wallet borrowed from a guy into a purse—and then it will turn out to belong to his date.

When I have the basic steps of the trick ironed out, I check my phone.

It's nine now. How long do meetings go for? An hour? More?

Why isn't he calling? Or texting?

Have I been ghosted?

A part of me knows I'm being a tad unreasonable. I blame the fact that Tigger is my first at pretty much everything related to sex.

Unless… could it be a sign of having caught feelings?

Crap. Must stay sane. Must get back to the illusion—specifically, a big problem I can foresee with it: people will assume the wallet/purse couple are stooges on my payroll.

Sighing, I grab a mentalism book from my bookshelf. Proving your spectator isn't a stooge is a big part of that branch of magic.

By ten, I've chosen a spectator-picking procedure that should look completely random, but there's still nothing from Tigger.

Grrr. I guess I'll work on the next aspect of this new illusion: how to make the purse appearance as flashy as possible.

Should I use a cool fire effect that utilizes special chemicals?

Nah. That could trigger a fire alarm at the venue.

I pull another book from the shelf and see what else I can do—then get yanked out of my reading by a ding on my phone.

My heart leaps.

Is it Tigger?

Nope. It's just a reminder about the eleven o'clock meeting with Waldo that I almost forgot about.

It's ten-thirty now, so I'd better go.

This will be good. Hanging out with a friend should keep my monkey mind away from stalking my phone for Tigger's messages. And from questions such as, "It's ten-thirty now, why hasn't he texted or called?"

Unless... should I call him myself?

No. Waldo is waiting.

I dress and head out to the coffee shop.

By the time I get there, Waldo is already at our usual outdoor table, the same one where we met Tigger and His Royal Hardness.

"Hi," I say cheerfully.

Waldo's expression is somber. "Greetings."

"Is something the matter?"

He avoids my gaze. "I spoke to a colleague the other day. His camera was illegally confiscated near Crispy Mushroom after he took a picture of a certain prince. Any of this ring a bell?"

Oh. So that paparazzi from the other day works for the same magazine as Waldo? I didn't realize that.

"Let me guess," I say. "Your colleague described the woman who was with that certain prince, and you realized it was me?"

He nods. "More like my chum already knew who you are from the article I wrote. I thought I warned you about Anatolio. What are you doing?"

"He's just a client," I say. "I'm teaching him how to breathe."

Waldo arches an eyebrow. "Breathe?"

"Underwater," I say. "He wants to go free diving. This is off the record by the way."

"Why you?" he asks.

I shrug. "Why not me? You wrote that article, remember? Called me Amazing Hyman."

He blinks at me. "I thought that stunt wasn't for real."

"How would you know?"

He pulls out his phone. "Just to clarify… you're not dating him?"

I frown. "Why?"

"This." He thrusts his phone at me.

I study the image on the screen. In it, Tigger is standing in front of a gorgeous blond woman. He looks like he's just let go of her hand—a hand with its ring finger covered by a diamond the size of Prince Regent.

My stomach fills with liquid nitrogen. "What am I looking at?"

"She's his betrothed," Waldo says. "She's also a royal from—"

I don't hear the rest because the word "betrothed" renders me deaf, blind, and mute all at the same time.

Betrothed?

Fucking *betrothed*?

It can't be, can it? I mean, after he got tested, he told me that he *doesn't* sleep with everything that moves. He said he usually only has sex when he's in a relationship, and that his constant travels aren't conducive to that.

How does that compute with "betrothed?"

I squeeze my hands into fists until they hurt.

Was it all a lie? If he's got a fiancée, clearly that's a relationship.

This is so much worse than my original worry that he was a manwhore. Though, if he has a fiancée but slept with me, it's proof that he *is* a manwhore. A cheating manwhore.

But seriously, is there some other explanation?

I check my phone.

It's eleven-twenty. He should've called me by now.

Is this proof? Has he ghosted me now that he's gotten what he wanted?

"Are you okay?" Waldo asks, his voice reaching me as if from a distance.

"Can you send me that picture?" I say hoarsely.

I'm going to print it and make Tigger eat it.

Or shove it up his ass.

Or train every cat I know, from Hannibal to Machete, in the principles of terrorizing—

"I'm sorry," Waldo says. "I can't. It's going to be published as part of—"

I don't bother listening to the rest. I need that picture and I don't have the energy to argue with him about journalistic integrity.

"I have to go," I say. "Sorry."

He looks at me, eyes wide. "So you *were* dating him?"

"No. I wasn't." I stand up, trying to look as miserable as I can, which doesn't take much acting skill at all. "Can I have a hug?"

He looks stunned for a moment. He knows I'm

touchy about touching. "Of course," he finally says and envelops me in his spindly arms.

"Thank you," I say as I pickpocket his phone. "I needed this."

I sneak his phone into my pocket and make a mental note to apologize for this later. Also, to bathe in bleach.

"Of course," he whispers.

I pull away. "I'm sorry to cut things short like this."

"I understand," he says.

Turning on my heel, I sprint away.

When I'm far enough from Waldo, I take out his phone and put in the PIN I spied him using not long ago.

Whew.

For a second, I was worried that he changed it, but no. I'm in.

I forward myself the picture, and as soon as it's on my phone, I forward it to Tigger with a terse:

Care to explain this?

Chapter Twenty-Nine

Minutes that feel like centuries pass with no reply from Tigger.

By the time I get home, I'm fuming, as angry with myself as I am with him. How could I have let myself get so close to someone when I had such reasonable reservations? What made me think I can be with a guy in the first place? Me, with all my issues?

Then again, I should give myself a break. I did overcome my germ fears and sleep with him—and this is what I get for my bravery.

Fucker.

Seething with anger, I dial his number.

The phone rings and rings until it goes to voicemail.

"Are you ignoring my calls?" I growl. "Fine. Don't bother calling back. I never want to see you or speak to you again."

There. If only I could convince myself of the same thing.

Feeling dirty in part from the message I left, but mostly from the hug with Waldo earlier, I take a shower. It soothes me temporarily. But by the time I put on a fresh set of clothes, I'm back in crazy town and berating myself for letting my guard down with Tigger.

Unable to think of anything better to do, I video-call Blue and explain the whole situation.

"Wow, I'm so sorry," she says when I'm done. "Is there any way this could be a misunderstanding?"

"Sure," I say bitterly. "And you know who could clear it up? Tigger! But he's incommunicado."

"Why don't you send me the picture," she says. "I can run the image through our facial recognition database to see what I can learn about the fiancée."

I do as she says and watch her type away on the laptop.

The doorbell rings.

"Who's that?" she asks. "Tigger?"

"I don't know," I say, my pulse jumping. "Let me go check. I'll call you back."

Could it be Tigger? If so, did he forget to check his phone before coming back? Actually, why would he be back at all? Does he want to use me for sex a few more times before going back to his fiancée?

If it's the latter, could I bribe Hannibal to bite His Royal Hardness?

"Who is it?" I ask when I reach the front door.

"Waldo," says a familiar voice.

I open the door and look at my friend in confusion.

"Hey," he says, stepping inside. "After you left, I got increasingly worried, so I came to check on you. Sorry I didn't call—I seem to have lost my phone. You haven't seen it, have you?"

"Nope," I lie. I'll have to sneak it back into his pocket ASAP. "And I'm totally fine. Like I said, there was nothing between me and the prince."

Waldo looks relieved. "Really?"

"Really really. Now if you don't mind, I need to—"

"Hold on." Waldo shifts from foot to foot. "I have to tell you something."

I frown. "More bad news?"

He takes a step back. "No. Well, I hope not."

I look at him expectantly.

"I've... been meaning to ask you. Do you want to get coffee sometime?"

I look at Waldo like he's about to shoot coffee from his eyes. "Isn't that something we do all the time?"

"Maybe dinner then," he says. "Or lunch."

Wait a second. "Waldo," I say incredulously. "Are you asking me out on a date?"

Taking another step back, he sheepishly nods.

"You're asking me—your *friend* friend—on a date? Asking me, knowing full well how vulnerable I am right now?"

He takes another step back. "I thought you said you didn't care about him."

"I lied." I step toward him menacingly. "Was this your brilliant plan from the start? Reveal to me that the guy I'm seeing has a fiancée, just so you can ask me out yourself?"

I know I'm shooting the messenger to some degree, but I don't care. Waldo's privates are in as much danger as Tigger's would be if he were here.

Waldo must read some of this on my face because he backs all the way into the doorframe and turns partially to hide said privates. "I wanted to ask you out long before he came into the picture, ever since we first met, in fact, when I interviewed you for that article."

I shake my head slowly, too flabbergasted for words.

"Should I leave?" he mutters.

I take in a deep breath. "Yes, please. I don't want to date *anyone* anytime soon."

His expression crestfallen, Waldo turns and shuffles away.

I return to my frantic pacing, now equal parts confused and angry, with a smidge of guilt. It almost hurts to admit it, but it seems like on top of everything else, Tigger was right about Waldo.

My friend wasn't happy to be just friends.

I halt in my tracks.

Wait a second.

Is that why Waldo emphasized that Tigger was,

and I quote, "a total playboy?" Was he badmouthing the competition?

That would mean he not only looks like the Green Goblin, but is driven by a green monster as well.

Then again, Waldo didn't force Tigger to get engaged. Unless—

A videocall from Blue lights up my phone.

"I have news," she says without preamble.

"Tell me," I growl, the dule of doves performing somersaults in my belly.

Blue brings the phone close to her face and enunciates every word as she says, "That picture is fake."

Chapter Thirty

Fake?

Even though that's where my mind was about to leap right before she called me, hearing it said out loud sounds pretty nutty.

"What do you mean?" I up the volume on my phone so I don't miss a single syllable.

"What I mean is the picture was extracted from a video you can find on the Ruskovian version of YouTube. In that video, your boyfriend merely kissed the blonde's hand. He never put a ring on her finger. And, according to the research I've done, I don't believe he'd met her before that day, or since. She's a Ruskovian singer, and kissing her hand was either just a sign of respect or a minor flirtation that didn't lead anywhere."

Blue's every word is like a slap in the face. "She's not a royal?" I mutter.

"No more than you and I."

"But the ring—"

"Photoshopped in," she says. "It's done well, but at my agency, we have tools that let us see through such BS."

Fuck.

The jealous text I sent Tigger. And that voicemail. If he hadn't ghosted me before that, he certainly will now.

"Will you take this from here?" Blue asks. "Or do you need my help getting back at Waldo?"

"What do you mean getting back at Waldo?" I ask, but I already know what she'll say.

Waldo did this.

He Photoshopped a picture of Tigger.

Made up a fake engagement to break us up.

In fact, he's been pretending to be my friend for the entire year and a half that we've known each other, just waiting for a chance to pounce—and not in the sexy Tigger way.

"Oh, sorry," Blue says. "I forgot to mention. It was him. Since he was the source of the image, I took a look at his work computer and saw the Photoshop files."

I grit my teeth. "In that case, no, thanks. I won't need any help getting back at Waldo. Trust me."

She nods solemnly. "Let me know if you change your mind."

"Will do," I say and hang up.

If Waldo hadn't been a friend until today, I would let her help me—and she could do something really evil, like put him on a no-fly list.

Not that I'll be much kinder, given what he did.

Feeling almost dizzy from all the revelations, I text Tigger once more:

Can we talk?

No reply.

I call him and leave a new voicemail. "I'm sorry about before. Call me."

As I wait for Tigger to call back, I hurry over to my computer and locate a picture I've been saving for a particularly evil prank—a huge collage of micropenises with various STDs.

Gagging, I email the image to Waldo. Then I unlock his phone and save the image locally before selecting everyone on his contact list and texting them the micropenises with the following caption: "Where is Waldo's?"

I email the same thing to everyone he knows, with the exception of contacts that have the same work email as he does—because I'm not a total monster—and then I use the social media apps on his phone to tweet it, post it on his Instagram, pin it on his Pinterest, and make it his profile pic on Facebook.

Taking a break from revenge, I check my phone.

Nothing from Tigger.

Where the hell is he? It's afternoon now, and his meeting was at eight. Any meeting, no matter how long, would be over by now—which means he's purposefully not giving me a chance to explain.

Put another way, I blew it.

Chapter Thirty-One

I totally blew it. Tigger is not responding, and I'm not sure if I would either if I were in his shoes.

Fuck.

Images of our epic sex session flit though my mind, followed by our pseudo dates and training exercises and everything else until I feel like my head might burst.

Well, fuck this.

If I broke it, I can fix it.

If he wants to ignore me, he can do it to my face.

Gritting my teeth, I summon a ride.

Destination: The Palace Hotel.

Chapter Thirty-Two

The lobby of The Palace is again teeming with parrots and peacocks.

Sprinting over to the concierge, I ask to see Anatolio Cezaroff.

She looks me over snootily. "And you are?"

"Gia Hyman," I say. "His trainer."

She types something into the computer, perhaps checking me against some "approved visitors" list. Nodding at the screen, she says, "May I see some ID?"

I show her my driver's license.

"Thank you. Let me give him a call."

She dials a number and waits. And waits.

"He doesn't seem to be in his room," she says. "I'm sorry."

Shit. Is she telling me the truth, or did he ask her not to let me up? The latter seems kind of unlikely given the ID and name rigmarole—unless she's a magician-level liar.

"Can you give me a copy of his room key?" I ask. "I'd like to go up and see if he's okay."

"I'm sorry," she says. "That's against our policy."

"Can I at least go up and knock on his door?"

"I'm sorry," she says, reminding me of the nearby parrots. "That's against our policy."

I eye the room key cards in the box on the counter. Even with all of my prodigious pickpocketing skills, there's no way I could grab one and get it coded for Tigger's room without her noticing.

I heave a sigh. "In that case, I'd like to visit his brother, Kazimir."

Her eyes widen. "Is he expecting you?"

"Yes," I lie.

"Hold on." She dials another number and rattles out something in Ruskovian. All I can make out is my name and her overall dubious tone.

Whatever the person says on the other end surprises her enough to widen her eyes to comical levels.

Straightening her spine, she says, "His Royal Highness will see you now."

Wow, Kaz. Power trip much? Also, will I always associate that mighty title with Tigger's cock?

The concierge waves at a nearby pantalooned bruiser and says something in Ruskovian.

"This way," the guy booms with a heavy accent and begins walking.

I follow him through the lobby and up a fancy staircase. Then we take a sharp right and enter a huge theater.

I look around with envy. Kaz could host a Broadway show in here if he wanted. I'd give my left pinkie—and maybe my left earlobe—to perform magic on that stage even once.

"What do you think?" Kaz asks, appearing out of nowhere.

Clutching my chest, I take a calming breath. "I think your employees should call you Your Royal Ninjaness."

"I meant the venue," Kaz says, and there's not even a hint of a smile on his face.

The pantalooned guy, on the other hand, looks on the verge of tossing me out of the hotel.

Okay, got it. Henceforth, there will be no joking with His Royal Seriousness.

"What do you mean, the venue?" I ask.

Kaz gives the pantalooned guy a slight but very imperious nod.

The man bows and backs away for a few feet before turning around and rushing away.

There's deference, and there's that. Seems like someone's taking the Palace theme a little too seriously.

Kaz gestures at the stage. "Are you not here to check out the venue?"

I blink at him. "Why would I be?"

His forehead creases. "This morning, Tigger

convinced me to host your show here. I figured it was only a matter of time before you wanted to see if it's acceptable."

"Acceptable?" I stagger back, gaping at the curtains, the stage lights, the seats for thousands of people…

Is he jerking me around, or is this for real?

"I don't understand," I say. "Tigger talked to you on my behalf? This morning?" Then it hits me. "You're his secret eight o'clock meeting?"

"Secret?" His lips form a disapproving line. "I didn't realize."

I flap my arm. "Never mind that. You said yes?"

He nods curtly. "I thought it was a great idea. We could use more variety of performances here, and illusions fit well with the hotel theme."

Holy Houdini.

Would I look unprofessional if I did a few cartwheels?

I'm even tempted to give Kaz a grateful hug—except he seems like a person who'd welcome it even less than I would.

I can't believe Tigger did this for me.

It's amazing.

Unbelievable.

Mind-boggling.

Actually, I take it back. I *can* believe he did this. He's always gone to extraordinary lengths for me. That's why it hurts so much to think I've lost him.

Assuming I have. It's less clear now—at least

insofar as he hasn't yet pulled the plug on this initiative with his brother.

"Where *is* Tigger?" I ask. "I've been unable to reach him."

Kaz blinks. "I don't know. Our meeting didn't start until nine, as there was an emergency at the hotel that delayed me. After we spoke, he said he was going to talk to some people in the media. He thinks he can leverage his notoriety to get publicity for your show. He didn't give me much detail, but I figured it'd be something along the lines of taking pictures of you cutting him in half, like in the classic illusion."

Huh. Cut a royal hottie in half. I totally could do that—and maybe pull the same trick as Penn and Teller where I make it seem like a gory accident at the end.

"So he's talking to the paparazzi?" I ask, my excitement tempered by caution.

Even if what Kaz says is true, what are the chances he hasn't seen my texts or heard my voicemails?

Frowning, Kaz pulls out his phone and glances at the screen. "It's been many hours. He should be long done by now."

There goes that hope.

Tigger *is* ignoring me, just not from his hotel room.

Kaz's phone rings in his hand.

Looking at it disapprovingly, he picks up. "Speaking."

Whatever someone tells him on the other end causes his features to grow as stormy as the sky in Mordor.

Is that Tigger telling him to cut off my access to this hotel?

"When?" Kaz growls.

That question doesn't fit my theory.

Kaz squeezes the phone in his hand. "Repeat the name of the hospital again."

Ice floods my stomach.

Someone is talking about a hospital. To Kaz.

Blood leaves my face as I realize there's a theory I hadn't yet thought of.

What if Tigger isn't ignoring me? What if he can't take my call because—

"What happened?" Kaz's question is an imperious demand.

I want to rip that phone from his hand so I can also learn what happened.

If expressions could kill, Kaz's would slay the speaker on the other end of the line. "I'm his fucking brother. Tell me what—"

He stops with a growl, and I can see he's on the verge of smashing his phone into bits.

"They hung up," he says, staring incredulously at the device. "Didn't like my fucking language."

"What happened?" I yell, just barely resisting the urge to choke the information out of him.

He meets my gaze. "It's Tigger. He's in the hospital."

Chapter Thirty-Three

"What?" I exclaim. "What happened? Did he—"

"The fucker on the phone wouldn't tell me," Kaz growls. "Said to come down in person. Something about proof of identity."

A strange numbness comes over me. "Which hospital?"

He tells me, and it sounds familiar.

Very familiar.

"My friend was just there with an allergic reaction," I say unsteadily. "Let's go."

"Right. Let's." Jaw clenched, he strides out of the room so fast I have to sprint to keep up, which I don't mind in the least.

The faster we get there, the better.

"Is Tigger allergic to anything?" I ask breathlessly, catching up to him.

He shakes his head without turning.

"Did he practice underwater breathing without me?"

He shrugs, also without turning.

Fuck. Is it possible Tigger has drowned? That would make me complicit in—

No. Makes no sense. The pool is in this hotel, and if he'd gotten hurt here, Kaz would've known. Whatever happened must've happened after Tigger went to speak to the media on my behalf.

A horrific scenario occurs to me as I picture him driving in his cursed Lambo. With the way he drives, if he were in an accident, he might not even survive.

No.

Please let it not be that.

Anything but that.

We reach the hallway, and Kaz barks orders at his people like a general on a battlefield.

In an eyeblink, a limo's tires screech outside.

"That's us," Kaz says tersely and hurries out.

As soon as we climb in, the limo torpedoes forward.

Through the haze of panic, an idea comes to me, and I pull out my phone to call Blue.

Kaz gives me a disapproving glare.

"My sister might be able to help us learn what happened," I explain while the call connects.

"Hey," Blue says. "Did you—"

"No time for pleasantries. I need urgent help."

"What's up?"

"Tigger is at the same hospital Clarice was at the

other day. They didn't tell us what happened to him. Can you find out?"

"Of course," she says. "Let me get back to you."

I hang up and explain the situation to Kaz, whose expression is no longer disapproving.

"Thank you," he says just as the limo comes to a screeching halt.

We rush out and Kaz heads for the familiar hospital entrance.

I follow him until I reach the automatic doors.

The doors slide open.

He rushes in, but my feet stop moving.

Fuck.

Not this again.

Chapter Thirty-Four

I psych myself up to go in.

Tigger is inside. He might be on his deathbed.

Why can't I be normal just this once? Why do I need a hazmat suit to enter a hospital?

Actually, the last time, even the suit didn't help.

I'm not just the worst friend, I'm also the shittiest girlfriend ever—and yes, I just upgraded myself to girlfriend to make this argument.

How about just one step?

I will my feet to move and shuffle a few inches toward the door.

Okay, this is the farthest I've gotten yet, but I'm still not inside.

Kaz comes back, holding a surgical mask. "Here." He thrusts it at me. "I figured the clean pool and your reluctance to enter might be related."

"Thank you." I grab the mask gratefully and put it on my face.

"I'm going," he says. "See you inside."

Sure. Inside. So simple.

I clench my fists.

My feet don't move.

I clench my teeth.

My feet stay glued to the ground.

I clench my sphincter and Kegel muscles and everything else that's clenchable, and take a step.

And another.

Then one more.

By Houdini's immune system, I'm actually doing it.

I clear the door.

Yes!

I'm inside the hospital now.

My next step is more surefooted. The one after that is almost confident.

Before I know it, I'm speed walking—except I have no idea where I'm going.

Crap.

Where is Kaz?

I guess I'll have to circle back to the administrative—

My phone dings. It's a text from Blue:

He was admitted because of food poisoning.

I nearly bump into a passing nurse.

Food poisoning? I bet it was that bitch Matilda

with her unpasteurized milk. Fucking cow. Wait, is that fat shaming? No, she is a cow, so it's okay. All I know is, she'd better hope we never meet, or I just might punch her cow face. And if Tigger doesn't make it, I'll eat her liver with some fucking fava beans and a nice Chianti.

I shoot Blue a text back:

Where is he?

She replies immediately:

Second floor. Room 2E.

I sprint for the elevator and stab the second-floor button.

"He should be okay," I tell myself.

Then again, maybe not. Only the most severe cases of food poisoning require hospitalization, especially so soon after he was perfectly fine.

No.

He's okay.

Has to be.

When I exit the elevator, a new text arrives:

This is weird. He just checked out.

A wave of relief hits me, hard.

You don't check out if you're not okay.

I look down the corridor, and the wave of relief grows into a tsunami. There is Kaz with a couple of pantalooned bodyguard types—and with them is Tigger.

He looks faintly green but is able to walk on his own—something his entourage seems to be arguing with him about.

I rush forward.

Spotting me, Tigger narrows his eyes, and I realize I might be hard to recognize because of the mask.

"Gia?" he asks.

"It's me," I say breathlessly. "Please tell me you're okay."

"I'm fine." He gives the pantalooned guys a querulous look. "Someone overreacted by bringing me here. You go into a coma once, and everyone starts to treat you like you're made of porcelain."

I lunge forward and tackle-hug him. "No more unpasteurized milk," I say sternly. "Ever."

He chuckles weakly. "That's easy. I don't think I'll ever want to eat or drink anything that I've had today."

Huh. So far, he's acting like he hasn't gotten my insane messages.

If that's the case, I could make it so he never finds out.

Entering pickpocket mode, I snatch his phone from his pocket as I pull away. "When did this happen? I was trying to reach you."

"I'm not sure how long it's been," he says. "I haven't had a chance to check my phone on account of all the unmentionable activity I've been engaged in." He looks even greener at the memory. "Let's just say I'm never watching *The Exorcist* again."

"Say no more." Since we're by the elevator, I summon it for us. "I'm just happy I didn't lose you."

There. If he's listened to my messages, his reaction will show it.

"No, myodik, you can't get rid of me so easily."

As I hoped. He has no idea about the messages.

We walk into a crowded elevator, and I stand behind everyone.

This is my chance.

I know his pin and I've got his phone.

I can unlock the phone, delete what I need, and he'll never be the wiser.

Except something stops me.

Guilt.

And not the dismissible magician's guilt.

This guilt is of the kind that's hard to ignore.

Given everything Tigger's done for me and how I feel about him, I shouldn't invade his privacy like this. Or lie to him.

I don't want our relationship to be based on deceit.

By Houdini's conscience. It seems like I'll have to give him the phone back—as well as come clean about my lack of breathing expertise.

Which means I might still lose him.

The elevator opens and I walk through the hospital lobby in tense silence as the others converse in Ruskovian.

Once we're outside, I spot not one but two limos.

Tigger looks at his pantalooned companions. "Go with Kaz, please."

They nod.

Great. We have some privacy.

"Bye, Kazimir." I remove my surgical mask. "Or should I say, 'Bye, Your Royal Highness?'"

For the first time in our acquaintance, a hint of a smile touches the man's eyes. "After today, you may call me Kaz."

Tigger whistles mockingly. "What an honor."

Ignoring his brother, Kaz gives me a courtly nod and disappears into his limo.

Tigger opens the door for me. "Ready?"

"Thanks." Using a kiss on his cheek as misdirection, I put-pocket the phone back into his pocket.

Just because I've grown a conscience doesn't mean I'm a saint.

Climbing in, Tigger cozies up next to me and asks the driver to put up the privacy partition.

"So," he says when the thing is up. "As much as I appreciate you coming to check on me at the hospital, I'm not sure how you knew to do so. Kaz was my emergency contact, and he doesn't have your number."

I sigh. "I've got something to tell you."

He cocks his head. "I had a feeling you might."

I take off my glove and grab his hand. The tingly pleasure of his touch makes me braver. "After you left and didn't call for a while, I thought we were over."

His eyebrows shoot up. "Over? Why?"

I squeeze his hand. "I thought I was an Everest."

"What?" He looks at me like said mountain has just landed on my head. "What are you talking about?"

My grip tightens further. "I was worried that once we had sex, you'd lose interest in me. You never climbed Everest for a second time, so I thought maybe—"

"Stop." He covers my hand with his. "You couldn't be more wrong, myodik. With you, it's more like I got to the top of Everest, planted the Ruskovian flag there, and decided to stay for good."

The dule of doves in my belly throws a tantrum. "In that case, can you ignore the messages I left you? There was this thing with Waldo and—"

I stop at the dark expression on Tigger's face and hasten to clarify, "Nothing happened. It's just that you were right. He did come on to me—but first, he tried to trick me into thinking you were engaged."

"What?"

He looks ready to rip Waldo to shreds, so I explain what happened and how I exacted my revenge.

That seems to appease him slightly. He no longer seems ready to commit homicide.

"Here." He unlocks his phone and hands it to me. "Delete whatever you want."

Wow. I'm sure glad I didn't do this stealthily before. This is so much better.

I wipe my slate clean and hand the phone back. Now for the real toughie. I gather my courage. "There's one more thing you should know."

Wait, should I go through with this? What if he breaks up with me after all?

I have to say, if I were a psychopath, my life would be so much simpler.

He pockets the phone and gives me a concerned look. "What is it?"

"It's about the training." Dropping my gaze, I examine the fancy floor mat. "You know how you thought I could hold my breath for twenty minutes?"

Cautiously, I look up, only to find him smirking.

"Did I?"

I narrow my eyes. "Well, yeah. You hired me because—"

"I hired you to be close to you," he says. "I knew your underwater stunt was just a trick. In your defense, you never looked me in the eyes and claimed otherwise."

I feel like a cow's just been removed from my shoulders. An evil one too, like Matilda.

He knew.

All this time, he just wanted an excuse to be with me.

And what a perfect excuse. He made me feel good about one of my illusions.

"Wait," I say. "What about free diving into that lake? Was that just a cover story?"

Should I be upset that he's been deceiving *me*?

Nah. That would be mega hypocritical.

He shakes his head. "I *would* like to do that one day. But if you don't mind, I'll get training from some real experts before I attempt it."

I grin. "I insist you do that. Most of my training

revolved around seeing you with as little clothing as possible."

The limo stops and he opens the door for me. His feline eyes gleam. "Want to stop by my place, watch some Netflix and chill?"

"Can Houdini pick a lock?" I grab his hand and leap out of the car.

We step into The Palace hand in hand, though I feel like I'm floating through the lobby.

Which reminds me: I'll be putting on a show in this very hotel soon. Tigger made it possible.

With the hospital scare and the rest, I haven't gotten a chance to fully process that fact, but I do now—and if it weren't for his hand, I'd float to the ceiling like a helium balloon.

That gives me an idea. I should dedicate an illusion to today. Do my take on a classic—flying. I already have some ideas heavily inspired by David Copperfield's version of this amazing illusion.

When we face the door of his suite, I realize I've been lost in my magic fantasies the entire way here.

I turn and scan Tigger's face.

"You're looking better," I say and mean it. That green hue is gone without a trace.

"Thanks." He opens the door. "I guess one good thing about that trip to the stupid hospital is a quicker recovery."

Loud barking stops me from a reply.

Mephistopheles is at our feet, wagging his tail and body with enough energy to power all of Manhattan for a week. Caradog is also happy to see us, but his tail-wagging is very tempered in comparison to the younger bear—I mean, dog.

The strange part of this welcome is that Caradog is holding a stick in his maw. Walking over to me, he stands on his hind legs, his body language clear as crystal: *take the stick, human.*

"You want to play fetch?" I grab the stick and look at Tigger. "Is it safe to toss?"

He grins. "Do it here in the corridor. My flower arrangements are fragile."

I throw the stick.

Caradog doesn't move, but Mephistopheles chases the stick like the fate of the world depends on it.

I look at the bigger dog. "Are you teaching him to fetch?"

Those intelligent eyes behind the goggles seem to say, *Yup, fetch.*

"Can you play with them while I shower and brush my teeth?" Tigger asks.

I nod, and Tigger hands me a few dog cookies before he departs.

I toss the stick a few more times, then repeat my coin-magic moves using the dog cookies—to the delight of both canines.

"How do you do that?" Tigger asks, catching me just as I vanish another cookie.

"Expertly," I say, looking up.

Instantly, my mouth fills with saliva, Pavlovian-dog style.

Tigger is only wearing a towel, and his sickliness is but a distant memory. In fact, he's the epitome of health… and virility.

"Raincheck, guys," I say to the doggies.

Tigger leads me to the bedroom, locks the door, and puts on music.

I grin and begin to strip. "Is that 'The Final Countdown?'"

"Yeah." He drops the towel. "I figured it helps you."

I point at His Royal Hardness. "That works better."

He grins back, then yanks me to him and crushes his lips against mine.

Before I know it, he does his magic move, getting me on the bed in a heartbeat. Pausing only to cover His Royal Hardness's nudity with a latex surcoat, we join as one, and this time, his thrusts into me are slow and contemplative. Covering me with his body, he interlaces his fingers with mine, like the day I first touched him, and what we're doing doesn't feel like sex but rather something that starts with the letter 'L'.

We come together, and my orgasm is more potent than all the prior day's combined. As we lie there, spent and deeply content, he pushes up onto his elbow and tucks a strand of hair behind my ear before curving his palm over my cheek. His hazel eyes are soft and warm as he murmurs, "I have to tell you something."

My heart rate skyrockets again, the adrenaline

from before still coursing through my system. "What is it?"

"The day we met, you didn't just steal my belt," he says softly. "You also stole my heart."

By Houdini's oxytocin production.

My chest feels like it's going to burst from joy.

"When I thought I lost you today, it felt like I'd lost oxygen," I admit, turning my head to kiss his palm.

The warm glow in his eyes intensifies. "That's because you and I fit together. Like lupines and peonies."

"No," I say breathlessly. "Like top hats and rabbits."

He nods. "Like base jumping and parachutes."

I cover his hand with mine. "I love you."

I hadn't admitted it to myself until I said it, but it's true.

Wholeheartedly true.

"I love you too," he says. "You're the only mountain I want to climb."

Beaming, I glance at His Royal Hardness as it awakens anew. "Actually, it looks like you'll be mounting me, and I'll be climbing you."

Epilogue

TIGGER

The stage is huge, the biggest in Ruskovia and one of the largest in the world.

Gia is doing her world-famous flying illusion, and as usual, I'm overcome with awe and wonder.

Also, maddeningly, I have no idea how it's done. We're in the open air, so she doesn't have any place to attach wires to, not unless there's a silent helicopter above the clouds.

Actually, she claims not to use wires, and she usually doesn't lie about how she's *not* doing a trick.

I'll be honest. As this theme park's owner, I asked the staff to tell me if they see any hint of a wire or another explanation for how Gia does what she does, but so far, they've given me zilch. Same is true for Kaz's hotel staff.

Hey, I don't mind. Not much anyway.

I figure if my ignorance makes my myodik happy, I can live with that. Of course, if I do figure something out on my own… Well, if all is fair in love and war, all is fair without the war too.

Finishing her last aerobatic maneuver, Gia lands gracefully on the stage next to a spectator who's acting as the eyes for the rest of the audience. Her raven hair billows dramatically around her, highlighting the pale glow of her face.

She lets the spectator check for wires once more and takes a graceful bow for the larger audience.

The spectators—all one hundred thousand of us—leap to our feet and give Gia the most enthusiastic standing ovation. The applause is thunderous. Like the others, I clap so hard my palms hurt, and even my parents, who sit next to me, give a few grudging claps.

I can't describe in words how much I love this woman. I fell for her right away. By the time she stole my belt, it was like that Bryan Adams song: I was seeing my unborn children in her eyes… and she was one of those tiger moms to my tiger dad.

When the excitement dies down and the curtain falls, I hurry backstage.

Gia greets me with a passionate kiss. Since our first time together, she's been completely worry-free when it comes to bodily fluid exchanges with me. In fact, she's eager for them.

As is usual in her proximity, my cock—or My Royal Hardness as she's dubbed it—goes fully erect, reacting to her sleek curves. With her porcelain skin, dark hair, blue eyes, and black leather outfit, she reminds me of the sexiest vampire ever, and though

I've never told her this, I had a major crush on Kate Beckinsale in *Underworld*.

I readjust myself as best I can. "Another great show."

She beams at me. "You really think so?"

"Oh, yeah. And the best part is, I could tell my parents had no clue how you did any of it. I'm sure they didn't like that one bit."

Her grin turns devious. "You think they'll order the Ruskovian CIA to find out my secrets?"

"I wouldn't put it past them." Also, not a bad idea. Maybe I could do that.

As part of this trip to my motherland, Gia met the king and queen—and didn't break up with me afterward, which is a miracle on par with the things she does on stage.

My parents aren't exactly nice people—especially to those they view as beneath them, which is just about everyone.

"I have a surprise for you," I say. "Come, let me show you."

Actually, I have two surprises: one huge and one enormous.

She lets me lead her to the room where the first "surprise" said she'd wait.

I open the door with a flourish. "Gia, I want you to meet a Ruskovian national treasure. The great, the amazing… Rasputina."

Gia's eyes widen as she takes in the female figure who is dressed similarly to her—not a surprise, really, as Rasputina was a major influence on Gia's stage persona.

I can't even imagine how my myodik is feeling right now. Meeting this famous magician for her is like meeting Evel Knievel for me.

"I'm not worthy," Gia mutters.

"Nonsense," the other woman says with an infectious smile. "I saw your show. I'm honored to meet you."

Gia shakes her head. "Mrs. Rasputina, you're—"

"Please, call me Sasha," she says.

"Sasha." Gia looks like she tastes the word and finds it delicious. "Can I get your autograph?"

Sasha gladly obliges, and I watch everything closely because I'll never forget something Gia said to me once: "If I had to sleep with a woman—gun to the head situation—I'd sleep with Rasputina."

For that reason, I've made triple-sure that there are no guns in my park today. I'm too jealous to have my woman sleep with anyone, even another woman.

"So," Sasha says. "You know how I do predictions?"

Gia nods. "Yeah. They're amazing."

If you ask me, they're borderline creepy. My mother has spent a fortune and bestowed noble titles on this woman in exchange for her "prophecies," which, to my knowledge, have somehow come true.

A bolt of lightning seems to shoot from Sasha's hand into her eyes—a magic trick, obviously.

"You will be together your entire lives," she says,

looking at each of us in turn. "And it will be a joyful union."

At first, I'm as stunned as Gia is.

Then it hits me.

Rasputina is ruining my enormous surprise—which was supposed to take place at the ballroom in the royal palace, with our dogs playing their adorable roles and all that.

Fuck.

I'll have to improvise now.

In fact, given the momentousness of this occasion, maybe this will be just as, if not even more, memorable for Gia.

Pulling a playing card case from my pocket, I drop to one knee.

Her expression devilish, Sasha points Gia's attention my way.

Gia turns and freezes, looking comically stunned. "What is happening?"

"This." I ceremonially open the card box the way Clarice taught me.

Slowly and majestically, the diamond ring floats out of the box and lands on my palm.

Even though Gia might know how this trick is done, she gasps and clutches her chest.

A good start.

I take the ring between my thumb and index finger. "Gia Hyman, being with you has been the greatest adventure I've ever undertaken." I pause to make sure my voice doesn't catch in an unmanly fashion. "I've climbed Everest. I've surfed Cape Fear. I've base jumped from Burj Khalifa. But none of those feats compare to just holding your hand." Gently clasping her wrist, I pull her stage gloves off and hover the ring over her finger. "Would you do me the honor of becoming my wife?"

Gia looks at me, then at the ring, before turning to her idol. "Did you know this would happen?"

Sasha winks, and Gia turns back to me.

"Yes," she says and jams her finger into the ring. "By Houdini's balls, yes. Of course I will marry you."

I leap to my feet and give Gia a proper kiss. Meanwhile, Sasha hums Beyoncé's "Put a Ring on It."

"I'm going to be a princess?" Gia asks when we finally disconnect. "A fucking princess? Me?"

"No," I say with a grin. "As far as I'm concerned, you're already a queen."

Sneak Peeks

Thank you for participating in Tigger and Gia's journey!

Looking for more laugh-out-loud romcoms? If you haven't already, you've *got* to meet the Chortsky family from the *Hard Stuff* series! Read Vlad's story in *Hard Code*, Bella's story in *Hard Ware,* and Alex's story in *Hard Byte*.

Also, you'll definitely want to pick up a copy of *Femme-Fatale-ish*, featuring Blue, one of Holly and Gia's sextuplet sisters, and a sexy (possible) Russian spy.

Misha Bell is a collaboration between husband-and-wife writing team, Dima Zales and Anna Zaires. When they're not making you bust a gut as Misha, Dima writes sci-fi and fantasy, and Anna writes dark and contemporary romance. Check out *Wall Street Titan* by Anna Zaires for more steamy billionaire hotness!

Turn the page to read previews of *Femme-Fatale-ish* and *Wall Street Titan*!

Excerpt from Femme Fatale-ish by Misha Bell

My name is Blue—insert a mood-related joke here—and I'm a femme fatale in training. My goal is to join the CIA. Unfortunately, I have a tiny issue with birds, and the closest I've come to my dream is working for a government agency that's disturbingly up-to-speed on everyone's sexts, rants in private Facebook groups, and secret family chocolate-chip cookie recipes.

I know I'm a spy cliché, that agent who works at a desk but craves fieldwork. However, I have a plan: I'm going to infiltrate the secretive Hot Poker Club, where I've spotted a mysterious, sexy stranger who I'm convinced is a Russian spy.

And once I'm in? All I have to do is seduce the presumed spy without falling for him, so I can expose his true identity and prove my femme fatale bona fides to the CIA. I never lose concentration at work, so that'll be an absolute breeze for me. Oh, and did I mention he's sexy?

I'm doing it for my country, not my ovaries, I pinky swear.

WARNING: Now that you've finished reading this, your device will self-destruct in five seconds.

I stick my finger into Bill's silicone butthole.

"What the hell?" Fabio exclaims in a horrified whisper. "That's poking. You have to be gentle. Loving."

Grunting in frustration, I jerk my hand away.

Bill's butthole makes a greedy slurping sound.

"See?" I say. "He misses my finger. It couldn't have been *that* bad."

"Look, Blue." Fabio narrows his amber eyes at me. "Do you want my help or not?"

"Fine." I lube up my finger and examine my target once more. Bill is a headless silicone torso with abs, a butt, and a hard dick—or is it a dildo?—sticking out, at least usually. Right now, the poor thing is smushed between Bill's stomach and my couch.

"How about you pretend it's your pussy?" Fabio's nose wrinkles in distaste. "I'm sure you don't jab *it* like an elevator button."

"I usually rub my clit when I masturbate," I mutter as I add more lube to my finger. "Or use a vibrator."

Fabio makes a gagging sound. "You're not paying me enough to listen to shit like that."

With a sigh, I circle my finger seductively around Bill's opening a few times, then slowly enter with just the tip of my index finger.

Fabio nods, so I edge the finger deeper, stopping when the first knuckle is in.

"Much better," he says. "Now aim between his belly button and cock."

I cringe. I hate the word "cock"—and everything else bird-related. Still, I do as he says.

Fabio dramatically shakes his head. "Don't bend the finger. This isn't a come-hither situation."

I pull my finger out and start all over.

My digit goes in rod straight this time.

"Huh," I say after I'm two knuckles deep. "There's something there. Feels like a walnut."

Fabio snorts. "That *is* a walnut, you dum-dum. I shoved it in there for educational purposes. The prostate—or P-spot—is around where you are now, but the real one feels softer and smoother. Now that you got it, massage gently."

As I pleasure Bill's walnut, Fabio shakes the dummy to simulate how a real man would be acting. Then he starts to voice Bill as well, using all of his porn-star acting ability.

"Bill" moans and groans until he has, as Fabio puts it, "a P-gasm to rule them all."

I remove my finger once again. I have mixed feelings about my accomplishment.

Fabio grabs my chin and tilts my face up. "Show me your tongue."

Feeling like I'm five, I stick my tongue all the way out.

He shakes his head disapprovingly. "Not long enough."

I retract my tongue. "Long enough for what?"

"To reach the walnut, obviously." He sighs theatrically. "I guess I'll work with what I've got."

Ugh. Can I slap him? "How about we work on his peen?"

With another sigh, he turns Bill over. "Did you take those lozenges, like I told you?"

Not for the first time, I field doubts about my instructor. The goal for this training is simple: I want to be a spy, which means gaining skills as a seductress/femme fatale. Think Keri Russell's character in *The Americans*. According to her backstory in that show, she attended a creepy spy school that taught seduction. In fact, such schools are common in movies about Russian spies—the latest was featured in *Anna*. Alas, these schools are harder to find in real life. So I figured I'd hire a professional instead, but the prostitute I solicited for help refused. Ditto with the female porn stars I reached out to on social media. As my last resort, I turned to Fabio, a childhood friend who's now a male porn star. Being in gay porn, he claims he's able to please a man better than any woman can.

"Yes, I sucked on the lozenges," I say. "My throat is numb, and I can barely feel my tongue."

"Great. Now get that whole shlong down your throat." Fabio points at Bill.

I scan Bill's length apprehensively. "You sure about this? Wouldn't the lozenges make the penis numb? If Bill were real, that is."

He lifts an eyebrow. "Bill?"

I shrug. "Figured if I'm having relations with him, he shouldn't be anonymous."

Fabio pats my shoulder. "The lozenges are just to give you some confidence. Once you see that it fits, you'll be more relaxed for the real thing and won't require numbing. Don't worry. I'll teach you proper breathing and everything. You'll be a pro in no time."

"Okay." I take off my sexy wig and put it on the couch. Before Fabio says anything, I assure him I'll keep it on during a real encounter.

Now comfy, I lean over and take Bill into my mouth as far as I can.

My lips touch the silicone base. Wow. This is deeper than I was able to swallow any of my exes—and they weren't this big. My gag reflex is sensitive. Typically, even a toothbrush gives me issues when I use it to clean my tongue. But thanks to the numbing, the silicone dildo has gone in all the way.

This is interesting. Could lozenges also help one withstand waterboarding? If I'm to become a spy, I need to learn to withstand torture in case I'm captured. Of course, waterboarding isn't my biggest concern. If the enemy has access to a duck—or any bird, really—I'll spill all the state secrets to keep the feathery monstrosity away from me.

Yeah, okay. Maybe the CIA did have a good reason to reject my candidacy. Then again, in *Homeland*—another one of my favorite shows—they let Claire Danes stay in the CIA with all of *her* issues. Which reminds me: I need to practice making my chin quiver on demand.

Fabio taps my shoulder. "That's enough."

I disengage and swallow an overabundance of saliva. "That wasn't so bad. Should I go again?"

He shakes his head. "I think you need a motivation boost."

I know what he's talking about, so I take my phone out.

"Yeah." He rubs his hands like a villain from the early Bond films. "Show me the picture again."

I pull up the image of codename Hottie McSpy.

An undercover FBI agent took this photo because he was after one of the men in it, but not my target. No. Everyone thinks Hottie McSpy is just a rando—but *I* believe he's a Russian agent.

Fabio whistles. "So much premium man meat."

It's true. In the image, a group of extremely delicious-looking men are sitting around a table inside a Russian-style *banya*—a hybrid between a steam room and a sauna—wearing only towels and, in the case of Hottie McSpy, a pair of non-reflective aviator sunglasses that must have some kind of anti-fog coating. With the sweat beading on everyone's glistening muscles, they look like a wet dream come to life.

"They're playing poker," I say. "That's why I've been taking poker lessons."

"Yeah, I figured as much, since the picture is called Hot Poker Club." Fabio giddily enunciates the last three words. "You realize that sounds like the title of one of my movies?"

I shrug. "An FBI agent named this image, not me. They were after another guy who was in that room, and I was helping out as part of the collaboration between the agencies."

Fabio taps on the screen to zoom in on Hottie McSpy. "And he's the one you're after?"

Nodding, I drink in the image once more. Hottie McSpy has the hardest muscles of this already-impressive bunch, and the strongest jaw. His chiseled masculine features are vaguely Slavic, a fact that first made me suspicious of him. His hair is dark blond and shampoo-commercial healthy. Not even my wigs are as nice.

If I were to learn that this man was the result of Soviet geneticists trying to create the perfect male specimen/super-soldier/field agent, I wouldn't be surprised. Nor would I be shocked to find out that he was the inspiration for the Russian equivalent of a Ken doll (Ivan A. Pieceof?). Even if I didn't think he was a spy, I'd infiltrate that poker game just to rip those stupid glasses off of him and see his eyes. Though I picture them—

"You're drooling," Fabio says. "Not that I can blame you."

I nearly choke on the treacherous saliva. "No, I'm not."

"Yeah, sure. Be honest, are you going after him because he might be a spy, or because you want to marry him?"

"The first option." I hide my phone. "Spy or not, marriage is out of the question for me. My current attitude toward dating shares an acronym with the name of the agency I work for: No Strings Attached. But that's not what this is about, anyway. If I single-handedly expose a spy, the CIA is bound to take notice and rethink their rejection of my candidacy. And even if they don't take me, I will have made America safer. Russian spies are still among the biggest threats to our national security."

"Sure, sure," Fabio says. "And his hotness has nothing to do with you focusing on him, specifically."

I frown. "His hotness is why he's the perfect agent. Think James Bond. Think Tom Cruise in *Mission Impossible*. Think—"

Fabio raises his hands like I'm threatening to shoot him. "The lady doth protest too much, methinks."

I gesture at the silicone phallus. "Should I go again? I think the numbing is wearing off."

For some unknown reason, I feel super motivated to deep-throat someone.

Go to www.mishabell.com to order your copy of *Femme Fatale-ish* today!

Excerpt from Wall Street Titan by Anna Zaires

A billionaire who wants a perfect wife…

At thirty-five, Marcus Carelli has it all: wealth, power, and the kind of looks that leave women breathless. A self-made billionaire, he heads one of the largest hedge funds on Wall Street and can take down major corporations with a single word. The only thing he's missing? A wife who'd be as big of an achievement as the billions in his bank account.

A cat lady who needs a date…

Twenty-six-year-old bookstore clerk Emma Walsh has it on good authority that she's a cat lady. She doesn't necessarily agree with that assessment, but it's hard to argue with the facts. Raggedy clothes covered with cat hair? Check. Last professional haircut? Over a year ago. Oh, and three cats in a tiny Brooklyn studio? Yep, she's got those.

And yes, fine, she hasn't had a date since… well, she can't recall. But that part is fixable. Isn't that what the dating sites are for?

A case of mistaken identity…

One high-end matchmaker, one dating app, one mix-up that changes everything... Opposites may attract, but can this last?

I'm all but bouncing with excitement as I approach Sweet Rush Café, where I'm supposed to meet Mark for dinner. This is the craziest thing I've done in a while. Between my evening shift at the bookstore and his class schedule, we haven't had a chance to do more than exchange a few text messages, so all I have to go on are those couple of blurry pictures. Still, I have a good feeling about this.

I feel like Mark and I might really connect.

I'm a few minutes early, so I stop by the door and take a moment to brush cat hair off my woolen coat. The coat is beige, which is better than black, but white hair is visible on anything that's not pure white. I figure Mark won't mind too much—he knows how much Persians shed—but I still want to look presentable for our first date. It took me about an hour, but I got my curls to semi-behave, and I'm even wearing a little makeup—something that happens with the frequency of a tsunami in a lake.

Taking a deep breath, I enter the café and look around to see if Mark might already be there.

The place is small and cozy, with booth-style seats arranged in a semicircle around a coffee bar. The smell of roasted coffee beans and baked goods is mouthwatering, making my stomach rumble with hunger. I was planning to stick to coffee only, but I decide to get a croissant too; my budget should stretch to that.

Only a few of the booths are occupied, likely because it's a Tuesday. I scan them, looking for anyone who could be Mark, and notice a man sitting by himself at the farthest table. He's facing away from me, so all I can see is the back of his head, but his hair is short and dark brown.

It could be him.

Gathering my courage, I approach the booth. "Excuse me," I say. "Are you Mark?"

The man turns to face me, and my pulse shoots into the stratosphere.

The person in front of me is nothing like the pictures on the app. His hair is brown, and his eyes are blue, but that's the only similarity. There's nothing rounded and shy about the man's hard features. From the steely jaw to the hawk-like nose, his face is boldly masculine, stamped with a self-assurance that borders on arrogance. A hint of five o'clock shadow darkens his lean cheeks, making his high cheekbones stand out even more, and his eyebrows are thick dark slashes above his piercingly pale eyes. Even sitting behind the table, he looks tall and powerfully built. His shoulders are a mile wide in his sharply tailored suit, and his hands are twice the size of my own.

There's no way this is Mark from the app, unless he's put in some serious gym time since those pictures were taken. Is it possible? Could a person change so much? He didn't indicate his height in the profile, but I'd assumed the omission meant he was vertically challenged, like me.

The man I'm looking at is not challenged in any way, and he's certainly not wearing glasses.

"I'm… I'm Emma," I stutter as the man continues staring at me, his face hard and inscrutable. I'm almost certain I have the wrong guy, but I still force myself to ask, "Are you Mark, by any chance?"

"I prefer to be called Marcus," he shocks me by answering. His voice is a deep masculine rumble that tugs at something primitively female inside me. My heart beats even faster, and my palms begin to sweat as he rises to his feet and says bluntly, "You're not what I expected."

"Me?" *What the hell?* A surge of anger crowds out all other emotions as I gape at the rude giant in front of me. The asshole is so tall I have to crane my neck to look up at him. "What about you? You look nothing like your pictures!"

"I guess we've both been misled," he says, his jaw tight. Before I can respond, he gestures toward the booth. "You might as well sit down and have a meal with me, Emmeline. I didn't come all the way here for nothing."

"It's *Emma*," I correct, fuming. "And no, thank you. I'll just be on my way."

His nostrils flare, and he steps to the right to block my path. "Sit down, *Emma.*" He makes my name sound like an insult. "I'll have a talk with Victoria, but for now, I don't see why we can't share a meal like two civilized adults."

The tips of my ears burn with fury, but I slide into the booth rather than make a scene. My grandmother instilled politeness in me from an early age, and even as an adult living on my own, I find it hard to go against her teachings.

She wouldn't approve of me kneeing this jerk in the balls and telling him to fuck off.

"Thank you," he says, sliding into the seat across from me. His eyes glint icy blue as he picks up the menu. "That wasn't so hard, was it?"

"I don't know, *Marcus*," I say, putting special emphasis on the formal name. "I've only been around you for two minutes, and I'm already feeling homicidal." I deliver the insult with a ladylike, Grandma-approved smile, and dumping my purse in the corner of my booth seat, I pick up the menu without bothering to take off my coat.

The sooner we eat, the sooner I can get out of here.

A deep chuckle startles me into looking up. To my shock, the jerk is grinning, his teeth flashing white in his lightly bronzed face. No freckles for him, I note with jealousy; his skin is perfectly even-toned, without so much as an extra mole on his cheek. He's not classically handsome—his features are too bold to be described that way—but he's shockingly good-looking, in a potent, purely masculine way.

To my dismay, a curl of heat licks at my core, making my inner muscles clench.

No. No way. This asshole is *not* turning me on. I can barely stand to sit across the table from him.

Gritting my teeth, I look down at my menu, noting with relief that the prices in this place are actually reasonable. I always insist on paying for my own food on dates, and now that I've met Mark—excuse me, *Marcus*—I wouldn't put it past him to drag me to some ritzy place where a glass of tap water costs more than a shot of Patrón. How could I have been so wrong about the guy? Clearly, he'd lied about working in a bookstore and being a student. To what end, I don't know, but everything about the man in front of me screams wealth and power. His pinstriped suit hugs his broad-shouldered frame like it was tailor-made for him, his blue shirt is crisply starched, and I'm pretty sure his subtly checkered tie is some designer brand that makes Chanel seem like a Walmart label.

As all of these details register, a new suspicion occurs to me. Could someone be playing a joke on me? Kendall, perhaps? Or Janie? They both know my taste in guys. Maybe one of them decided to lure me on a date this way—though why they'd set me up with *him,* and he'd agree to it, is a huge mystery.

Frowning, I look up from the menu and study the man in front of me. He's stopped grinning and is perusing the menu, his forehead creased in a frown that makes him look older than the twenty-seven years listed on his profile.

That part must've also been a lie.

My anger intensifies. "So, *Marcus*, why did you write to me?" Dropping the menu on the table, I glare at him. "Do you even own cats?"

He looks up, his frown deepening. "Cats? No, of course not."

The derision in his tone makes me want to forget all about Grandma's disapproval and slap him straight across his lean, hard face. "Is this some kind of a prank for you? Who put you up to this?"

"Excuse me?" His thick eyebrows rise in an arrogant arch.

"Oh, stop playing innocent. You lied in your message to me, and you have the gall to say *I'm* not what you expected?" I can practically feel the steam coming out of my ears. "*You* messaged *me*, and I was entirely truthful on my profile. How old are you? Thirty-two? Thirty-three?"

"I'm thirty-five," he says slowly, his frown returning. "Emma, what are you talking—"

"That's it." Grabbing my purse by one strap, I slide out of the booth and jump to my feet. Grandma's teachings or not, I'm not going to have a meal with a jerk who's admitted to deceiving me. I have no idea what would make a guy like that want to toy with me, but I'm not going to be the butt of some joke.

"Enjoy your meal," I snarl, spinning around, and stride to the exit before he can block my way again.

I'm in such a rush to leave I almost knock over a tall, slender brunette approaching the café and the short, pudgy guy following her.
